1

NIGHTFALL

Blood Magic Book One by L.H. Cosway

Because I could not stop for Death –
He kindly stopped for me –
The Carriage held but just Ourselves –
And Immortality.

Emily Dickinson.

1.

"I'm the one who eats actual food here, so I know what I'm talking about."

"Well, I might not eat, but I know for a fact that you don't put chorizo in paella. I was once invited to dinner at Salvador Dalí's house in Figueres. Paella was served, and I remember a distinct lack of the spiced sausage."

I might not eat?

Salvador Dali?

Who the hell were these oddballs?

I was at work, mindlessly sticking price tags on tins of baked beans, when I overheard the oddest conversation. It wasn't way out of the ordinary for me to see or hear weird crap when working the night shift at Hagan's 24-hour grocery. I was kind of desensitised after witnessing one woman crack open a box of tampons before pulling down her pants in the middle of the aisle and, well, you know the rest.

People could be really disgusting sometimes.

I leaned closer to the shelves and strained my ears to listen.

"Hey, if she wants to put chorizo in the dish, then let her," another voice said. This one male. "What difference does it make? I'd like to get out of here sometime in the next century."

"Ugh, fine," the woman groaned. "I'll pass on the chorizo. I can't believe I gave Ethan the opportunity to name drop. I'll never learn."

"When you've been alive as long as I have, you meet a few historical figures along the way," the first man, Ethan, said casually.

9

I furrowed my brow. These three were definitely on drugs. The Yellowbranch Forest, just outside the city limits, was famous for its psilocybin. I shook my head, chuckling to myself, as I refocused on pricing tins. Head down, I continued to listen to their bizarre conversation when I heard them come my way.

"Did you ever cross paths with Da Vinci?" the second man asked. "I heard he was partial to handsome young gentlemen like you."

"He was sadly before my time, but unlike some, dear Lucas, I've never felt myself swayed by the same sex." A pause. "Actually, I tell a lie. I did once consider letting Bosie go down on me. He was terribly pretty and very persuasive."

I arched an eyebrow. Maybe they were role-playing, or practicing lines for a TV show. Chancing a quick peek, I spotted a red-haired woman, a tall, blond man, and a dark-haired guy idling by the jarred sauces. Hmm, they were definitely attractive enough to be actors.

"I'm sure you only considered it," the dark-haired man scoffed. "I've never known you to turn down oral pleasure."

"I do have some restraint," the blond man shot back before going markedly silent. His nostrils flared like he was sampling the air. It reminded me of my dad's Pitbull, Bruiser, and how he used to stand by the back door, sniffing the air before he decided to go outside.

A moment later the blond man's eyes met mine, and I gasped, dropping the tin of beans I'd been holding. *Were his eyes gold?* Acting on instinct, I bent to pick up the tin but found he'd gotten there before me. He was *fast*. He lifted the tin and handed it to me. "Here you go." His eyes drifted down to the name tag on my uniform. "Tegan."

"Thanks," I whispered, blinking rapidly. Up close he was even more attractive. I'd go as far as to say he was beautiful.

"She smells unusual, doesn't she?" the red-haired woman commented, tilting her head as she took me in.

"Yes, rather unusual indeed," the blond man agreed. I noticed a slightly Eastern European lilt in his accent.

His curious eyes wandered over me, and for a second, I felt like I couldn't breathe. The tiny hairs on my arms stood on end and some weird part of my brain yelled that I should get away from him fast.

Then, the glass sliding doors at the entrance of the store opened and a voice shouted, "I have a weapon. Come out here and open the till NOW!"

The blond man raised an eyebrow, muttering blandly, "That is quite the threat."

"Quite," I agreed as my stomach turned over in fear. It was just my luck that someone decided to rob the place when I was the only one on shift. *Again.* This was why I hated working at night. The dark brought out all the crazies. I'd also left my phone in my locker at the back of the store.

"Excuse me," I said to Mr Blond and Beautiful as I stood and went to confront the piece of shit who just threatened me. The first time this happened, I froze and the thief got away with all the money from the register, as well as what was in the safe. Mr Hagen said he'd fire me if I let the store get robbed again, and I couldn't afford to lose this job right now.

A greasy looking guy in a sweat-stained T-shirt and torn jeans stood by the counter, knife in hand. He wore a balaclava, but I was fairly certain I recognised him as the same scumbag who'd robbed us the last time.

"You again. I see the Tribane Police Department is

11

doing a stellar job keeping the city safe."

"Shut up and open the till, bitch," he hissed, thrusting the knife towards me in an unwieldy manner. I quickly sidestepped out of the way.

"As you can see, I'm on my way to open it now," I said, keeping my voice neutral as I passed by him and went behind the counter. The thief shoved a plastic bag at me. "Put it all in there."

Over his shoulder, I saw the blond man appear. He placed his finger to his lips, and I furrowed my brow. I thought he might've done me a solid by calling the police. Instead it looked like he was going to try and take this guy on directly. Well, better him than me.

I tried to act normal as I opened the till and shoved cash inside the bag. "I didn't realise thieves were so environmentally friendly these days."

"What are you talking about?" the robber asked impatiently.

"You brought your own reusable bag," I said. "Very forward-thinking. It's nice to know there are people out there making an effort to tackle global warming."

Behind him, Blondie smirked in amusement.

"Just put the money in the bag and shut your mouth," he snapped.

"Sure thing," I said with false politeness. As I spoke, Blondie reached out and swiped the knife from the thief's grip. He moved fast, just like he did when he picked up the tin of beans. Maybe I was extra-tired, but his speed didn't seem natural …

"Hey!" the thief exclaimed, grasping for his knife. Blondie was tall enough that he could easily hold it out of reach. Looking the thief dead in the eye, he said, "You're going to leave now and never come back."

12

The thief stilled, a strange look coming over him almost like he was in a trance. Then to my shock, he quietly turned and left the store.

Confused, I placed my hands on my hips and looked back at Blondie. "Eh, what the hell? How did you do that?"

Taking his time, Blondie pocketed the knife before turning his attention to me. I was vaguely aware of the red-haired woman and the other man standing a few feet behind him. Blondie pulled a fifty from his wallet and placed it on the counter. "For the food." I glanced at the woman, who was holding a basket full of items. "I'm sorry to have to do this, Tegan, especially since you smell so very interesting, but I must insist you forget this ever happened."

I stared at him blankly, intending to sound sarcastic, but my suppressed nerves from the attempted robbery made the word come out stilted. "Ooo—kay."

"Until next we meet."

With that, he left, the other two following behind him.

"Just take the basket with you then," I muttered, shaking my head. Bunch of weirdos. I glanced down at the bag of cash and swore loudly. I was going to have to reorganise it and put it all back in the register.

"Fantastic. Just bloody fantastic."

2.

It was just past 6 am when I arrived back at my dingy little sixth-floor apartment. Exhausted and weary, I was ready for a shower and a long nap, but my plans were derailed when I found Florence, my seventeen-year-old neighbour, sitting outside my door.

Florence's dad, Terry, was a violent alcoholic and an absolute waste of oxygen. I often let her hang out in my apartment when she needed space from him. I'd even given him a piece of my mind once or twice, but he still refused to change his ways.

"Hey," I said softly. "Are you okay?"

Florence glanced up. "Can I sleep on your couch for a few hours? D-d-dad's been a nightmare. He brought a lady friend home last night, and they've been drinking, smoking, and playing loud music in the living room ever since."

I gritted my teeth at what she said, then pulled my keys from my pocket and nodded. "Sure, come on in."

"Thank y-y-you," she replied quietly. Florence had a stammer. I'd noticed it the first time we met, but I never mentioned it, which I think she appreciated. I wasn't generally in the business of befriending teenagers, but there was just something about Florence that called to me. We were kindred spirits and had a lot in common since we'd both been raised by single dads, though mine was far nicer than hers. Growing up, my dad worked a lot, leaving me the epitome of a latchkey kid. He wasn't around much, but he tried his best.

"Do you want some tea?" I asked as she settled on the couch, her long brown hair tied back in a dirty ponytail. It looked like it'd been a while since she'd last showered.

"Yes, please."

I hung my bag up on a hook in the entryway then went to turn on the kettle.

"You can use my shower after your nap," I told her casually. "Oh, and there's some change on the coffee table if you want to go downstairs to the laundry room and wash your clothes."

There was no response. I turned and found her staring glassy-eyed into her hands. "Oh, Flo. What's the matter?"

She sniffled and blinked away her tears. "You're always so nice to me. I'm not used to it. And thank you f-f-for offering for me to use your shower. Dad smashed the mirror in our bathroom a few days ago when he was drunk. There are shards of glass everywhere, and he won't let me clean them up."

I stared at her, anger bubbling inside me. "That's it, I'm going to have a strong word with him."

Florence vehemently shook her head. "No! Please don't. There's no changing him. Besides, I only have a few more months before I turn eighteen. Then I'll legally be able to go out and find my own place. I've been saving every penny. That's w-why I haven't washed my clothes in a while."

I blew out a breath, hands on my hips. "Well, like I said, you're free to take whatever change is on the table." I tried to keep from sounding angry. God knew she had enough of that to deal with at home. But my heart broke for her. Florence was a kind, bright young kid. She deserved so much better than the shitty hand she'd been dealt.

I finished making the tea and grabbed two bars of Turkish Delight from the fridge. I placed a cup and a bar down on the table for Florence before taking mine into my bedroom. Chilled Turkish Delight was one of my favourite

15

treats. I knew it wasn't the healthiest thing to eat right before going to sleep, but after the night I'd had I needed the pick me up.

After washing and changing into a baggy T-shirt to sleep in, I climbed under the covers, sipping on tea as I replayed the events of the night. I was incredibly lucky the store hadn't been robbed, otherwise I'd be out of a job. I was also lucky that those three weirdos were there, especially Blondie. If he hadn't intervened, then that scumbag would've gotten away with an entire register's worth of cash for the second time.

I thought about his odd golden eyes and wondered where he was from. The faint Eastern European lilt in his accent told me he wasn't from around here. I wondered how exactly he'd gotten the thief to walk out of the store without a single protest. Then again, he was tall, broad-shouldered, and quite intimidating looking, not to mention he'd gotten hold of the knife. My would-be thief didn't have a leg to stand on.

It was after midday when I woke up, feeling groggy. I rarely woke up refreshed anymore, haunted by one too many bad dreams. Florence was no longer in my living room, but she'd tidied up and left a thank you note on the coffee table.

Thanks for letting me catch some sleep on your couch. You're my guardian angel. Flo. x.

My chest tightened at her heartfelt note. I was only twenty-six and she was almost a legal adult, but some days I seriously considered fostering her. Anything to get her away from her psychopath of a father.

Today was my day off. Normally, I'd take the opportunity to go out with friends and have some fun, but I'd been avoiding socialising the last few months. My boyfriend, Matthew, died earlier this year. The coroner deemed it a suicide, judging from the number of drugs in his system. At first, I'd refused to believe it. I refused to think he'd taken his own life. But now, as time went on, I was coming to accept that Matthew had a sadness in him nobody could fix. I'd loved him more than anything, but my love still wasn't enough.

This was why I was avoiding people. I hated how they looked at me, some with pity, others with thinly veiled suspicion. It was like they wondered if *I* was the reason he killed himself. If I was secretly an awful person who'd driven him to do what he did. It wasn't true though. I wasn't awful. But people were always going to think the worst.

Most of my day was spent watching TV, but later in the evening, I heard a knock on my door. Spying through the peephole, I found my friend, Nicki, all glammed up and clearly ready for a night on the town.

"I know you're in there, Tegan. Open up. I'm not leaving until you do."

I sighed and pressed my forehead against the door. Nicki was the one friend I hadn't completely cut out of my life. Mainly because she was stubborn and persistent and wouldn't allow it.

Reluctantly, I turned over the lock and opened the door. She gave me a quick once over, shaking her head as she walked inside. "You look like crap."

"Wow, thanks."

"I'm just being honest."

"Yeah, well, sometimes it isn't the best policy," I grumped, folding my arms and dropping back down onto the sofa.

Nicki removed two bottles of white wine from her bag

17

and placed them in the fridge before coming and sitting down next to me. "When was the last time you left this apartment other than to go to work?"

I shrugged. "Can't remember."

"Yes, you can. It was before Matthew—"

"Please don't talk about him," I begged.

Her eyes took on a sympathetic gleam. "You should come out with me tonight. Let off some steam. One of my co-workers gave me these free passes to that new Goth club, Crimson." She rifled through her purse and pulled out several tickets, waving them in my face. I eyed them a moment before shaking my head. "I'm really not in the mood."

"You will be once you're out. I heard this place is supposed to be *amazing*. Go shower and put some make-up on. I brought over that little black dress you love."

"The one with the straps on the back?" I asked, perking up a little. I did love that dress.

Nicki nodded. "I'll let you keep it if you come to Crimson with me."

I chewed my lip, considering it. "Okay, but if it's terrible you have to promise to leave with me."

Nicki smiled wide, knowing she'd gotten her way. "I promise."

***

Seated at the back of the bus, I shifted uncomfortably on our way to the club. Nicki's black dress was quite a bit shorter than I remembered, and my high heels pinched my toes since I was used to wearing comfortable flats these days. I'd blow-dried and straightened my long dark hair and put on some smoky eye makeup with nude lips. After a few stops, Nicki's friends, Dillon, Amanda, and Susan, got on.

Well, technically they were my friends, too, but I hadn't seen them in a while. They seemed amazed to see me—like I was a long-lost relative who they'd thought was dead. After a beat of awkwardness, Dillon came forward and wrapped me in a hug. "It's so great to see you, Tegan," he gushed while Amanda and Susan hung back, stiff, wary smiles on their faces. They clearly didn't know how to act around me.

"Hey, Amanda. Hey, Susan," I said with a little wave.

"Hi," Susan replied. "You look good. We haven't seen you in forever."

"Yeah, we thought you'd moved away or something," Amanda added.

"Nope, just living that hermit lifestyle," I said, and they all laughed politely.

Oh, man, tonight was going to be *fun*, and by "fun" I meant nightmarish.

"Look! This is our stop," Nicki announced, and we all lined up to get off the bus.

Nicki slid her arm through mine as we made our way down the street. I spotted the long line first, and then the club. There was a bright red neon sign over the entrance in fancy cursive font that read *Crimson*. I hoped Nicki's passes meant we didn't have to queue.

No such luck.

It took over half an hour to get inside, but as we entered, I was pleasantly surprised. The place was very tastefully designed for a Goth club. The expensive looking black velvet and dark red silk reminded me more of a high-end BDSM establishment than a place where sweaty rockers moshed out to heavy metal music.

19

"Would you look at this place? Very swish!" Dillon exclaimed.

I eyed Nicki, both of us quietly impressed. Maybe tonight wouldn't be so nightmarish after all.

A DJ stood on a high podium playing "White Rabbit" by Jefferson Airplane while attractive people dressed in black filled the dancefloor. Wearing Nicki's dress was a good idea because I fit right in.

"I'll get the first round," Nicki said while Amanda took me by the hand and led me to one of the booths centred around the dancefloor. Above the DJ podium were several steps leading up to a VIP section. A man sitting at the head of one of the tables seemed to be attracting a good deal of attention. I gasped in surprise, recognising him instantly. It was Blondie! I'd know those golden eyes and perfect head of hair anywhere.

Beside him sat the same redhead from last night. Her long, wavy hair shone under the club lights, and the deep purple dress she wore highlighted her flawlessly pale skin.

A wave of shock flowed through me when her head suddenly turned in my direction as if she'd sensed me watching her. Her eyes locked with mine and the second seemed to last an eternity. I quickly glanced away, but not before I saw a marked look of concern cross her delicate features. She leaned close to Blondie, whispering something in his ear.

"Are you okay, Tegan?" Nicki asked, arriving at the table with our drinks.

"Yeah," I said, frowning to myself. "I just saw someone I recognised."

"Oh? Who is it?"

I shook my head. "No one really. Just someone who came into Hagen's last night."

"I can't believe you're still working at that place," Susan remarked with disdain. "It's in such a dodgy neighbourhood."

Yeah, tell me about it. I lifted the gin and tonic Nicki placed in front of me and knocked back a long gulp. "Beggars can't be choosers."

"It's not like that nail salon you work at is so high end," Nicki scoffed at her.

Susan made a face. "It's better than washing dogs' buttholes all day."

"Dogs are the best. I have no problem washing their buttholes," Nicki shot back, defending her career as a pet groomer.

"I love this song! Let's go dance," Dillon suggested when the Eurythmics' "Sweet Dreams" came on. They all got up, but I remained at the table.

"Aren't you coming?" Nicki asked.

"I'll stay here and keep the table," I told her. The excuse came easy—I wasn't one for dancing.

She reached out and squeezed my shoulder. "I'm so happy you came out with us tonight."

I nodded and smiled, taking another sip of my drink as I watched my friends attract attention on the dance floor. Something about the flashing lights plunged me into a memory, twisting my stomach into knots...

Flashing ambulance lights. Paramedics.

I was the one who found Matthew when he died. Up until that point, I'd never seen a dead body. My blood ran cold whenever I remembered it. He'd been so ... still. I hated myself for not noticing the signs of depression in him sooner. Maybe then I would've been able to save him from taking his own life.

Matthew had messy dark hair and the deepest brown

21

eyes I'd ever seen. We'd met at a house party last year. He asked me for a lighter and I asked him to play me a song on the acoustic guitar he was holding. He might have asked me for my mortal soul, and I would have willingly handed it over. I was still trying to get used to the fact that he was gone.

I downed the rest of my gin and tonic and decided to make my way over to the bar for another. I drank my second one in record time and took a quick glance at the VIP section again. Blondie and the redhead were gone now. Maybe I'd imagined them. Last night's attempted robbery had left me with quite a bit of unresolved stress.

Suddenly, a wave of claustrophobia hit me. The club felt way too crowded, and I had an overwhelming urge to flee. It was the same feeling I'd gotten last night when I'd locked eyes with Blondie, right before the thief came into the store.

Someone brushed against me and I glanced up. *Well, speak of the devil.*

"Hello. I hope you don't mind me saying, but that is a stunning dress you have on," Blondie said, his voice oozing charm and charisma.

"Well," I deadpanned, "all you have to compare it to is my unflattering work uniform, which isn't a very high bar to surpass." His face dropped, and I frowned. Was it something I said? His entire being grew still as he stared at me, clearly confused.

"Um, are you okay?" I asked, gasping once I saw his gold eyes flash black.

"You remember me," he said. He sounded *pissed.*

A chill came over me and the urge to flee intensified. I took a tentative step back, edging away from him until I had enough room to turn and run. I had no idea why I was

22

running. I just knew I had to get away from him. Every cell in my body screamed at me to *move*.

I reached a fire exit and pushed it open, finding myself in a back alley next to several large waste bins. I began to run in the direction of the street but ended up walking right into a hard, impenetrable wall. No, not a wall, a chest, and a muscular one at that. Blinking, I stared up into Blondie's intense gold eyes. At least they weren't black anymore.

"We have to stop meeting like this," he said, the charming tone gone. His voice was low and somewhat disgruntled.

"I was just leaving," I said, moving to get by him only to be blocked. Frustrated and scared, I turned to go in the other direction, but the alley was a dead end. My only other option was to go back inside. Maybe I could lose him in the crowd. It was better than staying out here in a deserted alley alone with him. I pushed open the fire exit to go back into the club and came face to face with the redhead and the dark-haired man from last night.

"This part of the club is off-limits," the dark-haired man said, eyeing me up and down with a cruel slant to his mouth. "Trespassers will be prosecuted—I mean, *punished*," he continued with a mocking laugh.

"I didn't know. This is my first time here," I told him.

"Makes no matter to us," he said before taking a step toward me.

I looked at the redhead and found her glaring at me. "You remember us," she said, like it was the worst thing imaginable. What was wrong with these people? Of course, I remembered them. It was only last night that they came into Hagen's.

"Well, yeah, I'm not going to forget three weirdos like you in a hurry."

Behind me, Blondie re-entered the building. "Weirdos? That's not a very nice way to refer to the people who stopped a junkie from robbing you, now is it, Tegan?" he chided, the barest hint of reprimand in his tone.

A shiver ran down my spine at the way he spoke my name. My eyes surreptitiously moved from left to right, searching for an escape. "My apologies. You're not weirdos. In fact, I think you're all totally delightful. Now, if you don't mind, I'll be on my way."

"You're not going anywhere, prey," the dark-haired man said.

I shot him a dirty look. "Prey?"

"I can't think of anything else to call you. Coming in here smelling like that."

"Leave her, Lucas," the redhead said, an obvious warning.

"I'd oblige you, Delilah," Lucas replied, snapping his head back to her, almost too fast. "But this one is far too intriguing." I bristled when he reached out and ran a finger down my cheek. "Look at those eyes, so blue, such—what is it that I see? Ah, yes, pain."

I tried not to flinch at his accuracy. "Look, if you don't get out of my way, I'm going to start screaming, and believe me, I've got a hell of a set of lungs on me."

Blondie appeared in front of me then, his gold eyes overwhelmingly sharp. "We won't harm you. You have my word."

"Aw, come on," Lucas complained from behind him, and Blondie whipped his head around, his voice cutting. "You will not harm her, Lucas. That is a direct order."

Lucas gave a reluctant sigh. "Fine. I'll keep my fangs to myself."

My eyes went wide. *Fangs?* Blondie's tone turned

even more cutting. "I'll also remind you that she's seemingly impervious to compulsion so watch your words."

Okay, this was all getting way too strange. Blondie returned his attention to me, his voice suddenly courteous. "I'll let you go. I'd just like to try something first, if I might ask your permission?"

I folded my arms. "No, you don't have my permission. Now get out of my way."

He stared me down a long moment, before finally stepping aside, "Very well then. It was a pleasure to see you again, Tegan."

"Sadly, I can't say the same, Blondie," I replied then speed-walked the hell out of there.

I heard the redhead, Delilah, chuckling as I left. "Did she just call you Blondie?"

"I can't believe you let her leave. She smells like—"

"I'm well aware what she smells like," Ethan cut him off, and that was the last thing I heard before I was back in the main part of the club, thumping music filling my ears.

I found Nicki easily enough over by the bar. The other three were still out on the dancefloor.

"Tegan! I've been looking for you everywhere," she said, her relief evident.

"There was a really long queue for the bathroom. Listen, I'm going to head home. I'm not feeling this place."

She looked disappointed. "Oh, well, do you want me to come with you?"

I shook my head. "You stay and enjoy yourself. I'll grab a taxi and text you when I get home."

"Okay, don't forget to text when you get to your apartment. Otherwise, I'll worry."

"I won't forget," I assured her. We hugged, and I made

25

my way outside. I couldn't spot any taxis on the road, so I decided to save some money and take the bus instead. I walked the short distance to the bus stop and sat down on a bench, my mind reeling from the weird encounter back in the club. I shouldn't have been surprised though. This city was full of nutjobs. And besides, what else did I expect visiting a Goth club? That Lucas guy said something about fangs. Were they into vampire role play? It was the only thing that made sense.

I didn't know how long I sat there when a black SUV pulled to a stop in front of me. I looked up as the window rolled down, revealing Blondie sitting in the driver's seat.

Fuck my life.

"Need a ride?"

I tugged my coat tighter around myself. "No, thank you."

"Tegan, get in the car. There isn't a bus coming this way for another hour and it's freezing. You'll catch your death."

I scoffed. "You sound like someone's grandmother."

He smirked. "That's because I'm older than I look."

I arched a brow at his curious statement. "How old *are* you?" I asked. He looked about thirty, mid-thirties at a push.

"Get in the car and I'll tell you."

I glanced up at the screen showing the bus times. He was right. I'd be waiting an hour for the next one and I didn't fancy sitting on a damp, cold bench for that long. Besides, he'd let me go back at the club. He'd also given me his word he wouldn't harm me. Not that a virtual stranger's word was anything to trust, but still, he *had* helped me last night by disarming the thief at Hagen's.

Sighing, I stood and approached the car. "Fine. But just

so you know, I have pepper spray in my purse and I'm not afraid to use it."

"I promise there will be no cause for that," Blondie replied as I walked around to the passenger side. He threw the door open, and I warily climbed in. "My name's Ethan," he said, formally introducing himself as I strapped on my seatbelt. "Ethan Cristescu."

"Interesting surname."

"It's Romanian."

I glanced at him a moment. So that was where the unusual lilt in his accent came from. "And what brought you out to Crimson tonight?" I asked in an effort to make casual chitchat.

"I own the place."

3.

"I own the place."

Well. That was unexpected. Though, considering the car he drove, Ethan obviously had money.

"What do you think of it?"

"The club? It's very, um, *Eyes Wide Shut*," I answered honestly, soliciting an amused chuckle from him.

"That's exactly what I was going for." He glanced from me to the road ahead. "So, where to?"

"I live near Singh Square," I replied, avoiding giving my full address. Ethan was still a stranger, one I wasn't entirely sure of, and I had decided to reserve judgment until I knew more about him. We drove in silence for a few minutes, and I was a little annoyed that he didn't speak or give any explanation for his and his friends' odd behaviour back at the club.

"What's wrong?" he asked, clearly sensing my annoyance.

"I have questions."

"Ask them then."

Fiddling with the sleeve of my coat, I blurted, "Do I smell bad?"

He cast me a quick, disbelieving glance. "Do you smell *bad?*"

"Several comments were made by you and your friends about how much I stink. Obviously, it's difficult not to take offense," I explained, lifting my chin. Maybe it was Nicki's dress. I bent down to sniff the material, but there was only the faint waft of fabric softener.

"You don't stink. On the contrary, you smell wonderful. You smell like ... like ..." he faltered, as though he couldn't find the right word. When he spoke again, he sounded oddly bereft. "You smell like sunshine."

I shot him an arch look. "Sunshine?"

He nodded and stared back at the road. I frowned and bit my lip. I had no clue what sunshine smelled like, but maybe he meant fresh, like a Summer's day or something. He was Romanian so perhaps his true meaning was lost in translation.

"Okay, well, I'm glad I don't stink. Why were you so stunned that I remembered you from last night?"

"That is a question I can't answer. Not yet anyway." An intense, brooding expression came over his face, making him look rather fetching. Not that his good looks mattered. I wasn't in the market for a new relationship, not even for casual sex. After what happened to Matthew, my heart was still on the mend. It would be a long time before I opened myself up to someone new.

"I'm just going to put this out there so you don't go wasting your time," I said. "I'm not interested in anything romantic right now, so if that's what this ride home is all about—"

"I assure you, my intentions are purely platonic," Ethan cut me off.

"Oh." I was a smidge embarrassed by his blatant dismissal. "Well, what are your intentions then?"

His gold eyes flicked to mine. "Curiosity. Friendship?"

"A night club owner wants to be friends with a lowly grocery store clerk?" I asked, incredulous.

Ethan shrugged. "You seem like you could use a friend."

"I have plenty of friends."

"None like me."

"No," I agreed. "None like you."

A faint whisper of a smile graced his lips, "Now you do."

Something about the way he said it made me feel oddly touched. I didn't meet men like him very often, and certainly not ones who wanted to befriend me. I knew I should be suspicious, but for the moment, I chose to enjoy the feeling of being valued as a person.

We were almost at Singh Square when I commented, "You have the most unusually coloured eyes."

His hands tightened on the steering wheel. "What do you mean? My eyes are brown."

"No, they aren't. They're gold," I countered.

"They're brown, Tegan," he argued forcefully.

I cocked my head at him. "Um, I'm looking right at you, and it might be dark out, but your eyes definitely aren't brown."

His features hardened, and I grew tense. Why was he acting so pissed all of a sudden? After a moment, he relaxed and plastered on a neutral expression, but it looked like it took effort. "Sorry. I normally think of them as golden brown, but you're right, they're more gold than brown," he amended.

I swallowed tightly, a voice in my head saying I should get out of the car right now. "Oh, look. We're here. Thanks so much for the ride," I said as he pulled to a stop and I quickly vacated the SUV.

"You're welcome. Don't be a stranger, Tegan," he called, his voice unnervingly flat as I speed-walked down the street.

When I reached my place, Florence was there again. I'd never been happier to see her. Something in my gut told me I didn't want to be alone in my apartment tonight. I had no idea why, but I was beginning to suspect that my subconscious was warning me that Ethan Cristescu was bad news. Not to be trusted.

"Hey, come on in," I said, a little breathless as I slotted my key in the door.

"You look nice. Did you g-go out to a bar?"

"I went to that new Crimson club with Nicki and a few of our friends," I told her as I went to grab a glass of water. Why was I so thirsty? Maybe it was all the fight or flight responses Ethan brought out in me.

"Did you have fun?" Florence asked as she sat down. The pillow and blanket she'd used last night were still out, placed neatly over the arm of the couch.

"Not really. I think I'm getting too old for clubs. I'd rather stay in and watch a movie while eating Turkish Delight to be perfectly honest."

Florence laughed. "You really are obsessed with that stuff."

I smiled. "I know. It's becoming a bit of a problem." I opened my fridge to show her the stacks of magenta coloured foil-wrapped bars cooling in the side compartment.

"Oh, my goodness, you do have a problem. You need to enrol in TDA first thing in the morning."

"TDA?"

"Turkish Delight Anonymous," she explained, and I chuckled.

"You're right. I need help." Pausing, I studied her. "Are you hungry? I could make an omelette?"

Florence's cheeks pinked. "I am a little h-hungry," she admitted.

"Say no more. One omelette coming right up."

***

31

When I woke up the following morning, Florence was gone again. She never overstayed her welcome, which was ironic because I kind of liked having her around. The apartment was far too quiet when I was here by myself, especially after Matthew ...

I cut off the thought before I could get too morose.

I went to put on a pot of coffee when I saw a white envelope had been shoved under my door. Picking it up, I groaned. The letter was from my landlord informing me that my rent was being raised. I did the mental calculation and groaned again. Unless I got another job, I wasn't going to be able to afford to keep living here. I dreaded to think of the sort of place I *could* afford, considering this neighbourhood was far from fancy.

Yep. I was definitely going to have to search for another job, something during the day that didn't conflict with my night shifts. Then I could just sleep whatever hours were available in between. It would be hell, but at least I wouldn't have to move.

Over breakfast, I went online and made a list of all the places close by that were hiring. I sent out applications to a few, though I was particularly drawn to a listing for an assistant in a holistic store called Indigo. I felt a strange pull and a tingle in my throat. It was almost like some inexplicable force was urging me to apply. *Weird.* I opened a new email and sent off my resume, not thinking much of it.

Getting any of the jobs I applied for would be a long shot. I had no fancy education, no degree. I'd more or less entered the workforce the moment I finished school. I didn't have any other choice since my dad couldn't afford to pay for college.

I briefly thought of applying to work at Crimson but wasn't sure I wanted someone like Ethan Cristescu as a boss. He was beautiful, but was he a good person? The jury was still out. There was something sinister about the way he and his friends had acted around me. They were too ... eager.

Later that evening, I donned my work uniform and made the short walk over to Hagen's. I was several hours into my shift when the last person I wanted to see walked through the door.

Terry Vaine was Florence's dad and the biggest scumbag I'd ever met. I didn't understand how the very worst people could sometimes have absolute gems for children. Florence more or less raised herself.

"My daughter's been staying with you the last few nights and I'm here to put a stop to it," Terry spat. He reeked of whiskey and cigarette smoke.

"Your daughter doesn't feel safe in her own home. I won't deny her a safe place," I replied, doing my best to stay calm and stand my ground when all I really wanted to do was tell Terry exactly where to shove his threats.

The hairs on the back of my neck rose right before the doors opened and ... in walked Ethan Cristescu. *What the hell was he doing here again?* I spared him a brief glance as he picked up a basket and began shopping. Don't tell me he'd decided to make this his regular place for groceries.

"You're a grown woman allowing a teenager to sleep on her couch," Terry accused. "Don't you think people will wonder what's going on there?"

"Your daughter is my friend, Mr Vaine, and like I said, I allow her to sleep on my couch because your behaviour makes her feel unsafe. If you want her to stop staying with me, then maybe you should change your ways so that you aren't scaring the life out of your daughter."

"Listen here, you interfering little bitch, I'll behave whatever way I like, and you'll quit trying to lure my kid away from me, or I'll call the police."

Okay, now I was mad. "*You'll* call the police on me? How about I call child services and inform them about the bruises on Florence's arms? Don't think I haven't noticed them."

At this, Terry lunged for me. "How dare you accuse …" His words died on his tongue because suddenly Ethan was there. He grabbed Terry by the shirt collar and shoved him away like he weighed nothing.

"Leave. Now," he roared, and the look of sheer terror on Terry Vaine's face as he stared up at Ethan was a sight to behold. He practically stumbled over his own feet to get away from him, running from the store like a bat out of hell.

Once he was gone, Ethan turned back to me. "I'm making something of a habit of saving your bacon."

I didn't like the hint of smugness in his tone. "I was handling that just fine."

"He tried to attack you. Unless you're hiding some secret Kung-Fu skills, if I wasn't here, it wouldn't have ended well for you, Sunshine."

"I don't have to know Kung-Fu to be able to defend myself," I said, folding my arms in annoyance. Ethan was right. Things could've gotten pretty ugly if he hadn't shown up when he did. Terry wasn't just scum, he also had an unpredictable temper.

Ethan stared at me for a long moment, his features indecipherable, but then his expression softened. "That's very kind of you to let his daughter stay in your apartment. I don't know many people who would go out of their way like that."

I frowned. "How did you—"

"I have excellent hearing."

"You must. You were all the way over on the other side of the store. You also got to us pretty fast. Actually, I've seen you move a little too fast a few times now."

"I ran track at school," Ethan replied with a shrug. "I've always been faster than most."

"Well," I said, clearing my throat. "Thank you for defending me, again, but what are you doing here? I'm sure there are much nicer places in this city for you to do your shopping."

"Yes, but I wouldn't get to see you if I went somewhere else," he said with a charming smile. His perfectly styled hair practically glowed under the fluorescent store lights, and the angular, sculpted lines of his jaw and broad shoulders were the stuff of most women's fantasies. Even his clothes were attractive. He wore a pristine white T-shirt—the high-quality kind rich people overpaid for from designer brands—with a fitted navy jacket and jeans that encased his long, powerful legs. He was excessively tall but somehow managed not to appear lanky. And yes, those golden eyes were his crowning feature. I wasn't sure why he insisted they were golden brown. Some weird form of modesty perhaps?

I looked down at my worn uniform and scuffed shoes, thinking about my shit job and even shitter bank balance, and realised there was no logical reason for us to be friends. We came from entirely different worlds.

I was ninety-nine percent certain Ethan Cristescu had an ulterior motive, and I was just the right level of curious and reckless to play along.

"You aren't by any chance involved in human

35

trafficking, are you?" I asked casually.

His thick eyebrows drew together. "Of course not. Why would you ask such a question?" He actually sounded offended.

"Just trying to figure out your game." I reached out and took his basket of items, then proceeded to run them under the scanner.

His lips twitched. "You think I'm here to traffic you?"

"It's one of several possibilities, but just so you know, I won't be easily kidnapped. I've got a powerful kick and I'm not afraid to bite."

"Well, as intriguing as that sounds," he said, a hint of flirtation in his tone. "I won't harm you. I'm here for friendship. Nothing more."

"Forgive me if I find that hard to believe."

"I'd just like to get to know you, Tegan."

I cocked my hip, eyeing him sceptically. "Prove it."

He leaned his impressively large hands on the counter and examined me closely. "Were you born here?"

"In Tribane? Yes, I grew up in a suburb just outside the city."

"Parents? Siblings?"

"No siblings. My dad raised me, and my mother died when I was young. What about you?"

"Delilah is my half-sister."

"The redhead from the club?"

"Yes. I have a half-brother, too, but we're not close. You could say we're somewhat … estranged."

There was a flicker of sadness in his eyes, gone as quickly as it appeared. "That must be tough."

"It is."

"What about your parents?"

"My father died a long time ago, and my mother lives

back in Romania."

"I'm sorry about your father. Do you visit your mother much?" I asked.

"Oh, yes, at least once a decade," he deadpanned.

I gave a soft laugh. "Wow, that often?"

"It's often enough for me. How did your mother die?"

I swallowed tightly, a brief image of the dark-haired woman flashing in my mind's eye. "She had cancer," I told him quietly.

He reached out and placed his hand on mine. I emitted a tiny gasp at the feel of his cool, silky palm, the pleasantness of being touched taking over. I'd been living for the better part of a year without human affection, and I didn't realise just how starved I was for it until this very moment. I met his gaze, and curiosity lay in his golden irises. I pulled my hand away from his and returned my attention to scanning his items.

"You've bought quite a bit," I commented.

"It's for Delilah. She likes to cook," he replied, and before I could react, he reached out, his knuckles brushing just below my jaw. I froze, no idea what he was doing. Then I realised he was fixing the collar on my shirt.

"It was sticking out," he explained, his cool knuckles grazing my neck one last time before he withdrew.

"Thanks," I muttered, tingles running down my spine. I hadn't … disliked it when he touched me. In fact, his touch somehow managed to override my misgivings about him.

I packed his items into a bag and rang up the total. He handed me a credit card, and it felt intentional when his fingers skimmed mine. When the transaction was complete, he slid a small business card across the counter to me. "In case you're ever in need of rescuing again," he said with a suave little grin.

"Knights in shining armour don't exist. There's always a catch," I replied as he headed for the exit.

His eyes twinkled at me. "That sounds like another challenge to prove you wrong." With that parting line, he left, and I looked down at the small black business card, feeling an unreasonable amount of excitement that he'd wanted me to have his number.

4.

I woke up to the sound of my phone ringing. Sitting, I rubbed the sleep from my eyes as I answered groggily. "Hello?"

"Hello. May I speak with Tegan Stolle?" a prim, older-sounding gentleman asked.

"Speaking."

"Ah, how do you do, Miss Stolle? My name is Marcel Girard. I'm calling about the store assistant position at Indigo. I was wondering if you could come in for an interview?"

Just like that, my spirits lifted. I couldn't believe I'd gotten a call back. "Yes, of course. I'm free today, if that's convenient?"

"Today is perfect," Marcel replied. "Around two?"

"See you then."

I hung up with a renewed sense of purpose before hopping into the shower. I blow-dried my hair, tied it up in a bun, and dressed in my nicest white shirt and grey trousers with black ballet flats. I ate a large breakfast, feeling hopeful for the first time in a while. Indigo was in a much nicer part of the city than Hagen's. It'd be good to work somewhere that wasn't constantly being robbed. There was also that odd fizzle of urgency that seemed to push me towards Indigo. Maybe I just really wanted a nice, easy job that was free of stress.

Later that afternoon, I arrived for my interview with a few minutes to spare. Chimes rang above my head as I entered the store. It was the kind of place that sold crystals, incense, angel figurines, and books about Wicca. A man sat by the register drinking a cup of tea. He looked to be about sixty years old with his grey hair tied back in a ponytail. When he spotted me, he smiled widely, but as I finished climbing the steps of the mezzanine floor and came face to face with him, he narrowed his gaze, almost in suspicion.

Um, okay.

"Hi, I'm Tegan Stolle," I began, smiling despite his wary expression. "I'm here for an interview with Marcel Girard."

He stared at me for a prolonged moment before blinking and seeming to gather himself. "Right, yes, I'm Marcel. It's a pleasure to make your acquaintance, Miss Stolle."

"Please, call me Tegan."

"Tegan, if I may be so bold, might I ask a question?" His voice was tentative and unsure. "It's of a personal nature."

"Sure," I replied, no clue what he could possibly want to ask.

"Are you Wiccan?"

My eyebrows shot right up. "No, afraid not." Wait, did he only hire Wiccans? Because if that were the case, I could definitely fake an interest.

"So, you don't ever dabble in magic?" he went on.

The way he said "magic" gave me pause. He said it like it was a real thing. As real as horticulture or artisan bread baking. I shook my head.

"Do any of your friends practice? Perhaps a roommate or a family member?"

"Not as far as I know. I don't have a roommate. The only family I've got is my dad, and he's definitely not the magic and witchcraft type."

He inhaled a deep breath, exhaling slowly. "May I be frank?"

40

I nodded, feeling puzzled. Then again, you did run into all sorts in places like this.

"Well, it's just that there's a heavy magical aura all around you, my dear. It's almost as if someone cast a spell on you, a strong one, that has been permanent for a very long time."

A spell? I had to try hard not to laugh. I was seriously attracting all the crazies lately. This guy was clearly a loon, and I was about to tell him I'd changed my mind about the job when he went on, "Could you wait here a moment? I'd like to get a second opinion on this."

"Sure, why not," I replied, bemused. He rushed off to the back of the shop, walking through a door that must have led to a storage room. A minute later, he returned with a youngish, good-looking guy with dark hair and green eyes.

"This is Gabriel," Marcel introduced. "He works here and is a highly skilled, um, *Wiccan.*"

Highly skilled Wiccan, eh? I wondered sarcastically what that entailed. Why was I even humouring this? Gabriel had a silver earring in the top of his right ear. He wore black jeans, steel toe cap boots, and a loose grey shirt.

"Gabriel, this is Tegan," Marcel gestured towards me.

Gabriel gave me a shy nod, only meeting my gaze briefly while Marcel continued talking, "I'd like you to use your expertise to determine what exactly it is that surrounds her. I can sense it's magic of some sort, but she claims she doesn't practice, nor does she know anybody who does."

Seriously, I didn't know whether I should start believing this crap or get freaked out and leave. I was being way too indulgent with Marcel. He seriously seemed like a whack job.

Gabriel took a moment to study me, his eyes tracing the lines of my shoulders and arms and the top of my head.

41

"It's a spell," he confirmed. "It was cast a long time ago by my estimation. It's strong, perhaps even intended to last a lifetime." Then he stepped up close to me and asked, "May I?" holding out his hand.

"Knock yourself out," I replied, allowing him to take my hand into his. He closed his eyes, and a zip of electricity went from his palm into mine. I yelped and backed away. "Did you feel that?"

Gabriel nodded. "Sorry, I forgot to warn you. It's just my magic recognising yours. Nothing to worry about."

"I don't have any magic."

Marcel barked a laugh. "The aura surrounding you begs to differ."

"It's a lot to take in at first, I know," Gabriel said, and something about his kind, solid voice reassured me. "But you do have magic, or at least, someone gave it to you in the form of a spell. My instincts tell me it was your mother, but it could have been your grandmother, or maybe even an aunt. I can't determine what exactly it was intended to do, but I do know that its purpose is a combination of concealment and protection."

Suddenly, I felt a chill. "My mother died when I was three. I don't have any aunts, and both my grandmothers died before I was born."

"Well doesn't that render this all the more mysterious," Marcel interjected, sounding entirely too intrigued. "I do love a good mystery." He smiled at Gabriel in silent communication. I thought I saw Gabriel shake his head at Marcel ever so slightly, but I couldn't be sure.

Marcel turned his attention back to me. "Would you allow us to try and discover what this spell is? I'm sure you'd like to know, and I'd be grateful for the practice. I'm not half as experienced as Gabriel in this field, so it would be a first for me to unravel an old spell."

I would have thought Gabriel was the less experienced one judging from Marcel's seniority in age. They probably thought I was just dying to find out about this spell. But in truth, the only reason I stuck around was for the job I came to interview for. Speaking of which, maybe I could use Marcel's sudden interest in me to my benefit.

"That depends." I replied. "Are you going to hire me for the store assistant position?"

Marcel's lips curved like he grudgingly respected my brazenness. "Well, I'd still have to conduct an interview and do a background check, but I don't see why not. Can you start tomorrow?"

"I can," I answered, smiling. Marcel grinned back at me, but Gabriel looked a little concerned. I decided not to question it. Getting this job was a stroke of luck, and it meant I could afford to keep my apartment. As far as I was concerned, it was a win-win. I didn't believe in magic, so it couldn't hurt to play along with the whole spell unravelling business.

It wasn't until later that night, as I was drifting to sleep, that I remembered the spark of Gabriel's palm against mine and wondered, somewhere in the deep recesses of my mind, if there was truth to what they told me. If someone really had cast a spell on me a long, long time ago.

***

The next day, I arrived at Indigo bright and early. The shop door was locked, so I gave a few knocks, stopping once I saw a tired-looking Marcel make his way down the mezzanine floor to let me in.

"Not a morning person?" I asked with a grin.

"Not at all," Marcel replied, yawning. "I'm much more of a night owl. Would you like a cup of coffee before we begin?"

"Yes, I'd love one."

Marcel took me through the store and to the back, down a hallway which led to a tiny staff room with a small table and two chairs. Gabriel was sitting in one of them, reading a book while sipping on a cup of coffee.

He glanced up at me briefly. "Hello, Tegan. How are you this morning?"

"I'm good, thanks. And you?"

"I'm well," he replied before returning his attention to his book. I got the impression he wasn't big on small talk but I suspected it was due to shyness rather than him being rude.

"I'm just going to nip to the bathroom before we open," Marcel said as he handed me a cup of coffee. "Be back in a moment."

I took a sip, glancing back at Gabriel. His attention remained glued to his book, but I thought he sensed me studying him because his shoulders tensed a little. In an effort to make conversation, I asked, "Do you work mostly weekdays, or do you work weekends, too?"

Gabriel raised his eyes to look at me now, closing his book. His eyes were very green, like a lush forest. "Weekends and some weekdays," he replied. "Marcel likes to have Saturday and Sunday free, so I take those shifts."

"It must be hard on your social life."

"Not really," he shrugged.

"No?"

"I'm not much of a social animal," he said modestly.

"Yeah, me neither. You're probably better off, anyway. This city is full of crazies and weirdos. Better to be a

44

homebody."

He looked at me strangely for a moment and said quietly, "Yes, you're most likely right about that."

Marcel returned then and ushered me out to the shop floor. He started by showing me how to use the cash register, but it didn't take long since the one at Hagen's was similar. Then he showed me around the bookshelves, which were divided into several sections like Self-Help, Philosophy, Religion, and, of course, a whole bunch on Magic and Witchcraft.

Next he walked me through the section of the shop that contained the jewellery, healing stones, crystals, and little collectables like angel and fairy statues.

"Well," he said. "I think that's everything. I'll be gone for the rest of the morning, but if any customers come in looking for something specific, something that isn't out here in the main shop, just go get Gabriel and he'll deal with them. We've got a room in the back with some rarer, more expensive items. Our psychic Stephanie does her readings in there, too. She comes every Wednesday from four to seven, so if anyone wants a booking with her just consult this book." He pulled out a brown leather notebook from under the register. "If the date they want is free you pencil them down for an appointment."

"Got it." I nodded.

"Great, I'll be back before lunch."

"See you then."

After Marcel left, I sat down on the stool beside the counter and breathed out a sigh. There was something very peaceful about this place. Soft, soothing music, intermingled with nature sounds, like birds cawing and trickling streams, played over the sound system. A diffuser in the corner emitted the pleasant scent of lavender and jasmine essential oils.

Things were mostly quiet until ten when a steady flow of customers began to come into the store. It was almost lunch when a woman about my age, with a choppy bob and copious amounts of black eyeliner, strode in with purpose.

"Who the hell are you?" she demanded impatiently.

I looked her up and down, taking note of her black fishnet top, red tartan mini skirt, ripped tights, and chunky New Rock boots. Her dark brown eyes and furious expression told me she was angry, and that anger appeared to be directed at me.

"Hello, a pleasure to meet you. My name is Tegan, and I just started working here today," I answered dryly.

"*You're* working here? Oh, hell no. Get Marcel for me now!" she yelled.

"He's gone out."

"For crying out loud, then get Gabriel, and hurry up about it."

I stood there a moment, folding my arms and raising one eyebrow. "What do you want Gabriel for?"

"That's none of your business. Just go and get him."

"I will if you ask nicely," I said, standing my ground. I couldn't abide rudeness, especially from a stranger.

She sighed and rolled her eyes. "Fine. Could you please fetch Gabriel for me?"

"You don't sound nice. You sound sarcastic."

She scowled, her eyebrows two severe slanted lines on her forehead. After a long moment, she spoke again, and it sounded like she was making a real effort to keep her attitude in check. "Can I speak to Gabriel, please?"

"Much better," I said with a saccharine smile before turning and walking to the back room. I knocked first, then entered when Gabriel called for me to come in. He sat on the floor with a notepad open in front of him and a pencil in hand. There were stacks of books all around him.

"Hey, sorry to bother you. There's a girl out front asking for you, and she seems kind of pissed."

His lips formed an uneasy slant. "What does she look like?"

"Short brown hair, too much black eyeliner."

Gabriel chuckled at my description and sighed. "Right, that'll be Rita."

"Rita looks like she wants to punch me in the face."

He chuckled again and rose to his feet. "You don't need to be scared of her. She's all talk, believe me." He walked out the door, and I followed behind him. When we reached the counter, Rita was leaning against it with one hand on her hip.

"Why the hell haven't I been informed about *this*?" she asked, pointing at me.

"Marcel deals with the hiring, Rita. It's got nothing to do with me," Gabriel answered in a level voice.

"I thought you guys were finally going to let me work here, but then I come in to find *her* working at the job I was supposed to be given," she complained. *Oh.* Well, that explained her hostility. I'd be mad too if I were her.

"I never heard Marcel say he was going to give you the job," Gabriel countered.

"Don't give me that. You know as well as I do that I deserve it. I've been coming here for years. I know the place inside and out." She gave me another look up and down. "This one looks like she's never stepped foot in a place like this in her entire life."

"Don't be rude, Rita," Gabriel said, and for the first time, he actually sounded angry. For a brief second, he seemed older—older by *decades*. Rita clamped her mouth

47

shut at his scolding before changing her tack. "I'm sorry, Gabe. I didn't mean to be rude. You know how much I wanted the job."

"Yeah, well," he said, rubbing a hand over his jaw. "I don't think Marcel was ever going to hire you. You annoy him too much."

"Hogwash! He loves me really," she argued, her voice sweet and flirtatious. Gabriel didn't look charmed as he stepped away, intent on returning to his quiet room full of books.

"Is there anything else you wanted? I have to get back to work."

"What kind of work? Need some help?" Rita asked eagerly.

"Just research, and no, I don't need any help. Thank you."

At this, the door chimed open and Marcel appeared. "Hello, Rita. Here to cause trouble, I suppose," he said as he removed his coat and hat.

Rita gave a smile, but it wasn't as warm as the one she'd levelled at Gabriel. It was evident that she and Marcel didn't quite get along. "Good to see you, Marcel. I'm just getting acquainted with the new girl. I am one of your best customers after all," she said, glancing back at me now. "You'll have to familiarise yourself with my shopping list."

"Happy to," I said, plastering on a polite smile. I couldn't get a proper read on her, and I was still trying to decide if she was going to be a problem for me. She wanted my job, that much was obvious, and I sure as hell wouldn't be giving it up without a fight.

"How has your day been, Tegan?" Marcel asked.

"It's been great. I've been settling in just fine," I

replied, shooting Rita a look that said I wouldn't be gotten rid of easily.

"That's good to hear. Listen, I'm going to shut up shop for lunch so we can make a start on our little study. Is that okay with you?"

Our little study? It took me a second to figure out what he was talking about, but then I remembered. *The spell.* I'd been hoping he might miraculously forget about that. "That's fine by me."

"What study?" Rita asked, sounding annoyed to be left out of the loop.

"None of your concern," Marcel replied dismissively. "Now would you be so kind as to vacate the premises? We have business to attend to."

She frowned, her jaw working while she reluctantly turned and walked out the door. Once she was gone, Marcel breathed out a long breath, turned on his heel, and looked from Gabriel to me. "So, my darlings, are we ready for some magic?"

5.

Marcel and Gabriel led me to the back room, which was kitted out in Persian rugs and big beaded cushions. There were several alchemist-style chests of drawers, and shelves containing a variety of herbs and tinctures, as well as a large bookshelf.

"Please sit," Marcel said, gesturing to a cushion. I sat as he lit some candles and waved incense around. Gabriel sat down next to me and closed his eyes. When Marcel was done fussing, he came and sat down, too, making it so the three of us formed a circle.

"Now we'll take one another's hands to solidify the connection," Gabriel said, reaching out and taking my hand in his. His palm was warm, and it made me think of Ethan's cool, silky touch the other night at Hagen's. They were so opposite, and yet, something niggled at me about the two men. They strangely reminded me of one another, and I couldn't pinpoint exactly what it was.

"Close your eyes," Gabriel went on.

Marcel began a low chant in a language I didn't recognise. Latin, maybe? Gabriel joined in. The chanting went on for about twenty minutes before they wound it down. Marcel told me to open my eyes, and I stared at him expectantly.

"Well, did you manage to unravel the spell?" *Please say yes so I don't have to endure another one of these bizarre chanting ordeals.* He and Gabriel shared a glance, and Marcel replied, "Not yet. We'll need a few more sessions before we can make a definitive conclusion."

Wonderful.

When Marcel mentioned "magic," I was hoping for the

kind that you could actually see, but no. It seemed, conveniently, that Marcel's magic was as invisible as the air we breathe. Or, dare I say it, non-existent. I didn't want to be rude, but most sane people knew that magic was the stuff of fiction. That it was the kind of thing you made up to delight children during bedtime stories.

These two men seemed to think it was very real and took it all very, very seriously.

Several days went by and I started to feel the effects of working both a night and a day shift, only getting four or five hours sleep in between. It was survivable though. It just meant I was going to have to make friends with the tired bags under my eyes.

At least I didn't have to work the night shift on Saturdays at Hagen's, and I also had Sundays and Mondays off from Indigo, which meant I could use those days to get as much sleep as humanly possible.

On Saturday, I'd finished showering and eating dinner after my last shift of the week at Indigo when Nicki showed up.

"We're going back to Crimson tonight," she declared. "And I won't take no for an answer. You bailed early last time, so you owe me."

I was about to argue with her, but Ethan hadn't visited me at Hagen's again, and something about his absence bothered me. He said he wanted to be my friend, but I hadn't seen hide nor hair of him all week. Every time I thought of him, I felt this low, nagging pull in my stomach, like I was both drawn to and repelled by him all at once. It was confusing.

"Okay," I said, and she blinked in surprise.

"Okay? Well, that was easier than I thought it would be."

She sauntered into the apartment carrying a bag of cocktail ingredients and proceeded to make us both margaritas while I picked an outfit. I finally settled on a dark red dress with the black heels I wore last time. They were the only fancy shoes I owned. I also let my hair down and put on some make-up.

"You look fabulous!" Nicki exclaimed when I emerged from my bedroom.

"Thanks." She handed me a cocktail, and I took a thirsty gulp. I was both nervous and excited about the possibility of seeing Ethan again. He was so ... unlike anyone I'd ever met before. I wanted to tell him about my new job at Indigo and what a loon my boss was, thinking I had a spell cast on me. I thought he'd get a good laugh out of it.

We took the bus to the club, same as last time, and when we finally reached the entrance, my heart skipped a beat. Ethan's dark-haired friend, Lucas, the one who made me extra uncomfortable, was standing next to the bouncer. He was talking to someone on his Bluetooth, staring off into the middle distance. I ducked my head, hoping he wouldn't notice me.

The bouncer stepped forward and asked for our IDs. I fumbled in my bag, and when I looked up, I locked eyes with Lucas. His lips curved in a grin as he continued speaking into his Bluetooth.

"Hello, Tegan," he greeted. "How are you tonight?"

"I'm good, thank you," I replied while Nicki shot me a curious look, clearly wondering how I knew him.

Lucas patted the bouncer who'd been waiting for our IDs on the shoulder. "These are friends of the boss. You can let them in."

"Friends of the boss?" Nicki leaned in to whisper.

"Yes, I randomly met the guy who owns this place last week," I explained.

She looked surprised. "You did? How?"

"He was in Hagen's and helped me get rid of this scumbag who was trying to rob the place."

Her eyebrows shot right up into her forehead. "Really? That sounds intense."

"It was."

When we passed by Lucas, he touched me gently on the arm, bending down to murmur in my ear, "Ethan is pleased you're here. He'll come find you when he has the time."

I gaped at him. "How does he know I'm here already?"

Lucas tapped his Bluetooth as I walked by him, ushered into the club by Nicki. I replayed Lucas's words in my head and tingles skittered down my spine. *Ethan is pleased you're here.* Why was I so pleased that he was pleased? It seemed that I'd already forgotten my misgivings about him, revelling, instead, in my excitement over his interest in me.

"I'm just going to visit the ladies'," Nicki said.

"I'll go get us some drinks."

I made my way through the crowded club, spotting Amanda, Susan, and Dillon on the dancefloor. Nicki hadn't mentioned they'd be here. Amanda waved to me, and I waved back. At the bar, I asked for two gin and tonics before I sensed somebody standing behind me. Somehow, I knew it was Ethan. He lightly placed his hand on my lower back, appearing at my side.

"Hello, friend." His voice was a low rumble over the club music. "Did you come to see me?"

I shook my head. "My friend Nicki invited me."

"Ah, well, in any case, I'm glad you're here."

"You are?"

"I am." He turned his attention to the barman. "Her drinks are on the house."

"You don't have to do that," I protested.

"I want to."

He gazed down at me in a way that made my skin tingle. He was so close that we were almost embracing. Not dropping my gaze, he took my hand into his, sliding his thumb along the inside of my wrist. A small, exhilarated shudder went through me, and Ethan sucked in a harsh breath. Instinctively, I leaned in closer to him like I was in a trance. *What was I doing?* There was just something so mesmerising about his golden eyes.

"Tegan, there you are!" Nicki's voice cut through the unexpectedly intense moment. How had he done that? It felt like he'd hypnotised me.

Ethan dropped my hand and moved away. "I have some business to attend to, but I'll find you later." He drifted back into the crowd, disappearing a moment before Nicki was at my side.

"Oh, you got drinks already. Perfect. I'm thirsty," she said, picking up the glass and taking a long gulp. "Who was that guy?"

"The club owner. His name is Ethan."

"That guy owns this place? Wow. No wonder Crimson is so popular. People probably come just to get a look at him."

"Yeah, probably."

"It looked like he was flirting with you."

I glanced at her now. "It did?"

"Uh-huh. You should go for it. Clear out the cobwebs," she blurted then winced, realising her insensitivity. The last person I had sex with had taken his own life, and yes, it

54

was a sore spot and I still mourned for him, but I wasn't offended by what she said. "Sorry, that was rude."

"No need to apologise. You're right. I do have a few cobwebs to clear out. I'm just not sure Ethan is the man for the job. He'd eat me alive." A soft laugh sounded from behind me, and I turned, catching a flash of red hair. Delilah, Ethan's half-sister, had just walked by. She shot me a wink as she moved farther into the club, and I grimaced. She'd obviously heard what I said.

"What's wrong?" Nicki asked when she saw my embarrassment.

"Nothing. Do you want to go dance with the others? I'll sit here at the bar."

"No way. I'm not leaving you on your own. Let's down these drinks and go dance together."

And that was how I found myself on the dancefloor at Crimson, making an effort to have fun with my friends and be carefree for once. I hated dancing when I was sober, but I was a little tipsy, so I didn't mind.

After several songs, I spotted Ethan up in the VIP section. He stood by the railing, staring down at me. Every cell in my body tightened in awareness. The way he looked at me was just so all-consuming. He was way too handsome, so handsome he seemed to be able to transfix me, hypnotise me. Acting on instinct, I left the dancefloor and climbed the steps to the VIP section. Ethan waved at the bouncer to let me through, and I went to stand next to him. He didn't speak, but there was an energy radiating off him that had pleasant goosebumps rising in my skin. His arm brushed mine, and the contact seemed intentional.

I think he wants me.

The realisation was shocking. It seemed like a forever since I had last felt desirable. I decided to go with the flow, see where the night took me. I deserved to feel good for a change, let loose, go wild. But then, my body betrayed me when I let out a massive yawn.

"Tired?" Ethan asked, his lips twitching in amusement.

"A little," I answered honestly. "I had to take on a second job, so sleep has been elusive."

"Oh? Where's the new job?" he asked, turning to me with interest now.

"It's in this little holistic store. I actually really like it there, even though the hours are rough. But, get this, my new boss is so eccentric. He thinks I've had a magical spell cast on me," I said with a laugh.

Ethan didn't laugh though. He went incredibly still. "A spell?"

"Yes. It's so silly," I rolled my eyes, but Ethan didn't drop the seriousness.

"What's your boss's name?"

"Marcel Girard. He's this old hippy-type with a ponytail."

At this, a violent look came over him. "You're working at Indigo?"

My eyebrows rose. "You know the place?"

"Yes, I know it. Tell me what exactly Marcel said to you." I didn't like how pushy he'd become. I also didn't like his perturbed expression. Had I taken crazy pills? Why was everybody acting like this whole spell thing was plausible?

I backed away from Ethan. "You know what, I think I'm going to go find my friends now."

I'd barely taken two steps back when Ethan reached out and caught my upper arm in his grip. "Tegan, this is serious. Tell me what he said."

"Let go of my arm right now," I ordered, gritting my

teeth.

"No. *Talk*."

"I'll scream," I warned, the instinct to flee strong. How did I keep forgetting that Ethan was scary? It was like his beauty dazzled me and erased my memory every time I saw him.

We stared one another down, then finally, he let go. "I'm sorry. I shouldn't have grabbed you, but your new employer is not what he seems."

"What do you mean?"

"I'll explain when you tell me what he said about the spell that was cast on you," Ethan answered calmly. I didn't want to give him what he wanted, but I was curious to know why he thought Marcel wasn't what he seemed.

I let out an aggrieved sigh. "Fine. When we first met, Marcel told me I had a magical aura, but he couldn't tell what it was. So, he got this other guy who works there, Gabriel, to see if he could—"

"Gabriel?" Ethan questioned, and several indecipherable emotions passed over his face.

"Do you know him, too?"

"I do."

"Oh, that's odd."

"Why is it odd?"

"Well, it's odd that in a city this big I met two new people who just randomly happen to know each other in the same week. You two also remind me of each other for some reason."

At this, the barest flicker of pain entered Ethan's expression before disappearing. He cleared his throat. "Was Gabriel able to decipher the spell?"

"No. They still don't know what it is, only that they think it was cast by my mother. Now tell me what you know about Marcel."

"Let's just say, you cannot associate with both him and me. You will have to make a choice."

"Okay, well, that's easy. I choose my job."

I turned to walk away but Ethan moved to block me. "I wouldn't choose so hastily."

"No? Why not?"

Ethan glanced from left to right. "We can't discuss this here. Come with me." He took my hand, swiftly leading me from the main club floor and down a corridor to a tastefully decorated office. Ethan shut the door behind him and gestured for me to sit. I perched on the edge of the couch, not allowing myself to get comfortable. I was more than a little wary about being alone in an empty office with him.

"It might seem like Marcel and Gabriel are trying to help you, but they may have ulterior motives."

"And what about you?"

"What about me?"

"Do *you* have an ulterior motive? Because I still don't entirely understand your interest in me."

"I have no motive other than curiosity. Like I already told you, I mean you no harm."

"And what's so curious about me?" I asked, folding my arms and tilting my head.

"I find it curious that you were drawn to Indigo and that you made my acquaintance within the same few days."

Well, he had me there. I was curious about that, too. The strange draw that seemed to urge me to apply for the job at Indigo was also, well, curious.

"It's difficult because there's so much I can't tell you," Ethan said in frustration as he dragged a hand through his short, thick hair. "You're not ready for the whole truth, but you need to know that choosing to continue working at

Indigo isn't the right decision. I'll give you a job here. I'll even double whatever Marcel is paying you."

My eyebrows shot up. *Double pay?* It sounded too good to be true, which usually meant it was. "That's very generous, but no, thank you." A more trusting person might've jumped at Ethan's offer, but I wasn't trusting. Far from it. In fact, his offer only made me more suspicious.

I stood, but he moved fast, appearing in front of me. "Don't leave," he murmured, gently touching my chin and tilting my head so that our gazes met. "Do you know what it feels like when I'm near you?" he asked in a seductive, entrancing voice. It made me instantly forget why I was wary of him or why I should be leaving.

"What does it feel like?" I whispered.

He lowered his mouth so that it was hair's breadth from mine. "It feels like my entire body is vibrating with the undiscovered mystery that lies inside of you."

"There's no mystery in me."

"I beg to differ." Something flashed in eyes. Hunger? His hand moved from my chin to rest against the side of my neck. "Your heart beats so fast," he sighed like it was somehow devastating and his minty breath washed over me. "Can I kiss you?" he asked, and I was sure my heart beat even faster. I wanted to kiss him, but at the same time a voice in my subconscious screamed at me that it was a bad idea.

"I don't think that would be wise," I answered, sounding far too breathy. "Also, not very *friendly*."

Ethan moved away a few inches. "Be that as it may, I look forward to kissing you, and doing other things to you, if you ever allow it." The way he looked at me made me feel naked. Vulnerable, even. I didn't like it.

"Platonic friends don't kiss or do… *other things*."

59

He studied me a moment, a look in his eyes like my resistance both impressed and surprised him. "No, they don't," he finally agreed, giving me a confident smile that had me clenching my thighs together. *No. Stand your ground. Get out of here before he obliterates your self-control to shreds.*

I cleared my throat. "Right, well, I really should get back to my friends now."

He seemed disappointed that I remained intent on leaving, his face and tone turning flat. "Very well then."

He moved away and led me from the office. As we entered the corridor, I heard shuffling coming from down the hallway. I glanced in the direction of the noise and saw that the fire exit I'd gone through last time had been left open. For some unexplainable reason, I walked towards it, hearing a feminine shriek followed by a loud gasp outside.

"Tegan, where are you going?" Ethan called, but I was already at the exit. I peeked my head around the doorframe, and the scene I was confronted with literally froze me in place. I recognised my friend Amanda even before I saw her face. There was no mistaking her long blonde hair.

Lucas's mouth was on her neck, and it looked like he was giving her the hickey of the century. What they were doing just looked so … strange. It struck me as different, not the usual sight of two people necking in an alleyway. Tiny hairs rose on my arms.

"Oh, my God."

As soon as the words left my mouth, Lucas's head snapped up, and I fell back from the shock of it.

His eyes were pure black like he was possessed by a demon. A trickle of blood ran down his chin. Amanda's eyes rolled back in her skull, as though she were completely out of it, and there was a small, bloody bite mark on her neck. My back hit something solid. I was vaguely aware that Ethan was behind me just as everything became a blur. Seconds later, I was back in his office, sprawled on the couch. I shook my head, feeling a wave of dizziness, and looked up in time to see him lock the door.

6.

"What the hell did I just see?" I asked, my voice shaky. Ethan stood by his desk, his head tilted down as he stared at the floor in contemplation.

"It appears that Lucas and your friend have been getting to know each other better."

"Riiiight," I said, blinking rapidly. He'd bitten her like ... like a vampire. *Shit, she was still out there!* I rose, rushing to the door before remembering it was locked. I turned back to him, furious. "Open this door. *Now.*"

"I can't do that, but I assure you, your friend is quite all right. She's probably enjoying a nice little high right now courtesy of Lucas's bite."

"*His bite?*"

"Correct," Ethan affirmed. "I didn't want to tell you like this, but circumstances have forced my hand." He paused and heaved a frustrated breath. He looked conflicted, like he was trying to come up with the best possible way to break some very bad news. "We aren't human, Tegan. I'm beginning to suspect you aren't either. Not entirely, anyway."

I let out a loud, manic burst of laughter as I turned back to the door and futilely turned the handle over and over. "*Ha!* Hahaha! Not human. Very funny. Where are the hidden cameras?"

I was rambling now, on the verge of losing it completely. I just really needed to get out of here. Maybe I was having a manic break. Yes, that could be it. The grief of losing Matthew combined with the stress of my night shifts and trying to keep my head above water financially had caused me to snap.

Eventually, I gave up on the door handle and sank to the floor. This was all a little more than I could take right now. A comforting hand landed on my shoulder and then Ethan was helping me up and leading me back over to the couch. I swallowed thickly and met his gaze. I didn't sense any danger from him, not in that moment anyway. He looked down at me, his expression apologetic, like he was sorry to have turned my worldview upside down in the space of a few moments. I tried to think clearly. If this wasn't a dream and I wasn't having a nervous breakdown, then I needed to know exactly what Ethan was trying to tell me.

He said he and Lucas weren't human. Okay, well, there *could* be some truth to that. For one, Ethan Cristescu moved inhumanly fast, and for two, his eyes were a shade of gold I'd never seen before, and for three, Lucas had certainly looked far from human out in the alleyway with those black demon eyes.

"If you aren't human, then what are you?" I finally whispered.

Ethan gave a sad smile. "Isn't it obvious?"

I stared at him in disbelief. "A vampire?"

"That is the modern term, yes."

"And what do you think I am? A werewolf or something?" I asked in panicked bemusement.

Ethan gave a low chuckle. "I'd place my money on a witch, or at least the descendent of one."

Okay, now I felt dizzy. "There are witches?"

"There are many, many things in this world, Sunshine."

I swallowed, shaking my head as another wave of dizziness hit me. "This is a lot to take in." A tremble of fear shot through me as I grabbed the arm of the couch to steady myself. If Ethan really was a vampire, and this wasn't some surreal, exhaustion induced nightmare, then I had to play it cool. *Real cool.*

"I have no doubt," Ethan said soothingly as he came to kneel before me.

Was I losing my mind? Was my sanity slipping? If there was a Bible in front of me right now, I'd unhesitatingly place my hand upon it and swear that I saw Lucas transformed into a monster and feeding on one of my friends. Feeling a chill, I wrapped my arms around myself.

"You have nothing to fear," Ethan went on. "We don't kill people, Tegan. At least, it is our policy not to."

"What *is* your policy?"

"To feed and wipe the memory of those we drink from when we're done."

My eyes grew wide. "You can wipe memories?"

"Yes, though not yours, apparently."

My mind whirled, going back to the night we met. He'd stared at me all intense and insisted I forget what happened. I thought he meant the robbery, but he meant *our meeting.* That was why he was so freaked out when I came to Crimson the next night and remembered him.

"You tried to do it the night we met, didn't you?"

Ethan nodded. "It's called compulsion. We can compel humans to do and see what we wish." He gestured to his gold eyes. "If you were an average human, you wouldn't be able to see my true eye colour."

"That's why you insisted they were brown," I whispered. This was all making far too much sense, and I didn't like it. At least if things didn't make sense, I could pretend I was dreaming.

"Brown eyes are much less conspicuous. Mine mark me as … other."

And by other, he meant not human. A long stretch of

silence fell. I didn't know what to do, what to say. If Ethan and Lucas were vampires, then the world was a much scarier place than I thought. And believe me, I'd already given it some fairly negative reviews. Add vampires and witches and whatever else Ethan was referring to when he said there were many, many things out there, well, I was just about ready to pass out thinking about it.

"What happens now?" I asked quietly. "You can't keep me locked in your office forever."

"I wouldn't mind keeping you forever," he replied darkly, and my heart skipped a beat. Being kept by Ethan Cristescu would be a sweet prison, but a prison nonetheless.

"I can't believe vampires are real," I said, my mind racing. My entire fact-based, scientific system of belief teetered in the balance.

Ethan reached out and ran a finger along my bare forearm. I realised it wasn't merely a caress. He was tracing the line of a vein, which somehow managed to both arouse and put me on edge. "Have you ever heard of the saying, within every myth lies a grain of truth?"

"I'd hardly call this a grain."

Ethan chuckled, the sound a pleasant rumble vibrating through me. "You are taking this all rather well, I must say."

I was? Well, at least he thought so, because personally I felt like I was losing my marbles. "How do other people take it?"

"A lot of screaming and crying, pleas to God that it isn't so. Then I typically have to use my compulsion to calm them down. It's a good thing you're acting so calm since I don't have that option with you."

"At least now I finally understand why you want to be

my friend."

"It's not the only reason," he said, his tone teasing. "There's also your stubbornness and sassy attitude, which I'm becoming quite fond of. But on a more serious note, I need to explain things to you about our existence. If you are to be one of the few humans aware of us, then you need to know that we are not the killers portrayed in your stories."

"Please do." I sat back, making a gesture for him to continue and trying my best to maintain the calm he'd just been praising me for.

Ethan eyed me closely. "As you have already deduced, I am a vampire, as is Lucas ..."

"What about Delilah?" I interrupted, thinking of her otherworldly beauty.

"Delilah is neither one nor the other. She is a dhampir, half-human, half-vampire. We share a father but have different mothers."

"You share a father? Does that mean you were born?" The idea went against the visions of coffins and the undead swirling on the periphery of my brain.

"Yes, I was born," he replied. "We're not the dead things most myths say we are. We're simply another species. It's not known how we evolved. Nobody can trace our origins that far back. We're parasitic in nature—in that we survive off human blood. Animal blood will do in a pinch, but it doesn't provide the nutrients and strength we need to operate to our highest potential. We don't need to kill when we feed. We only take a small amount, the same as what you might donate to a blood bank, and the human falls into a state of euphoria from the chemicals released in our saliva when we bite. It's similar to taking a drug like heroin, but without any of the negative side effects. At least, there are no negative effects if we only feed once for a period of a few weeks. If we feed on the same human too often, they can become addicted to our bite."

"How many of you are there exactly? I don't get how you can exist and people haven't discovered you yet."

"Many have discovered us, but our use of compulsion allows us to prevent it from becoming widespread knowledge. In the grand scale of things, there are very few of us. We make up less than half a percent of the world's population. We normally live in cities because there are more people to feed on and it's also easier for us to blend in with the crowd."

I furrowed my brow, thinking about it before I replied, "That's still almost forty million vampires in the world."

He laughed at my estimation. "Did you just do the math?"

"Maybe."

"Cute." He paused to study me, a glimmer of affection in his eyes. "The number isn't so large when you consider that our kind is spread throughout the world. Here in Tribane, there are less than a thousand of us."

"A thousand vampires are living in this city?" I gaped at him. A thousand super-fast, likely super-strong beings with fangs. A chill ran down my spine. I wouldn't be getting the sleep I needed any time soon.

"There are, but remember, we don't kill to feed, so there's no need to look so startled. Do you have any other questions?"

I thought about it for a minute, trying to recall all the myths I knew about vampires. I decided to start with the obvious. "Can you go out during the day?"

Ethan shook his head. "Sadly, no. Sunlight is extremely uncomfortable for us, and our skin is highly sensitive to its rays. We don't burst into flame or anything quite so dramatic, but we do get sick if we stay in it for too long. Thus, we are nocturnal by nature."

"Do you eat regular food, too, or just blood?"

"Just blood." That sounded kind of depressing. Food made life so much more interesting.

"Don't you get bored consuming the same thing over and over?"

"On the contrary, every human's blood tastes different. Some are cheap sauvignon blanc, others expensive champagne. Going by how you smell, yours, I imagine, would be quite something."

"Well," I said, feeling a shiver. "You can keep on imagining because I'm never letting you drink it."

Ethan's eyes gleamed as though I'd just given him the most delicious challenge. "We shall see."

My shiver intensified as I swiftly changed the subject. "How often do you need it?"

He casually lifted a shoulder. "Once every few days normally, depending on the individual."

"Do you sleep in a coffin?"

His eyes were heated now and his voice unexpectedly sultry. "I sleep in a bed. Would you like to see it?"

I rolled my eyes as I tried to suppress the wave of desire washing over me. I wondered what his bedroom was like. Ugh, what was wrong with me? I should be screaming at the top of my lungs, begging to get out of this room, yet here I was, interviewing him like I was the host of some late-night talk show.

"That won't be necessary," I finally replied, and he smirked. "You said that Delilah is half-human. Does that mean vampires and humans can reproduce?"

Now he shot me a lazy grin. "Yes, we can reproduce. Although the infant mortality rate for vampire/human pregnancies is extremely high. Very few of the infants survive past their first year, even when they do make it to being born. Delilah is a rare and lucky case."

"Are you immortal?"

"No, but vampires can live very long lives. Sometimes up to a thousand years."

"Wow, that's ... incredible. How old are you?"

"Old enough," he stated, evading my question. I arched an eyebrow and folded my arms. He sighed. "I'll be two hundred and seventy-seven this year."

My mouth fell open. "What?!" That was old. *Too* old. I began to see him in a whole new light. "You're old enough to be my grandfather several times over," I blurted.

He moved closer, his voice washing over me as his breath hit the back of my neck. "Do I look like your grandfather, Tegan?"

Shivers encapsulated me as I swallowed thickly. "No, I guess you don't."

A moment of thick silence ensued, and my head filled with even more questions. Imagine living that long, through all of that history. The world must seem so different from his perspective. My eyes met his, and I saw his nostrils flare as he breathed me in. "Can I see your fangs?" I whispered. There was a flash in his eyes, then a low growl rumbled from the back of his throat. Wow, I'd never actually heard a person growl before.

I didn't dislike it.

"It is a very intimate thing for us to reveal our fangs. It's a sign that we're attracted."

My eyes practically bugged out of their sockets. "Oh!" I exclaimed. "Well, never mind then. Forget I asked."

"You may see them if you wish ..." he murmured.

I couldn't help but look at his mouth as two white

fangs elongated down and over his lips. A foreign urge made me want to reach out and touch them, but I resisted. I turned away, feeling overwhelmingly nervous and shy all of a sudden. "You can put them away now." Ethan gave a husky laugh, and the next time I looked at him his fangs had retreated inside his mouth.

"Now I must ask you for something," he said, his voice so quiet it was almost a whisper. "Will you promise to keep this to yourself, to not tell anyone of what we are?"

The way he posed the question made it seem like I could be all, *Sorry, no. I'm off to shout your secret from the rooftops,* and he'd be like, *Oh no, please don't do that.* In reality, he'd probably have to kill me.

And that right there was a sobering thought.

I levelled him with a steady look. "I promise. Your secret's safe with me."

He reached out and lifted my hand. I watched in fascination as he brought it to his lips and pressed a delicate kiss to my skin. The sexy yet gentlemanly gesture took me by surprise. I inhaled a sharp breath at the unexpected, pleasurable feeling of his mouth on me. "Thank you, Sunshine."

I shot him a sassy grin. "You're welcome, Blondie."

He grinned right back at me. "I'll take you home now if you'd like."

I nodded, and he led me from his office. My entire worldview had tilted since I entered this room. Now I had to come to terms with the fact that there were far more things out there than my small mind could even conjure. I pulled my phone from my pocket, finding several missed calls and a text from Nicki.

Nicki: Where have you gone? Amanda's completely out of it. We need to bring her home. Text me when you see this. I'm worried about you.

I typed out a quick reply.

Tegan: I'm so sorry! I was in the VIP section. Please let me know if Amanda's okay.

If what Ethan said was true, then she should recover well enough from Lucas's bite, so long as he didn't feed from her a second time. Ethan led me to his SUV, opening the passenger side door and helping me in. We got stuck in traffic on the way to my apartment, and I noticed Ethan kept glancing suspiciously in his rear-view mirror.

"Is everything all right?" I asked, wondering what had him so on edge.

He continued to frown at the mirror. "Do you see that green van behind us?"

"Yes."

"We're being followed."

"Followed by who?"

"Not sure, probably slayers."

I blinked several times. "Slayers? As in Buffy?"

"Not at all so palatable I'm afraid. I haven't had the chance to explain to you yet, but there are groups of humans aware of our existence, hostile groups whose sole purpose is to bring about our extinction."

I absorbed this information as Ethan made a sharp turn around the next corner. Followed by another and then another. All the while the green van made the exact same swift turns on the road.

So, we were being followed then.

7.

Ethan didn't drive to my apartment. Instead, he brought us to the outskirts of the city. It took about twenty minutes, but still that green van blatantly followed us. I grew more nervous by the second. There could be ten or more people huddled in there, and there was only one of Ethan. I doubted I'd be much use in a fight. And what if they mistook me for a vampire? Would I die with a wooden stake to my heart?

"Are stakes as lethal to you as the myths say they are?"

"Yes, that one is true. Although the problem for slayers is that we can move much faster than the average human. It's a momentous feat if they get to us in time. They might be aiming directly for our hearts one second, but in the same amount of time we could already be ten yards away." There was a pause as he looked from the road to me. "Are you worried?"

"No." I lied, a clot of fear clogging my throat.

He sent me a reassuring smile. "There's absolutely no need to worry, Tegan. I won't let anything happen to you." His voice was steel and undiluted power. I supposed a vampire could get fairly good at fighting off slayers with two hundred and seventy-odd years of practice.

If you told me earlier today that this was a thought I'd be having I would've laughed you out of the room.

"You see the licence plate?" Ethan asked.

"What?"

"The licence plate on the van. It contains the letters DOH. That's how I know they're slayers. They call themselves the Defenders of Humanity. DOH for short."

"There must be a lot of money in the slaying business,"

I joked anxiously. "It's only the big shots who can afford snazzy personalised licence plates."

Ethan laughed at that, loud and boisterous. "Lucas likes to call them Dickhead Onanistic Humans."

"Onanistic?"

"It means to be fond of touching oneself," he explained.

"Ah, I see."

"I find it amusing," Ethan said, chuckling away.

"Maybe that's because you developed your sense of humour back in the eighteenth century," I teased.

He smiled wide now. "I like it when you give me shit. It's fun. Hold on." Before I had a chance to ask why, he swerved the car around a corner and into an abandoned looking industrial estate. Ethan turned off his headlights, plunging us into darkness.

"I'm going to have to fight them," he said, turning to me. "You must promise me that you'll remain inside the car until it's finished. I'll make sure to keep them as far away from you as possible."

I gulped, my mouth suddenly sandpaper-dry. "Do you really have to fight them? I mean, do you even know how many there are?"

"They usually hunt in groups of five or six. Don't worry, I could handle twice that."

"You could?" I asked, stunned.

Ethan didn't answer. Instead, he deftly swung the car around in a circle and stopped so that we were facing the van of slayers. I started to hyperventilate. He placed his hand on the door handle, turning back to me a moment. "How about a kiss for good luck?" With his carefree attitude, you wouldn't think he was about to take on a group of slayers intent on his demise.

"How about a slap?"

He gave a devilish grin. "Next time then."

There was a blur of movement as Ethan emerged from the car, using his vampire speed. He stopped when he reached the middle-point between his SUV and the slayers' van. The full moon was the only source of light. I wrapped my arms around myself, clutching tightly to the seat belt strapped across my body. I had never been so on edge in my entire life.

Ethan stretched out his arms and flexed his hands in preparation as though to rile them. The van doors slid open and three men got out on either side.

Three and three equalled six against one. Each of the slayers was tall. Oh, and did I mention that every one of them had an array of weapons strapped to their chests? The slayers made a V-shaped formation around Ethan. He loosened his shoulders, readying himself for the challenge.

A second later, the first slayer attacked. He launched his blade at Ethan, who sped to the left, avoiding it. Next, the slayer grabbed something from his chest strap. It took me a moment to realise it was a wooden stake. He launched it through the air at Ethan, and a manic laugh escaped me when Ethan's hand shot out, snatching the stake in mid-air like a frisbee. He tossed it aside and flew at the slayer as two others tried to attack him from behind.

"Look behind you!" I yelled from my open passenger window.

He must've heard me because he turned around swiftly, grabbing one of the slayers by the throat. And then, well, things got a little too *real*. Ethan's fingers sank into the man's throat like they were sharp claws. Blood sprayed, the liquid a black ink in the dark. I yelped in sheer terror as he proceeded to rip his throat out.

Suddenly, my fear transferred onto Ethan. He wasn't the mysterious, mildly flirtatious vampire I thought he was. He was a cold-blooded killer vampire. He turned around swiftly to meet his next victim. For less than a fraction of a second, I could see him clearly in the moonlight. His fangs were out and his eyes were black as coal. Just like Lucas when he'd been feeding on Amanda.

I watched in terror as he sank his fangs into another man's throat before tossing his limp body aside. He made short work of most of the others, leaving only one. This slayer seemed to be the best fighter of the six, and he was fast enough to keep up with Ethan. Unfortunately, he was still human. Ethan caught up with him, punching the slayer right in the face, possibly breaking his nose judging from the spray of blood. The slayer sprawled unconscious on the ground as Ethan moved in for the kill. My heart pumped faster than ever before. Having witnessed more death tonight than I ever imagined I would in a lifetime, I opened the car door.

"Don't!" I shouted as I emerged from the SUV.

Ethan's shoulders tensed, stilling at the sound of my voice. "Get back inside!" he commanded.

"Don't kill him," I begged. "He's no threat to you anymore."

"I have to," he responded, sounding tired, pained, and a little remorseful. He hadn't planned to kill these men tonight. They were the ones hunting him, but their hunt backfired.

"Ethan—"

"I said get back in the car, Tegan. I have to finish this."

On instinct, I ran to him and placed myself in the way of the unconscious slayer. I couldn't bring myself to touch Ethan because I was still terrified after seeing him kill. I put my hands out, gesturing for him to stop and try to see things from my perspective.

"What difference will it make if you spare one life out of six?"

"You don't understand how this works. If I don't kill him now, he'll keep coming back for me until one of us is dead."

"Or maybe he'll see that you showed him mercy and change his perception of vampires," I countered.

"You're foolish if you believe that."

"Kill this man and you'll never see me again," I threatened and that seemed to strike a chord in him.

A long moment of quiet elapsed before he relented, "Fine. I'll let him live if that is what you want."

"It is," I said, my voice jittery from fear and adrenaline.

"Very well then." He turned slowly and began walking back toward his car.

"Are you just going to leave them here like this?" I asked, unable to look at the bodies littering the ground. If I did, I'd be in danger of throwing up. "Won't somebody find the bodies and call the police?"

"The DOH keeps tracking devices in all of their vehicles. Once they see that this van has been stationary in a remote area for a period of time, backup will come. Then they'll take away the bodies."

"You seem experienced with this kind of thing," I said, my stomach turning.

"I've been defending myself and my species for a very long time. It's only natural that I have also learned the procedures of my enemy."

We reached his SUV, but I hesitated to get in. Seeing him kill was terrifying, and though technically, I knew he was only defending himself, it still made me incredibly wary. Strike that, I was horrified. He said that vampires didn't kill to feed, but they still *killed*. At least, Ethan did. What he'd done tonight was the behaviour of a seasoned professional, not a novice.

I considered calling a taxi, but I doubted they'd come all the way out to this creepy abandoned place. No, the best course of action was to allow Ethan to drive me back to the city. Then I could figure out how to rid him from my life for good. Because I sure as hell wanted no part in a world that involved vampires and slayers, witches and mysterious spells. I wanted to go back to the safety and security of normality.

Reluctantly, I climbed into the passenger seat and strapped on my seatbelt, trying not to fixate on how Ethan was covered in the blood of the men he'd just murdered.

"I'll take you home now," he said in a quiet, solemn voice.

8.

For most of the journey back to the city I just sat there, unmoving. Maybe it was the overload of information that caused me to zone out.

In a single night I discovered that, one, vampires were real. Two, they drank human blood. Three, their eyes went black when they fed. Four, they were adept at killing humans when outnumbered. And five, there was an organised group of slayers which was actively trying to wipe them out.

A single image kept replaying over and over in my head; Ethan's hands gripping that slayer's neck. He quite literally tore the man's throat out. It was like something from a horror movie.

After several minutes of staring dead-eyed at the dashboard, I regained my focus and returned to the present. "Country Roads" by John Denver played on the radio. The song couldn't be more benign, but right then it was terrifying. Ethan's attention was fixed straight ahead like a serial killer who liked listening to country and western music after a kill.

He glanced at me out the corner of his eye, flecks of blood spattering his face. "You're in shock," he stated. "I can bring you to my home and take care of you there. You shouldn't be alone tonight."

"No, thank you. I want to go to my apartment. And I'm not in shock. I'm fine."

"You don't look fine. You look like you're about to be sick."

"I assure you," I told him calmly but firmly. "I'm perfectly well."

A while later, we arrived at Singh Square. I still hadn't given him my full address, and thankfully, he didn't ask for it. Despite my protestations of being fine, I wasn't. Far from it. But I needed to fake it for now, otherwise, I might break down and curl up into a distressed ball in the corner of his car and never leave. As soon as the SUV came to a stop, I was out of there. Ethan caught my wrist before I had a chance to fully escape.

"You don't need to fear me," he said, voice low.

I plastered on a tight smile. "I don't fear you."

"I can smell that you do," he countered, nostrils flaring. I stiffened in self-consciousness. He could smell how I felt? Obviously, there was a lot more I needed to learn about vampires than the small bit he'd told me tonight.

"Okay, I'm scared of you," I admitted. "But can you blame me?"

Ethan let out a frustrated sigh. "Did I not let that slayer live because you asked me?"

"Why yes, how charitable of you." I didn't mean to sound so sarcastic, but I tended to get bitchy when I was frightened or stressed.

"It *was* charitable. The man wanted me dead. He still does. And I'm going to have the headache of dealing with him when he comes for me again, something I will endure *for you*."

I swallowed tightly, not knowing how to respond. "I need some time to digest all of this. It's a lot to absorb in one night." My voice was quieter now.

Ethan let go of my wrist, his expression tender. "You're right. Go home. Get some rest, but please, don't try to run from me. We will achieve wonderful things together if you just give me a chance."

He sounded so certain. Could vampires see into the

79

future? I had no idea. Turning, I hurried down the street, making sure Ethan had driven away before I headed to my building.

I fumbled in my bag for my key and opened the lobby door, almost jumping out of my skin when I caught sight of him standing across the street.

"How did you ... You followed me!" I yelled accusingly at him. He glanced from left to right, then walked across the street, approaching me hesitantly.

"Please don't freak out," Ethan said, hands in the air. "I wanted to make sure you got to your apartment safely. The DOH doesn't take kindly to humans who associate with vampires. They might've had another vehicle following us."

"So those crazies could be coming for me next?" I could almost taste the sharp tang of fear on my tongue.

"They won't get to you. I won't let that happen," he reassured me, and my skin tingled with the protectiveness in his voice. I couldn't help it. One part of me feared him, while the other part ... *wanted* him. I had to keep reminding myself that the world's greatest predators were often quite beautiful.

"Okay, well, you can go now. I'm not inviting you in."

"That particular myth isn't true. I don't need an invitation. I would like one though."

"Why?"

"To ensure there are no slayers already waiting inside."

"So, purely for security reasons?"

"Purely," Ethan nodded.

My gut clenched. I wasn't a huge fan of letting him inside, but if some slayer was laying in wait for me in my apartment, then I certainly didn't want to face them alone.

I made a sweeping hand gesture. "In that case, come on

in."

Ethan walked ahead of me as I directed him to the sixth floor. I felt his eyes on my profile as I stared straight ahead, focusing intently on the doors of the lift. When they pinged open, Ethan emerged first. He paused outside the door of my apartment, sniffing the air and listening intently. He gave a nod for me to unlock it. I did, and he pushed it open. Ethan stood on the threshold, going freakishly still.

"What is it?" I whispered. "Is someone in there?"

"No," he replied, looking perturbed. "It's just that your apartment smells like ... death."

You'd know all about that now wouldn't you, I thought snidely.

"My boyfriend," I said, swallowing down a lump in my throat. "He passed away in here a few months ago."

Ethan's expression softened. He looked taken aback by what I said. "My condolences. How did he—"

"Drug overdose," I answered flatly as I went to put my bag and coat on the hanger. "The coroner said it was a suicide, most likely." I paused, my brow furrowing. "How can you smell death?"

"My senses are extremely heightened," he explained, crossing the threshold and stepping inside. "I can smell traces of things that occurred months and even years into the past."

Well, that was both impressive and unsettling. "Is that how you could smell my fear, too?"

"Yes."

I chewed on my lip as I went to turn on the kettle for my nightly tea and Turkish Delight ritual. Ethan didn't make any move to leave, even though he'd determined no one had broken into my apartment. Instead, he closed the door behind him.

81

"Would you mind if I used your bathroom to clean up?"

"Go ahead."

When he returned, the blood was gone from his face and hands. He lowered himself onto the couch, and I got the sense that he was taking everything in. Self-consciousness nipped at me. My place was small, so there wasn't a whole lot to take in. Would he judge how cheap and worn my furniture was? I'd never really made enough money to own nice things, but I suspected Ethan Cristescu lived in a place full of luxury.

Then again, he'd been alive for almost three centuries. That certainly gave you enough time to amass some wealth. He eyed my bookshelf. "You have varied interests." He scanned the weathered spines, from history to science to modern psychology. Most of my books were second-hand or borrowed from the library.

"I didn't get the chance to go to college, but I like to learn, so I read a lot. I try to learn about a few new topics each year."

"That's an admirable goal. Few people realise that learning is a lifelong pursuit."

"I agree," I said as I approached with refreshments.

"Turkish Delight?" Ethan asked as I placed two cups of tea down on the coffee table. He might've been a vampire, and a part of me might've been terrified of him, but I still had manners. I always offered guests tea. The hospitality was ingrained in me, whether or not my guest was a homicidal maniac who only consumed blood.

"I'm a bit addicted," I admitted.

"Thank you for the tea, but I don't drink it."

"Just let me pretend for a few minutes that everything is normal," I said, an edge of desperation in my voice.

"Normal is overrated, but I will feign drinking tea if it comforts you."

"It does," I said, taking a bite of the sweet, rosewater scented confection.

"I spent time in Constantinople as a young man," Ethan spoke quietly, his eyes on my throat as I swallowed. Despite everything, something was soothing about his voice. "Around the same time those candies became popular, funnily enough. It was an interesting period. The Ottoman Empire was nearing its decline, and there was much change in the air."

I couldn't help but stare at him in awe. Here was a man who'd lived through so much. Part of me wanted to stay awake all night and pick his brain. "What was the world like back then?"

"It was a lot less hygienic, that was for sure," he said, surprising a laugh out of me. "People were more savage, too, but the world required savagery then in a way it doesn't anymore. For the most part, at least. I've lived through periods of war and strife when to kill was necessary, rather than the depraved act of a psychopath." He eyed me pointedly, and I knew what he was trying to say. He was trying to show me that yes, he killed people, but not because he enjoyed it. And maybe I was being naïve, but I started to understand. If I'd lived through a period of violent war, perhaps I'd have killed people, too.

Several moments of silence passed before he spoke again. "With your permission, I'd like to try something."

"What do you want to try?"

His eyes flashed eagerly. "I want to level the full force of my compulsion on you and see if it works."

I clearly needed to get my head checked because that sounded kind of sexy.

I took a sip of tea because my mouth had gone decidedly dry all of a sudden. "Okay, but no funny business."

My answer seemed to please him because the hint of a smile graced his lips as he turned to face me fully. "No funny business," he promised before taking the teacup from my hand and placing it down on the table, his fingers a cool caress against my skin. Then he clasped either side of my face in his palms, and a flutter went through me at the connection. "Look into my eyes," he whispered.

I did as he requested, though it was hard to stare right into them. They were too overwhelming—like staring directly into the sun. There was a flash of mischief in his gaze when he spoke and his voice was mesmerizingly husky. "Tegan," he said. "Take off your dress."

At this, I gave a loud scoff, "No chance."

He grinned. "It was worth a try." His hands slid from my cheeks, briefly grazing my neck, before falling away completely. I instantly missed his touch. What was wrong with me?

"I really am immune." I wondered what exactly it was that made me resistant to his compulsion. Marcel and Gabriel might very well be right about my mother casting a spell on me. Did that mean she was a witch? I'd been so young when she died that I barely had any memories of her.

"It seems so," Ethan agreed. He didn't sound annoyed. He sounded impressed as he stared at me like I was some rare and precious gem on display in a fancy museum. "Come here," he whispered, and though his compulsion didn't work on me, something else did. There was something about him that drew me in, and his open arms were a comfort I couldn't seem to resist in that moment. I shifted closer, allowing him to envelop me in his solidity

84

and strength.

"Tell me about him," he murmured as he traced relaxing circles on my bare arm.

"About who?"

"The man who died here."

My heart gave a swift clench at his request. "His name was Matthew," I said quietly. "We weren't together long, but I did love him. It's still hard for me to believe that he killed himself."

"People commit suicide for all manner of reasons," Ethan murmured.

I closed my eyes, willing away the emotion threatening to clog my throat. "He was a sensitive soul, and he had a sadness in him. I just didn't realise the true extent of it until he was gone. We spend so much time being busy, working and trying to make ends meet, not paying full attention to the people we treasure most. All the while, there's this inner turmoil that they're struggling with and you're completely clueless." Unbidden, a tear fell down my cheek. Ethan reached out and wiped it away with his finger. I didn't open my eyes, choosing instead to enjoy the simple comfort of being held.

I didn't intend to fall asleep, but the next thing I knew it was morning and I was waking up alone on my couch as sunlight streamed in through the curtains. On the coffee table lay a note written in a beautiful cursive script.

Dear Tegan,

My apologies for departing before you awoke, but I needed to leave before sunrise. I'd like you to come to the club tonight at sundown to discuss some outstanding matters.

Yours sincerely,

Ethan.

P.S. You are even more delectable when you sleep.

Butterflies fluttered through me at that last line. But what did he mean by outstanding matters? It felt a bit ominous. After taking a shower and dressing in some leggings and a knit top, I found my phone and dialled Amanda's number. I needed to speak to her to see if she was okay. Nicki said in her text last night that she was out of it, but I wasn't entirely sure what that meant.

The phone rang a few times before she picked up, sounding tired. "Hello?"

"Hey, Amanda, it's Tegan. Um, how are you?" I asked awkwardly. We'd never been particularly close, so she had to think it was odd that I was calling her.

"I'm okay," she answered warily. "A little hungover from last night, but otherwise, I'm good."

"You are?" I said, my relief evident.

"Of course. What's going on? Why are you calling me? You never call me."

"Well, I just noticed that you went off alone with that guy last night and—"

"You mean Lucas? Yeah, we made out a little. He's hot. I gave him my number. Fingers crossed he calls."

So, they really could wipe memories. Amanda had no clue that Ethan's friend sank his fangs into her last night. "Yeah, fingers crossed," I said, not meaning it in the slightest. If anything, I had my fingers crossed that he wouldn't call. I didn't want Amanda getting addicted to vampire bites like Ethan said could happen. "Well, I better go. Talk soon, yeah?"

"Sure," she replied. "I'm really glad we're speaking again, Tegan. We all missed you."

There was a knock on my door as soon as I hung up the phone. When I opened it, I found Florence standing on my doorstep, glancing anxiously from side to side.

"Can I come in?" she asked, looking tetchy.

"Sure," I said, standing aside. She hurried in, and I closed the door behind her. "What's up?"

Florence chewed her lower lip. "I'm so s-s-sorry about my dad. He said he came to see you."

I reached out and clasped her shoulders, levelling her with a serious look. "Hey, you don't need to apologise. Not for him. Not ever. And if you want to hang out here today feel free. I'm off work so I was planning on making all my favourite comfort foods and having a movie marathon." After last night's world tilting experience, I needed a day of rest and indulgence.

Florence smiled. "That sounds amazing." Then she frowned, her eyes moving intently from my shoulders to the top of my head. "Are you okay?"

"Yes, why do you ask?"

She blinked, then shook her head. "Nothing. Don't mind me. Comfort food and a movie marathon sound amazing."

"Great. I'll go get started on the food."

***

Later that day, I left Florence napping on my couch as I headed out to meet Ethan. Whether I liked it or not, I'd taken a misstep into a brand-new world, and though it was scary, I needed to be a grown-up about it. Face whatever was to come head-on, even though a part of me just wanted to run away in terror.

As I waited at the bus stop, I locked eyes with a man standing outside a building across the street. He was handsome, with light brown hair in a crew-cut, dark eyebrows, and bright blue eyes. There was a sort of military vibe about him. He was tall and well built, and he looked familiar. He stared at me intently, as though he recognised me.

Then, just as my bus arrived, the penny finally dropped. A chill ran down my spine because I'd seen the man before. He was the slayer, the one I begged Ethan not to kill. The only man left alive in that industrial estate last night. And just like Ethan told me, he obviously wasn't going to quit hunting him until one of them was dead. Wait, was he hunting me now, too? Ethan said they didn't take kindly to humans who associated with vampires. His intent stare was creepily sinister, never leaving me as I climbed on the bus, paid my fare, and took a seat.

I glanced out the window and there he was, still eyeballing me. Some kind of intention lay in his eyes, and I worried it was a bad intention. I couldn't believe he was gunning for me after I convinced Ethan to spare his life.

Ungrateful bastard.

I was still on edge when I arrived at Crimson. I pressed the buzzer on the big steel door, and it opened a moment later, revealing Delilah. She wore tight pale jeans and a black string top with a pair of bright pink Sketchers. Ethan said she was half-vampire and half-human. I wondered how old she was.

"Hello, Tegan," she greeted, a knowing look in her eyes. Ethan had clearly filled her in on last night's events.

"Delilah, hi. I'm supposed to be meeting with Ethan."

"I know," she replied. "Come on in."

The club was empty. I imagined it didn't open for another hour or two. Delilah led me past the bar and to the corridor where Ethan's office was located. Just before we reached the room, she turned back to me, her expression serious. "A word of warning. We have guests."

Before I could ask her who the guests were, she pushed the door open, and I laid eyes on the last two people I expected to find in the office of Ethan Cristescu.

Marcel and Gabriel.

9.

They sat in the two chairs directly opposite Ethan's sleek, imposing desk, while Lucas and another man sat on the leather couch. A sliver of guilt ran through me. Had I gotten Marcel and Gabriel into trouble through their association with me? I felt like a walking, talking smashed mirror.

Seven years bad luck.

Delilah closed the door behind us once we'd entered the room. "What's going on here?" I asked cautiously. Ethan stood at the head of his desk, a hint of warmth entering his eyes when he saw me. I thought of last night and how I'd fallen asleep in his arms. Butterflies flitted through me at the memory.

"Tegan, please take a seat."

I took the empty chair next to Gabriel while I continued to eye Ethan. "Why have you brought Marcel and Gabriel here?"

Marcel didn't look happy, while Gabriel stared at Ethan with an expression that brought the phrase *if looks could kill* to mind. Ethan appeared unaffected by the obvious hostility in Gabriel's glare.

Ethan cleared his throat before addressing me. "As you have recently discovered, we vampires are not merely the creation of myth and legend. We are very real, and our kind has populated the city of Tribane for many centuries now. I've told you some things about our species, but not nearly all of it, and those are the outstanding matters that need to be addressed." He paused a moment, and I gave a little nod for him to continue.

"Through your discovery of our existence you have

inadvertently become involved in our society, and so, you must know what this involvement entails. There are rules to this world, and those rules need to be followed." Ethan's voice was direct and informative, devoid of the affection he sometimes showed. "For you, this city is open. As a human, you're not attached to our world, and therefore, are not obligated to obey our rules. You may come and go as you please. But for us, there is segregation."

"Segregation?" I asked, tensing. That word rarely had positive connotations.

"You're familiar with the Hawthorn I presume?" Ethan went on. "The river that runs through Tribane, splitting it in half."

"Yes."

"The south side of the Hawthorn is vampire territory, while that which lies to the north belongs to the slayers, the dhampirs, and," he glanced at Marcel with a wry expression, "the magical families."

My mind was a labyrinth of shock, amazement, and confusion. There were magical families? That meant witches and warlocks, right?

"Okay, so why exactly do I need to know all this?"

"Because," Ethan replied, "in a very short space of time you have caught the interest of two opposing parties and there has to be a reason for that. I don't believe in coincidence, not this sort anyway."

"Yeah, well, I didn't believe in vampires two days ago, but look at me now, all entangled in some sort of supernatural politics," I joked. Nobody laughed. *Wow, tough crowd.*

"Even so, we must get to the bottom of this and come to an agreeable conclusion. Now, if I might explain," he looked to Marcel seemingly for permission. Marcel gave a swift nod of his head. "Tegan, your new employer here, Mr Marcel Girard, proprietor of Indigo and a warlock of the Girard magical family, is loyal to the governor of North Tribane, Mr Siegfried Pamphrock. Pamphrock is a dhampir and leader of the DOH." Ethan addressed Marcel again, a vaguely satisfied expression on his face. "Tegan came into contact with your Defenders of Humanity last night, Mr Girard. A terribly messy business."

"Yes," Marcel said. "A team was sent to clean up that very mess early this morning."

"Good, good," Ethan replied with frightening cheeriness. "Now, where was I? Oh yes, so, Mr Girard's business partner here, Gabriel Forbes," he pronounced the name slowly, "is a dhampir and a warlock, and therefore his loyalties lie, too, with Governor Pamphrock."

Ethan gave him something of a weighted glance, while Gabriel frowned back at him. There had to be some sort of history there.

"Wait a minute," I said, my brow furrowing in confusion. "You said that all dhampirs are enemies of vampires and live on the north side of the river, but isn't Delilah a dhampir? And another thing, if dhampirs are the offspring of vampires, then why are they also your enemies?" I was proud of myself for picking up on the inconsistency.

"Delilah is an isolated case," Ethan replied, taking a moment to glance at his half-sister with genuine affection. "Our father was a very powerful man when he was alive, and she was his only daughter. That made her special, so she was raised with vampires on vampire territory. Normally, dhampirs are rejected by our race because their blood isn't pure. They're raised by their human parent after they're born, and in most cases, they're taught by their

92

human mother or father to despise vampires because their vampire parent rejected them. A lover scorned and all that. Once fully grown, a young dhampir is normally headhunted by the DOH and recruited into their organisation to kill vampires. It's highly important for them to recruit dhampirs since it's believed that they possess all of the strengths of a vampire with none of the weaknesses. For example, our sensitivity to sunlight is cancelled out in a dhampir by their human genes. Also, they only require a minuscule amount of blood to survive and can consume human food. The DOH was created by a dhampir, but it is largely made up of human slayers since dhampir births are few and far between." Ethan stopped speaking, and the room fell into silence.

I glanced at Marcel and Gabriel, both of whom sat tensely in their seats. I couldn't believe that Marcel was a warlock and Gabriel a dhampir warlock. Aside from their insistence about the spell cast on me, they just seemed so … normal.

The gap in conversation gave me a moment to clarify everything in my head.

"So, if this Pamphrock guy is the head of the DOH, then who is the leader of the vampires?" I asked.

"That would be Sir Howard Herrington. He would be akin to your city mayor. He governs over vampire territory, everything that lies to the south of the Hawthorn."

"Sounds sufficiently important and terrifying," I replied, unable to resist. When I was stressed, sarcasm just seemed to sputter out of me like a leaky pipe. Gabriel shot me a side glance, and I noticed his lips twitch ever so slightly in amusement. At least somebody found me funny. Ethan glowered at me, unimpressed.

"To get to the point," Ethan went on. "The problem

that arises here is quite the anomaly. In general, very few humans know of our existence. The exceptions lie mostly with those recruited into the DOH, or if they are a member of one of the twelve magical families. You, Tegan, are not a slayer nor a magic holder, and so, we must decide what to do about you. This gentleman here," he gestured to the man beside Lucas, "is David Rollans. He's one of our rare neutral vampires and is loyal to neither Pamphrock nor Herrington. Due to his position as neutral, David is to be our mediator here today. His presence is required for Marcel and Gabriel to come onto vampire territory. If he weren't here, their crossing the river would be seen as an act of open aggression and would have to be dealt with accordingly. In the same way that the presence of the slayers who followed us last night was a hostile act. When an individual or a group of individuals from either side crosses the river, they are, in essence, declaring war."

Jesus. That was … intense. I let the information sink in, finally understanding why Ethan acted so violently last night when he fought the slayers. I realised that my apartment was in vampire territory. Was that bad or good? I couldn't decide.

A gentle knock sounded on the door, and a leggy blonde entered wearing a mini dress with red high heeled boots. I recognised her as one of the club's bartenders. She carried in a tray of drinks and set them down on Ethan's desk, slower than necessary, as if she were giving him time to admire her plentiful assets. A bolt of jealousy shot through me. It seemed I was possessive of Ethan. Go figure.

Ethan picked up one of the drinks and offered it to Marcel. He took it, but when Ethan offered one to Gabriel, he declined. Next, he offered one to me, and I took it

94

gladly. I definitely needed a drink. It was some sort of whiskey cocktail, and it burned as it went down. The blonde sauntered out of the room, hips swaying from side to side.

"So, what now?" I asked, glancing around the room.

"If I might make a suggestion," David Rollans spoke up, addressing Ethan. "There may be a way for the young lady to continue her friendship with you *and* remain in the employment of Mr Girard. It would be an unusual case since she is human," he looked at me and smiled as one would at a child with ideas above their station. "But she could declare herself neutral, as myself and several others have done. Since she has connections to both sides of the river, it shows she's not one hundred percent affiliated with either party. To give my own case as an example, I work as a mediator for all supernaturals, and I maintain an unbiased position."

"How about I sever my connections with both sides? That way I can go back to my normal life and forget any of this ever happened."

"I'm afraid that is not an option, Tegan. You already know too much, and we're incapable of taking your memories from you. There isn't any going back to your old life now," Ethan said, almost consolingly.

I blew out a sharp breath. "Okay then, let's say I try this whole neutrality thing. What would I have to do exactly?"

"You would present your case in front of both governors, declaring your position as neutral," David explained. "Mr Cristescu and Mr Girard would have to accompany you to their respective superiors, stating your case as a human with special abilities, and that your relationship with both of them is one of importance."

"But before we do any of that," Marcel cut in, "we will first need to determine what exactly your special ability is, and there lies our conundrum."

"Surely, you two can manage it," Ethan interjected tauntingly. "Or are you not as skilled in magic as you would have us believe?"

Neither Marcel nor Gabriel rose to the taunt. "It should be a very simple procedure, except that the nature of the spell cast upon her is to conceal. It's a big task to break through that kind of barrier," Marcel replied.

As he spoke, my curiosity and excitement built. Now that I could plausibly believe that the spell was real, I was eager to discover more about it, especially since my connection to my mother had always felt so tenuous. I only had a handful of memories of her. I wanted to know more about her; if she was a witch in the same way Marcel and Gabriel were warlocks, and if it really was her who cast the spell.

I turned to Marcel. "What do you think the spell is concealing?"

"Truthfully, Tegan, I have no clue. But I do know that when a witch goes to the trouble of casting such a thick and impenetrable spell it is only for the most vital of reasons. That leads me to believe that whatever the caster had endeavoured to hide is something very valuable indeed."

Valuable? Me? It seemed implausible. I'd always considered myself so, well, ordinary. It wasn't that my self-esteem was low. It was just that I'd grown up working class in a sea of other working-class people, all of us struggling to make ends meet. I never once thought that I could have something special in me—something so special a witch would cast a spell to hide it.

"I wouldn't be so eager to unravel the mystery,

warlock," Delilah warned, speaking up for the first time. "For all we know, the spell could be hiding something detrimental if unveiled. Perhaps the caster performed such a powerful spell so that whatever is hidden within Tegan will never be permitted to cause harm."

"You think I could be some kind of Trojan horse?" I asked in alarm.

"What she's saying," Ethan put in, eyeing his sister a moment before levelling his gaze on me. "Is that you may very well be death wrapped in an undeniably tempting package." There was a flare of heat in his gaze, and I looked away, flushed. Gabriel glanced between us, as though putting two and two together and not liking the conclusion.

"And what if it turns out I'm not anything quite as special as you all think?" Would they let me go back to my ordinary life or—

"You are special," Delilah answered. "No average human can withstand our abilities as you can."

"And," Lucas put in, "no average human smells quite as appealing to us as you do."

"Lucas," Ethan warned.

"What? You know I'm right."

"Well," Marcel cleared his throat. "Are we all agreed? Gabriel and I will endeavour to unravel the spell, after which Tegan will declare her neutrality to the governors."

"Yes, I'm in agreement," Ethan replied before glancing at me expectantly. "Tegan?"

"Do I have another choice?"

"I wish I could offer you one." His tone was apologetic.

"In that case, yes, I agree, too."

With that, everyone started to leave. I made a move to

follow Marcel and Gabriel, but Ethan stopped me with a hand on my shoulder. "How are you?" he asked softly.

I turned and looked up at him, getting a little lost in his concerned eyes. "I'm coping."

"Have you eaten dinner yet? I could take you somewhere."

"I've eaten, but thank you. That's kind of you to offer."

He held my gaze, the hand on my shoulder lowering and stroking down my arm. I suppressed a tremble at his touch. "How about another drink then?"

"Sure, I could go for another."

He placed his hand on my lower back and ushered me out to the bar, where the blonde bartender from earlier stood wiping down the countertops. Ethan pulled out a stool for me to sit, and I didn't fail to notice the catty look she shot me, followed by a sultry smile for him. Somebody had a thing for the boss.

She approached and threw down two napkins, "What can I get for you, Mr Cristescu?"

"Nothing for me," Ethan answered. "Tegan?"

"I'll take a gin and tonic," I said with a confident smile. She cast me a vaguely irritated glance before turning to make my drink. I leaned close to Ethan. "I don't think she likes me."

He gave a soft chuckle. I always got a little kick out of making him laugh. The buzzer for the club door went off, and Lucas emerged from the back, shrugging into his jacket. "That's for me. I'll be back before opening time."

"Where are you going?" Ethan questioned.

Lucas flashed a devilish grin. "I have a hot date."

Something about the way he said it made me suspicious. "A date with who?"

He tapped the side of his nose. "Never you mind."

I pursed my lips. "Amanda?"

He cast me a challenging look. "And if it is?"

I turned to Ethan. "You said it was bad to feed from the same human twice, didn't you?"

"Hey," Lucas protested. "Who says I'm going to feed? I drank more than enough last night. Is it so hard to believe that I enjoy her company?"

I narrowed my gaze. Ethan reached out and placed his hand over mine, the touch bringing my focus back to him. "He won't feed on her."

"Can I have your word on that?"

"You have my word."

"Okay," I whispered, still unable to deny the bad feeling that Lucas dating Amanda gave me. Being plunged into this vampire world was one thing, but bringing my friends along with me was another matter entirely.

10.

"You shouldn't have let Lucas know you don't want him to date your friend," Ethan said.

We were alone aside from the bartender, whose hatred for me seemed to grow by the minute. I'd never been the recipient of so many dirty looks in my life. I eyed the drink she placed down in front of me, wondering if she'd secretly spat in it.

"Why not?"

"Because it will only make him more determined to do the opposite. Lucas is a good friend, but he's terribly contrarian."

"Can't you tell him to leave her alone?"

"I'm not his father."

"You're old enough to be," I grumbled under my breath, soliciting yet another soft laugh from him. I could get addicted to those laughs.

"Let's make a toast," he said.

"How can we make a toast if you're not drinking anything?"

"Humour me."

"Fine. What are we toasting?"

"You and I making each other's lives infinitely more interesting."

Well, I couldn't argue with that. I certainly hadn't been bored since I met him. I lifted my glass, clinking it to his imaginary one, and knocked mine back in a long gulp. I slammed the glass down, worry for Amanda still churning in my gut.

"What if he feeds from her again?" I whispered, unsure if the bartender was eavesdropping and wondering whether or not we could speak freely. Then again, the fact that she asked Ethan if he wanted something to drink led me to believe she didn't know he was a vampire. My suspicion was confirmed when he leaned close and spoke very quietly.

"It's unlikely he will. It's highly frowned upon to feed from the same human twice without leaving at least several weeks in between. Problems sometimes arise when one of us gets a taste for the blood of a particular human, especially if there's a romantic involvement. When that happens it's difficult to resist feeding from the same person again and again."

I blinked, not knowing what to say to that.

"And it works both ways," Ethan went on. "Our bite is addictive to humans since it comes with its own unique high."

"I wonder what that's like," I said absently, rolling my glass between my palms.

Ethan's elbow knocked against mine. "I'd be happy to show you."

"I'm sure you would," I scoffed, ignoring the bolt of intrigue and arousal that shot through me. "Me and my delicious smelling blood. Hey, maybe I could bottle and sell it."

"No. If anyone's having a taste of you it's me, and I don't like to share."

A warm, fluttery sensation took hold at his husky tone. "A little possessive, are we?"

His eyes blazed. "You have no idea."

I looked away then, unable to handle his intensity. I wondered what sex with a two hundred-and-seventy-seven-year-old vampire would be like. An image entered my mind of me in my underwear sitting astride Ethan. He was topless, his dark blond hair hanging over his face. His hand brushed over my thigh and his lips pressed against my neck. Then his fangs extended and softly grazed my skin. Goosebumps rose, and I felt a shameful heat flood my core. I blinked, breaking myself from the strangely intense daydream. Then I glanced at Ethan, and he had the most curious look on his face. There was a knowing glint in his eyes.

Wait a second, had he freaking planted that image in my head?

"It seems I have one power that works on you," he murmured huskily.

"How did you do that?" I demanded.

"It's a skill of mine. I can make humans see images. Not many vampires can do it, only the older ones."

"Well," I huffed and folded my arms. "It's not nice."

His eyebrow arched. "It isn't? I thought it was *very* nice."

I shot him a scolding look. "Don't do it again."

"I shall endeavour not to," he said, but he didn't sound like he meant it. He sounded entirely too amused.

I picked up my drink and downed the rest of it. "Thanks for the drink, but I better be going."

"May I have the pleasure of driving you home?"

"I'd prefer to walk," I replied. "I need some time to think everything over."

"Then I will walk with you."

I eyed him firmly. "Thank you, but no." I was finding I liked Ethan far too much, and I needed to put my foot on the brake. His ability to give me sexy daydreams aside, I still knew next to nothing about his world. Plus, developing feelings for someone so soon after Matthew probably wasn't a wise idea.

There was a brief flash of unhappiness in his eyes at my refusal, but then it was gone. "Very well, I'll walk you out."

He led me from the club, and I exited through the same steel door I'd come in through. "I'll be seeing you, Tegan," Ethan called as I walked away.

Full dark had descended on the city, but I decided not to take the bus. I needed to walk. It always helped me think. As I made my way past busy bars and restaurants, something niggled at me. I was halfway to my apartment when I realised I'd forgotten to tell Ethan about the slayer. A chill skittered across the back of my neck as I glanced behind me, making sure I wasn't being followed. It was a longer path home than I normally took, and as I turned a corner at the end of the street, the oddest thing occurred.

I heard the faint tinkling of off-beat piano music playing an unfamiliar and antiquated tune. The sort of music you'd see a flapper dancing the Charleston to in old black and white footage from the 1920s.

I looked around, realising how completely empty and deserted the street had become. Hadn't there been people a second ago? All the businesses were shuttered, which didn't make sense because Tribane wasn't a city that shut down early. No matter the street, you could always find someplace open.

A sense of eeriness pervaded, driving me to quicken my step. Something in the back of my mind told me this wasn't the slayer. My speedy steps transformed into a run, and the music grew louder and louder until finally I turned a corner and it faded out. Life returned to the city. The streets filled with people, the restaurants and bars, too.

Okay, that was some freaky shit.

Under any other circumstances I might have

immediately brushed off the music and the empty street, but there was something about the encounter that chilled me to my very core. When I reached my building, I was eager to get inside, so eager that I didn't immediately notice the strange man sitting in my kitchen. I recognised him instantly.

The slayer.

Every cell in my body tensed at the sight of him sitting there like he owned the place. He didn't even look my way as he casually peeled the skin off an apple with a pocketknife; a red apple that he'd obviously appropriated from *my* fruit bowl.

His body language was completely laid back. He even had the gall to take his time popping a neatly cut slice of apple into his mouth before deigning to cast his eyes to me.

"I'm calling the police," I announced sharply, slipping my hand inside my pocket and retrieving my phone.

"I wouldn't do that," he warned in a thick Irish accent.

"Just try and stop me." I proceeded to dial the numbers, but before I got to the last digit something knocked the phone straight out of my hand. It flew to the other side of the room and landed on the floor. The slayer had flung something at me. I looked down to see what he'd thrown and sputtered a laugh. A banana? How on earth do you knock a phone from a person's hand with a banana?

I stood there for a second, phone-less, as he ate another slice of apple.

"Are you going to explain why you've broken into my apartment?" I asked. "Or have you just come to steal my fruit?"

"Good apples." He wiped the excess juice from his lips onto his sleeve. I couldn't help but notice he was attractive in a rough and ready sort of way. What was wrong with me? This man was an intruder. I shouldn't even be thinking about his looks. "And don't play dumb, Missy. You know why I'm here."

"Because of the vampires? Wait, you don't think *I'm* one of them, do you?"

"What do you take me for? Of course I don't think you're a vamp. I'm here because you saved my life last night, and I'd like to say thank you."

Oh. That was unexpected. "Well," I sniffed. "In that case you're welcome. Also, you can go. I don't take kindly to home invaders, and I still plan on calling the police."

"Call away." He gestured to where my phone lay on the floor. Thankfully, it appeared undamaged.

I hesitated. "You're not going to throw another banana at me, are you?"

He seemed to suppress a smile. "I can't make any promises."

I eyed him now, from the heavy-soled boots he wore to the dark jeans and cargo jacket. He looked like some sort of mercenary. A hitman for hire maybe. *So why aren't you screaming from the top of your lungs?* Somehow, I sensed he wasn't here to hurt me.

"How do you know I saved your life? Weren't you unconscious last night?"

"I was, but I came to in time to hear your little speech to the bloodsucker. I think that's the first time I've ever seen a vamp look guilty."

"Yeah, well, it would've been wrong for Ethan to kill you while you were incapable of defending yourself." A pause as I worried my lip. "How did you find out where I live?"

"I followed you two home last night. I kept well behind so the vamp wouldn't cotton on to being tailed again."

Ethan had been right to insist on accompanying me up to my apartment.

"So," the slayer went on. "What's a nice girl like you doing driving around in cars with vampires, eh?"

"Wrong time, wrong place," I deadpanned.

He eyed me studiously now. "Well, shit," he exclaimed.

"What?"

"You haven't been compelled."

"No, I haven't."

"Then why aren't you running a mile? Most people freak out when they discover the truth, then the vamps use their mind voodoo to put them under a thrall and make them forget why they should be scared. Sneaky bastards."

"Sadly, I'm already too entangled to run a mile. Also, the mind voodoo doesn't work on me."

Disbelief coloured his features. "It doesn't work on you." Now he laughed. "And how, pray tell, do you manage that?"

"I'm still trying to figure that one out."

His expression sobered, his thick eyebrows drawing together. "You're human, right?"

"As far as I know, yes."

"Interesting."

I blew out a heavy sigh and kicked off my shoes before removing my coat. Might as well get comfortable while entertaining an intruder. "Yes, everyone finds me so terribly interesting these days."

"I've never known anyone immune to the compulsion of a vampire. It takes years of training to withstand them even a little bit," he said, a hint of awe in his voice.

"I've had no training. Two weeks ago, I didn't even know vampires existed."

106

Now he frowned. "How did you come into contact with them?"

I was about to relay the details of the night Ethan and I met but reconsidered. I still had no clue if I could trust this guy. I didn't even know his name and breaking into my apartment didn't make the best first impression.

"I think I've told you enough for one night. Also, shouldn't you be on the other side of the river right now? I thought crossing it was considered an act of aggression."

He seemed impressed that I knew about the Hawthorn, a hint of a grin shaping his lips. "What can I say, I'm an aggressive son of a bitch."

"Aren't you scared you'll come across vampires? They're so much stronger than humans."

"I'm good at sticking to the shadows."

"I'm sorry about your, um, fellow slayers. Ethan didn't need to kill them."

A dark look crossed his features. "Yes, he did. If he hadn't, we wouldn't have stopped until we killed him. But not to worry, I'll take him down eventually."

Something tugged at my chest. I didn't like the idea of this guy setting his sights on Ethan. I might've still had my reservations about him, but I didn't want him to be killed.

"I think it's time you left."

He shot me a challenging look. "I'll leave when I'm ready."

I placed my hands on my hips, staring him down. He chuckled. "That's some glower you've got on you, Missy."

"I've got some right hook on me, too," I threatened, even though I had no clue how to throw a punch. This guy didn't know that though.

"The vamps are only interested in you because you pose a threat. If their compulsion doesn't work on you, they'll want to ensure it isn't something that can be replicated. The fact that they can erase people's memories is the whole reason they can remain hidden."

"I don't think it can be replicated," I said, not telling him about the spell.

"How do you know? You could be the answer to the imbalance of power between vampires and humans. No longer would they be able to control us with no more than a glance of their eyes."

Suddenly, I wondered if I'd made a terrible mistake by talking to him. He was looking at me like I was the answer to all his problems, and I was pretty sure I wasn't.

I folded my arms. "I'm sorry, but I can't help you. Now you really need to leave."

He narrowed his eyes, his expression flat. "I see you've already been swayed by the vamps. You know very little of the species you're aligning yourself with."

"I'm not aligning myself with anyone. Whatever friction there is between vampires and slayers is none of my concern. But if I *were* to pick a side, I'm not sure it would be with a group of people who set out to destroy an entire species, even if they are predators. Would you shoot a lion just because its nature is to kill? It's the way of the world for one species to prey upon another. You're extremely gullible if you think that a group of slayers with a mission is going to change any of that."

"No," he said, his voice cold. "I wouldn't shoot a lion under normal circumstances. But if that lion were to murder my entire family, then I wouldn't bat an eyelid before ending its life."

His words sank in, and my stomach twisted. "Did a vampire kill your family?"

He didn't answer, remaining quiet for a long moment.

Then he pulled a small business card from his pocket, setting it down on the table before he rose. "I'll see myself out. My number's on the card if you ever need help. You might be silly enough to trust a vampire now, but you'll soon learn his true nature."

With those parting words, he left. I walked over to the table and picked up the card to read it.

Lt. Finn Roe. DOH. 980561230

11.

As soon as Finn Roe left, I turned over all the locks and sank onto the floor, my legs curling beneath me. I held my head in my hands and rubbed my temples. What had I gotten myself into?

This crap was becoming way too complicated.

I wasn't sure how long I sat there before I finally dragged myself into my bedroom. I opened a drawer and removed the old shoebox where I'd placed the few things I had left that belonged to Matthew. There wasn't much, just a guitar pick, a notebook of song lyrics, the silver chain he always wore, and a half-used bottle of his favourite cologne. I smoothed the pick between my fingers, then took a quick sniff of the cologne.

Ah, memories. They cut deep even while they soothed.

My hand brushed over the notebook. I'd only ever managed to read the first few pages. Reading it made me feel guilty—like I was intruding on his most personal thoughts and feelings. But tonight, I needed a distraction, something to take my mind off everything and bring me back to a time when my life was normal, or what most people deemed normal.

I flicked through several pages before my eyes latched on a title. I wasn't sure why it drew my attention, but I felt a pull. It was titled "Nightfall". Most of Matthew's lyrics portrayed his feelings of loneliness and depression, his frustrations with life. But this one was different. There was an eery quality to it that made the small hairs on the back of my neck stand on end.

No one knows it but I do.
No one sees it but me and you,

110

And I don't know if anyone would believe it.
But when the day turns to night,
And all I see is a speck of light,
Nightfall comes to drain my soul away.

The lyrics stole my breath. It was almost like Matthew was speaking to me from beyond the grave. My heart hurt as I wondered what he felt when he wrote this. What had been happening in his life? Were we together at the time, or was it written before we met? The part about when the day turned to night really struck a chord in me. My life had been turned upside by Ethan, a person who I only ever saw at night.

I touched my finger to the page, letting it drift over the indentations made from his pen. Then a sharp pang of grief hit me, and I closed over the notebook. I couldn't read any more. It brought up too many feelings, too many questions that I'd never get the answers to.

Carefully, I placed the shoebox back in the drawer and went to get ready for bed.

The next night I was back to my regular shift at Hagen's, which was blessedly uneventful.

When my day shift at Indigo came around, I was a little hesitant. Now that I knew the truth about Marcel and Gabriel, things were going to be different. For one, I'd started to believe the spell was real, and for two, I *needed* them to untangle it for me. I didn't fancy going through life with some invisible magic hanging over my head.

As I arrived at the store, I bumped into Gabriel.

"Morning, Tegan," he greeted.

If I wasn't mistaken, he seemed a little wary of me. It was a wariness he hadn't shown before, and it had to be down to my friendship with Ethan. I still wondered what happened to make them dislike one another so much.

111

"Marcel and I will be out all morning," Gabriel went on. "Will you be okay taking care of things on your own?"

"Sure," I answered. "No problem."

When he left, I settled in and spent some time fixing the bookshelves before I heard the chimes ring over the door. I turned to check who it was and saw Rita, my possible nemesis, aka, the girl who was after my job. Just like before, her wardrobe choices were … interesting. She wore a sleeveless, knee-length black dress with bare gaps on either side where the front of the garment was secured to the back via long rows of safety pins. Her short hair was messy, her make-up heavy.

Chewing on a wooden toothpick, she approached, stopping to lean against one of the display shelves. Her black-rimmed eyes looked me up and down, and for a moment, I felt an intense pang in my chest. It was a pleasant pang, almost like a hum, and for some reason it caused most of my wariness about her to fade. I couldn't explain it, but I suddenly felt a connection to her, a feeling of sameness, which was odd because we were nothing alike.

"So, are Tweedle Dum and Tweedle Dee not around today?" she asked.

I arched an eyebrow. "Marcel and Gabriel? No, they're out."

Now she grinned. "Right, well, I'll just be in the back."

"Wait a second," I called, chasing after her as she made her way to the back of the store.

She pretended she didn't hear me, disappearing into the room containing all the specialty items. When I entered, I found her rifling through a chest of drawers, stuffing various herbs and glass dropper bottles into her bag.

"You better be planning to pay for those," I warned

112

sternly.

She cast me a glance. "Don't worry about it. Gabriel lets me borrow stuff all the time." I shot her a disbelieving look, folding my arms. "I'm not lying. Ask Gabriel when he gets back."

Walking around her, I peered inside the drawer she had open. "What are you taking?"

Rita bristled when I got close but continued to speak casually. "A bit of this, a bit of that."

"Are you a witch?" I blurted.

She froze before turning to face me fully. "Who've you been talking to?"

"I just presumed, since Marcel and Gabriel are warlocks, maybe you were a witch."

Rita heaved a sigh, and for a second, I saw a flicker of vulnerability in her. "Technically, no, I'm not a witch, since according to the backwards, arcane rules you've got to be from one of the twelve families to use magic. But I've got the ability, same as my mum does, and we practice, too. No offence to Marcel and Gabriel, but we're a whole hell of a lot better than they are. We're just younger, less experienced. And because they happen to have the right last names, they get all the respect. But I'm telling you, if ever a time comes when one of *them* has to go up against one of *us*, they won't know what's hit them."

"Who's "them" and "us?" I asked, suddenly very curious. Rita was more interesting than I gave her credit for. Plus, the weird draw I suddenly felt to her persisted, sitting right in the centre of my chest.

"*They* are the Marcel Girards of this world. In other words, born into magic with silver spoons in their mouths. *We* are those who practice magic, but don't belong to one of the magical families."

113

"Oh." I said. "So, who exactly are these families then?"

"You're telling me you know Marcel and Gabriel are warlocks, but you don't know who the families are. How does that work?" She tilted her head questioningly.

"I'm extremely new to all this."

"How new?"

"Two weeks new."

Rita let out a low whistle. "That's sort of unheard of. Why would Marcel and Gabriel tell you what they are just because you're working for them? They've had employees before who never knew."

"They weren't the ones who told me. It was, um, someone else."

"Who?"

I took a second to consider whether to answer her or not, but since she practiced magic it shouldn't come as too much of a shock. "A vampire," I said finally.

Both her eyebrows shot up. "You know a vampire? No way. Marcel would never give someone even remotely associated with the vamps a job."

"Special circumstances, I guess."

Rita closed the drawer she'd been looking through. "What kind of special circumstances?"

I went and sat down on one of the beaded cushions. I wasn't sure why, maybe it was the pulse in my chest or maybe I just wanted an outsider's perspective, but for some reason, I told Rita everything. How I met Ethan. How I was drawn to Indigo where I met Marcel and Gabriel, their theories about the spell cast on me. She stood still and listened, and when I was finished, she looked flabbergasted.

"Girl, you've had a hell of a fortnight."

"Tell me about it."

114

She drew closer, shutting the door as she approached. "You want my advice?" I nodded. "I wouldn't trust anyone if I were you. Not the vamps and not Marcel or Gabriel. Once they've discovered what's different about you, they'll either use you up 'til there's nothing left if it's anything of worth, or they'll throw you away and forget about you if it's something useless. They're all being nice to you because of the mystery, the possibility that you're something they've never seen before. You saw how Marcel was with me last week?"

"Yeah, he was kind of dismissive," I admitted.

"You probably thought that was because I'm some sort of bitch, right?" Reluctantly, I nodded again. "Well," she smirked. "I am kind of a bitch, but that's not why Marcel treats me like crap. It's how the warlocks and witches behave with anybody not from one of their precious families. Kind of incestuous if you ask me. They think me and my mum are pretenders, trying our hardest to be one of them. We aren't though. My mum taught me everything I know about magic, and we practice it with more integrity than Marcel's got in his baby finger."

"What about the vampires? Do you think I can trust them?"

I wasn't sure why I was asking her for advice. Maybe it was because Rita had no skin in the game. She didn't want anything from me, which meant she was more likely to give an honest opinion.

"I don't deal with the vamps, so I can't really advise you on that. But they've probably only befriended you for the same reason Marcel and Gabriel have. They're all after power, and if you can give it to them, then they'll treat you like the Queen of fucking Sheba."

I rested my chin on my palms, my forehead crinkling

with apprehension. We were both silent for a few moments, my brain considering what I'd just learned. Rita's mention of there being others like her piqued my interest.

"So," I ventured. "Exactly how many of you are there—unofficial magic users that is?"

Rita glanced away, her cheeks flushing ever so slightly as she gave a cough. "Three."

"Only three?" Given the way she'd been talking, I was expecting a much larger number. "Is that including you and your mum, or after?"

Her lips pursed. "Including."

"Oh."

"Look, it's not all about numbers you know. We aren't trying to build an army. We practice magic to better ourselves and our quality of life and to further our understanding of the universe. Not for power or accolades or status."

I started to smile. "That sounds very admirable."

She cast me a glance, looking surprised by what I said. "You think so?"

I nodded. "Your reasons for practising magic sound noble and honest. A lot more so than a bunch of elitist families who refuse to let in outsiders."

"I was wrong about you," she said then.

"You were?"

"I thought I wasn't going to like you, but I was just annoyed that Marcel gave you the job over me."

"So, you do like me then?"

She smirked. "Maybe." A pause before she went on. "So, what are you going to do about your situation?"

"Not a clue." I answered truthfully.

"Can I be frank?"

"Please."

She sucked in a big breath before letting it out. "If I were you, I wouldn't let Marcel and Gabriel break your spell. Whatever they discover, they'll either try to profit from it, or they'll try to use you against the vampires. Well, maybe not Gabriel, but Marcel will. Don't let the aged hippy thing fool you. Underneath the ponytail is a shark, and a ruthless one at that."

"If he's so awful then why do you shop here?"

"Because it's the only place in the city that sells good spell ingredients. Though I do take a five-finger discount whenever I can as a secret fuck you." She shot me a wink.

"I'm still making you pay for what you took."

She rolled her eyes. "Spoilsport."

"Are you better than them at magic?" I questioned.

"Marcel and Gabriel?" she scoffed. "Hell yes. Like I said, I don't have as much experience, but I definitely have more natural talent. No offense to Gabe or anything, because I know he's old as shit, but in a few years' time I could magic him under the table."

Gabriel was old as shit? I wondered how long dhampirs lived for.

"So why don't you unravel my spell for me?" I suggested impulsively.

Rita stared at me in surprise. "You'd trust me to do that?"

"If you're right about everyone only being interested in me for what they can gain, then yes."

"And how do you know I'm not exactly the same as everyone else?"

"I don't," I said, not mentioning the whole chest hum connection thing. "But it's a chance I'm willing to take." Besides, this way I could discover what sort of spell had been cast on me without Marcel, Gabriel, or Ethan finding out, and I could then decide whether or not it was something I wanted to share with them,

Rita stepped toward me, her hand out. "Give me your phone." I pulled it from my pocket and handed it to her. She fiddled with it for a moment and gave it back to me.

"There you go," she said. "My number's in your contacts. Call me when you want to do this."

She turned to walk out the door, but not before laying some money on top of the dresser for the herbs she'd taken.

12.

Later that night, after I began my shift at Hagen's, I was stacking packets of candy onto the shelf near the register when Ethan strode in.

"You know, for someone who doesn't eat food, you visit this grocery store surprisingly often," I commented as he approached.

Ethan flashed me a devilish smile. "I come for the company, not the food."

I dipped my head down, feeling weirdly shy at his compliment. "Right, well, I'm working so ..." I made a gesture around the completely empty store. That was the problem with working at night. Customers were few and far between, which meant Ethan had me all to himself.

"You do look incredibly busy," he agreed sarcastically, picking up a chocolate bar and scanning the contents before placing it back on the shelf. "The things humans find appetising has always confounded me."

"Because blood is so yummy," I deadpanned.

His eyes flashed hungrily. "It is. Especially when drunk from the right person."

Something in his cadence made me shiver. "Uh-huh."

He sighed, as though I was terribly troublesome. "Why do you do this to yourself? Come and work for me. You look exhausted." He reached out to caress my cheek, and the shivers intensified.

I stepped back, a little scared of how his touch affected me. "I'd still be exhausted if I worked for you. Your club opens at night, too, remember?"

"I'd pay you enough so that you could quit working at Indigo. More than enough."

119

"No, thank you. I like working at Indigo. It's an interesting place."

"Oh?" Ethan looked displeased.

"Yep. I even made a new friend there today."

"You don't need any new friends. I am your friend."

"Right. Or at least until you find out what's different about me. What if it's nothing interesting? Will you cast me aside? Disappear out of my life like we never even met?" I challenged. I tried to keep my voice even, but a part of me was upset by the idea that Ethan may be hanging around me only for what he could potentially gain.

He moved closer. "Is that what you think?"

"It's what I suspect."

"Then I must not be doing a very good job."

"Of?"

His eyes blazed as he advanced forward, backing me up into the wall. "Of showing you just how much you have bewitched me," he rasped, lowering his mouth and pressing his lips to the hollow of my neck. I let out a tiny, surprised squeak, butterflies wreaking havoc with my insides. Then, just like in the fantasy he'd planted in my head the other night, he dragged the barest tips of his fangs across my skin. I undulated before closing my eyes and trying to gain the sanity he'd robbed me of. The mixture of danger and enticement was a heady combination.

"If I bit you right now, would you let me?" he whispered curiously.

"Try it and see," I warned, levelling my knee with his crotch.

He gave a low, husky chuckle, pressing his lips to my neck just before someone flew into the store.

"Tegan! Help!" A familiar voice called. It took me a moment to break through the sexy fog Ethan put me under to realise it was Florence. I drew away from him and hurried to her. She looked out of sorts, holding a bunch of tissues to her nose. She was *bleeding*. I cast Ethan a nervous glance, unsure if he had control over his blood lust or if the very sight of it would drive him crazy.

He stood stock-still next to the cash register, his eyes focused intently on Florence. "You good?" I asked him warily.

I saw his throat bob as he swallowed. "I'm fine."

I turned back to Florence, my attention running over her in search of other injuries. It seemed her nose was the only part of her that was bleeding. "What happened to you?"

"My dad," she sniffed. "He was drunk and accused me of stealing cash from his wallet. I told him I didn't, but he wouldn't b-believe me. He punched me."

I stared at her in horror. "In the face?"

She nodded, a tear rolling down her cheek. "Come here. Let me see." I pulled away the tissues to check the damage, wincing when I saw her nose needed to be reset. Anger swirled in my gut. I was going to break Terry's jaw for this.

"I can do it," Ethan said, and I jumped in fright. He'd moved so silently, coming to stand close behind me. I couldn't tell if he was talking about setting Florence's nose or breaking her father's jaw.

"W-who are you?" Florence asked. Her eyes darted all around Ethan, an expression of unease and fascination shaping her features as she took him in.

"I'm Tegan's friend. Your nose is broken. I can reset it for you if you'd like."

She turned to me, her eyes round as saucers. "Is he really your friend?"

"Yes."

Now she leaned in close and whispered quietly, "There's something very wrong with him."

I looked at Ethan. As far as I could see there wasn't anything amiss. He'd seemed to have gotten a hold of himself and was no longer frozen by the blood. "What do you think is wrong with him?"

Florence seemed to reconsider her statement. "Nothing. I think it's just blood loss making me see things." She looked at Ethan. "Will it hurt?"

"Resetting your nose? Yes, but it's better than allowing it to heal incorrectly."

She sucked in a harsh breath. "Okay, please try to be fast."

"That won't be a problem." Ethan reached out, his movements a blur. I heard a sharp yelp of pain from Florence and then it was done. I stared at him in awe. It seemed there were many benefits to vampire speed.

"Thank you."

"You're welcome," Ethan replied. "Now, about your father—"

"Don't worry about him. I'll deal with it," I said, cutting him off. I didn't need Ethan getting involved in Florence's fraught home life.

The vampire turned his attention to me. "Let me help. I can bring the girl back to your place, clean her up, deal with her father, and be back before you've finished your shift."

"I don't think—"

"It's okay," Florence interjected, her attention focused on Ethan. "Your friend is t-trustworthy. I can see it now."

I frowned at her, wondering at the odd certainty in her eyes. Ethan studied her, and he seemed intrigued. I blew

122

out a tired breath. "Okay, well, be careful with Terry. He's a wild card."

"I'm always careful." Ethan leaned down to press a quick kiss on my cheek. My eyebrows rose at the sweet gesture as I handed him the keys to my apartment. He was the perfect gentleman as he offered Florence his arm and helped her outside.

A little over an hour later he returned just as I was shrugging into my coat. My co-worker, Debbie, had arrived to take over. I met him outside the door, my eyes expectant.

"How is Florence?"

"She's fine. Right now she's asleep on your couch."

"And Terry?"

"I used my compulsion. The next time he has the urge to hurt his daughter he'll feel the most explosive pain shatter through his skull."

"You can do that?"

"The human mind is a fascinating thing, but it's easily manipulated. Well," he allowed, shooting me a wry smile. "Most human minds are."

"Thank you for doing all that. You didn't have to."

"I wanted to. I know you don't want to believe it, but I'm your friend, Tegan. You can lean on me whenever you need."

Man, that sounded good. I'd love to lean on him, but my naturally suspicious nature still kept me wary, kept me questioning things. Then again, I kind of already did lean on him, not to mention gave him the keys to my place. Was I acting recklessly out of exhaustion, or did a subconscious part of me actually trust him?

"Your keys," Ethan said, offering them to me. I took them and slotted them in my pocket. Ethan slid his palm along mine, interlocking our fingers as we made the short walk to my building. *He was holding my hand?* Okay, Ethan was behaving seriously sweet tonight, and I wasn't sure my heart could handle it.

"About the girl," Ethan said, catching my attention. "She smells different, too. Not quite as intoxicatingly different as you, but different nonetheless."

Florence smelled different to him? "But she's just a teenager."

"A teenager who isn't quite normal. Didn't you notice how she looked at me?"

I frowned because I had noticed that. "Yeah, it was weird. She seemed wary of you, then all of a sudden she decided you could be trusted."

"It's quite curious, especially since the two of you found each other."

"I've always felt a draw to her, a protective instinct," I admitted.

"Even more curious," Ethan replied, his expression thoughtful.

We reached my building, and he stopped at the lobby door. "I have to go, but I'll try to come visit you tomorrow night. And of course, you're always welcome to come see me at the club."

"I don't have a lot of free time for clubbing."

"The job offer still stands. You don't need to suffer unnecessarily."

"Then you'd be my boss, which would be entirely too problematic."

"And how is that?"

"Well, you're dying to sink your fangs into me for a start."

"I'm not—" He was about to argue with me, but I cut him off with a cynical look. "Even if that were true," he amended. "I'm adept at resisting the urge to feed, even when the blood is as succulent as yours surely is."

"Even so—" Before I could finish my counter-argument, Ethan swept me inside my building. I spun on my heels, blinking rapidly as I tried to steady myself.

"What the hell!"

"There's a slayer outside, hiding in the shadows. He thinks I can't see him, but he underestimates my night vision."

A slayer? *Oh, shit.* Don't tell me it was Finn Roe again. I scratched the side of my jaw. "Yeah, about that. I might know who it is."

Ethan turned to me, eyes narrowing. "Who?"

"Remember the slayer you let live? He broke into my apartment the other night."

Just like that, Ethan looked murderous. "*What?*"

"Relax. He didn't hurt me. He came to thank me for saving his life."

His eyes flashed black. "I suppose he tried to sway you to his side, too?"

I bit my lip. "He might've, but don't worry, he didn't convince me."

Now he gave a sharp laugh. "Wonderful." He went quiet, stepping past me to peer out the window. "We'll discuss the fact that you're only now deciding to tell me a slayer broke into your apartment later. Right now, I have an enemy to deal with."

"You're not going to kill him, are you?"

Ethan didn't reply, only shot me a dark look that didn't bode well for Finn Roe. He opened the door and stepped back out onto the street. "I hope you've made peace with your maker, slayer," Ethan announced loudly. "Because this night is going to be your last."

There was no response. Then, out of nowhere, a stake came sailing through the air. Ethan moved fast enough to dodge it, and then he was gone, disappearing around the side of a building in search of his adversary. My heart got stuck in my throat. Though I knew next to nothing about Finn Roe, I didn't want him to die. He was a zealot, sure, but he seemed to believe he was fighting for the side of good. But if he didn't die, that meant Ethan might, and my stomach grew ill just thinking about it.

I'd grown fond of the vampire, and that was an unsettling thought indeed.

13.

I took the elevator up to my apartment, reassuring myself that it would be daylight soon. Finn Roe just had to escape Ethan's clutches for another half an hour before my vampire friend would have to hurry back to wherever it was he hunkered down during the day.

Florence was still asleep on my couch when I entered the apartment. I stroked my hand over her long brown hair, her face remaining peaceful while she slept. I wondered what was different about her. Judging from what Ethan said, and how she acted when she met him, she wasn't an ordinary human.

Was that why I was drawn to her? Were we the same? I'd felt a similar, though different, draw to Rita, too. This was all way too confusing. Maybe I just needed some rest so I could look at things with a clear head in the morning.

I changed out of my work uniform and crawled into bed, but I was too on edge to sleep. About an hour passed before I caved and grabbed my phone, using Ethan's number for the very first time.

Tegan: What happened? Are you safe?

Several minutes went by before my phone buzzed with a reply, and my heart leapt. He couldn't be responding to my message if he was dead. I opened it eagerly.

Ethan: Damned slayer managed to get away. I'm home and safe. Glad to know you worry about me. I was beginning to wonder...

Tegan: Of course I worry. I'm very much against needless death.

Ethan: Admit it. You'd be terribly upset if I died.

Tegan: Maybe. Just a little.

Ethan: Get some sleep. You'll be seeing me soon. xxx

I fell back into my pillow, heaving a shaky sigh. Oh yeah, I was definitely starting to be charmed by Ethan, which was cause for *great* concern.

My alarm woke me way too early. These back to back shifts were going to be the death of me, but I was too stubborn to take Ethan up on his offer.

I was on my own for most of the day at Indigo. Gabriel dipped in and out once or twice, but there was no sign of Marcel. I wondered what he did when he was out all day. Did maintaining the segregation between the two opposing sides of the city take a lot of work?

It was just all so … divisive. Ethan swayed me toward the vampires, but was my attraction to him clouding my judgement? Maybe I needed to keep my feet on more neutral ground like that vampire David Rollans.

With these thoughts swirling in my head, I pulled out my phone, staring at Rita's name in my contacts list. I'd been hoping she'd stop by again so we could talk more about my spell. Impulsively, I hit 'call' and waited while her phone rang.

"Knew you'd be in touch," she said when she answered.

"Rita, hi. Are you free this evening?"

"Free as a bird. Do you want to come over?"

"To your house? Um, I guess so—" Before I could finish speaking, she rattled off her address.

As expected, her house was on the north side of the Hawthorn, the same as Indigo, on magical family/dhampir/slayer territory. I hopped on a bus and headed straight there after my shift. Rita lived in a small, terraced house on a residential street just outside of the cramped city centre. Approaching her house, I spotted three cats sitting on her doorstep. One of them waltzed up to me, purring and rubbing against my leg.

"Hey there, kitty," I said, reaching down to pet its head. It purred louder, rising to my touch with a curve of its back and a lifting of its behind. "Aren't you friendly."

I reached for the heavy brass knocker, and a moment later the door flew open. I wondered if I'd come to the wrong house. A man stood before me. He had thinning black hair styled into a quiff, a nose piercing, and a velvet shirt with the first few buttons undone to reveal a pale, birdlike chest. He was also barefoot.

"May I help you?" he asked.

"Hi, I'm Tegan. I'm looking for Rita."

His eyes flashed with recognition. "You're Tegan! Oh, I'm so excited to meet you. You're much prettier than Rita described."

"Thanks … I think. Is she home?"

"She is. Come in," he said, standing back and motioning me inside. "I'm Alvie, by the way. Rita and I are besties." He led me to the end of the hallway and through a door, which opened into a kitchen that might have been spacious once but was now so full of things that it was nearly impossible to determine its original size. Shelves lined every wall, packed to the brim with random items. Crockery, antiques, dozens of yellowed paperbacks, and of course, all manner of jarred herbs, oils, and tinctures. There was also an endless array of green, leafy house plants that made the place feel like a living, breathing thing.

The back door was open, leading out to a rear garden. "Reet!" Alvie called. "Tegan is here. Come inside so we can get our spells on!"

Get our spells on? I was starting to rethink my decision to come here.

"Be there in a minute, Alvie," I heard her call back from somewhere out in the garden.

Alvie gestured to the kitchen table. "Please, take a seat."

I sat, still taking the place in. Alvie went to the stove, where there was a large pot simmering. He lifted the lid, took a sniff, then stirred whatever concoction was inside with a big wooden ladle before replacing the lid.

"Get your filthy paws off that," Rita snapped playfully when she entered the house. There was an older woman behind her who I presumed was her mother. The woman had chestnut hair with a few greys peeking out at the temples. She also wore a long purple skirt that pooled around her bare feet. They weren't fond of footwear in this house.

Rita grinned when she saw me, her brown eyes a mixture of excitement and mischief. The mischief could be cause for concern, but I didn't detect any ill intent.

"Tegan, I'm so glad you came. This is my mum, Noreen."

"Pleased to meet you," Noreen said with a smile. She had kind eyes.

"You, too. You have a wonderful home."

She laughed. "That's very kind of you to say. I know it can be a lot to take in." She glanced around at the endless shelves. "Rita told me all about your predicament. I would have liked to stay and take part in the casting, but I have a house call with a client."

"Mum's a healer," Rita put in.

"Oh," I replied, intrigued.

"I've been flat out lately," Noreen said as she grabbed her coat and slid her feet into a pair of flats. "I'll be back before midnight, Rita. Don't make a mess."

Once she had left, Rita came to sit across from me and clasped her hands together. "Are you sure about this?"

"Not really, but I want to get to the bottom of things, and I want to do it without Ethan, Marcel, or Gabriel being involved. Then I can decide for myself if it's something I want to tell them."

"I like it," Alvie grinned. "It's like supernatural female empowerment."

"We don't know if she's supernatural yet," Rita countered as she settled her gaze on me. "But from what you've told me I'd be surprised if you weren't. Since we talked at Indigo, I've been working round the clock to devise a clairvoyance spell for you."

"You have?"

She nodded eagerly. "I'm pretty excited to see if it works."

I glanced at Alvie, who was reaching up to retrieve a large bowl from one of the shelves. "And are you a warlock?" I asked him.

His expression turned sheepish. "Not officially."

"So, you don't come from one of the magical families?"

He scoffed. "No, and thank goodness for that. Those stiffs couldn't handle all this." I laughed as he made a swooping hand gesture down his body before handing Rita the bowl.

"How confident are you that your spell will work?" I questioned, watching as she threw various herbs into the bowl.

Rita pressed her lips together. "Pretty certain, but you always have to leave room for error. I can give no guarantees, but even if we fail, we won't do any harm. The spell is benign, not malevolent."

"There are malevolent spells?"

"Oh yes. I consider myself a good witch. My magic is only ever used to help people. But there are some who practice the dark arts, and those spells are drawn from dark power. You'll know a good witch from a bad one based on the ingredients used in their spells. Good witches use herbs and flowers, things that come from the earth, while bad ones use blood and death and sacrifice."

A shiver ran through me at that last part. "Are Marcel and Gabriel good or bad?"

She thought about it a moment. "Marcel is ambiguous. He often plays both sides. But Gabriel is good. If it weren't for his association with Marcel, I'd say you could trust Gabriel."

Well, that was interesting. I thought of the day I first met the two men and how Gabriel seemed somewhat reluctant to work with me while Marcel was quite eager.

Rita went about gathering her implements and readying them for the spell. I glanced at Alvie when he joined us at the table. "Has Rita told you everything about me?"

He nodded. "I hope that's okay. I need to know all the details if I'm going to be the third member of the circle. You couldn't have done this kind of spell with just the two of you—not unless one of you was a sorceress or a very experienced witch."

"Oh, right."

"You don't have to worry about me telling anyone," he went on, touching my arm in reassurance. "When it comes to magic Rita and I keep everything strictly confidential."

"Thank you. That puts my mind at ease."

Rita stood and walked over to the stove, where she removed the lid from her pot and ladled some of the concoction into her bowl. The scent of mint and cloves hit my nose. Then she returned, placing the bowl in the centre of the table with steam rising from it. Next, Alvie placed three smaller bowls filled with water in front of each of our place settings.

They both dipped their hands in the water then began rubbing herbs into their palms. "Thyme," Rita said, handing some to me. "It purifies the skin. There can't be anything on our hands that might corrupt the spell."

"Right," I replied as I copied her movements, first placing my hands in the water, then rubbing in the thyme. There were a further four bowls in front of Rita, containing various herbs and berries. I eyed them curiously. A slow, calming breeze flowed in from the garden, the air crisp. I noticed a marked difference in the way Rita practiced magic compared to what I'd seen Marcel and Gabriel do.

Rita reached out and took my left hand, while Alvie took hold of my right. My stomach tensed. This was it. Tonight, I might actually find out what made me, well, different.

Rita gestured to the largest bowl. "This is a neutral bath. It contains a base from which to start. What we put into it after we begin determines the nature and function of the spell." I nodded along as she continued speaking. "We'll take several moments to clear our minds before we start."

Rita and Alvie both closed their eyes, and I followed suit, trying my best to clear my head. The quiet seemed to close in around me. I allowed myself to fall into a meditative state.

"Okay," Rita said after a few moments of quiet and I opened my eyes. "Let us begin."

"I call on the Goddess to watch over our proceedings here this night," Rita said. "And to secure the success of our casting. Into the formula, I add aniseed." She lifted some flowery, leafy green herbs and threw them into the bowl. "This will banish any negative energy or negative thoughts and will ensure that no person within the circle is present for deceitful or insidious reasons."

Next, she plucked another bunch of herbs and tossed them in. "Secondly, I add bay leaf, for protection from the seeping in of the dark arts and purification of our intentions. But most importantly for clairvoyance, so that we may see that which has been hidden."

Rita took a breath, making eye contact with both me and Alvie. "Finally, I add euphrasia, more commonly known as eyebright, for it will serve in pulling out lost and forgotten memories from within the depths of my circle sister's mind. It will seek the truth, which is our purpose here tonight." She tossed a cluster of small white flowers with a dash of yellow into the bowl and more steam started to rise. My grip on both Rita and Alvie's hands tightened. The concoction began to swirl, and a sliver of golden light shone through.

Wow.

The gold faded, replaced with a rainbow of dazzling colours. I could feel the magic pulling at me, dragging, *demanding* my attention. Rita was right. She was far more naturally talented than Marcel or Gabriel because this already surpassed what I'd seen them do.

The colours started to converge. My eyes were drawn closer to the bowl before the most bizarre thing happened. I fell into the colours. They merged, forming a picture …

There was a room with cream painted walls and pine floors. My childhood bedroom. There was a cot, above which hung a fairy mobile that twirled around and around. A baby cooed from the cot, reaching up with pudgy hands.

The door opened, and my mother walked in. Was I that baby? My mother set a variety of objects down on the rug in the middle of the floor. Then she picked the baby out of the cot and set her down on the rug. She organised the objects into a circle. There was a wide bowl containing a broth, and several smaller bowls containing different varieties of herbs. There was a small silver knife to the left of the bowl. It looked old, like an antique. To the right lay a glassy red stone.

Was she casting a spell?

My mother spoke, invoking the Goddess just as Rita had. She requested that she watch over her child, sheltering her from malevolent intrusions. Next, she began picking up bits of leaves, flowers, and berries, sprinkling them all in. The way she did it seemed so effortless, like second nature.

My mother was a witch. Seeing her now, it was undeniable.

She lifted the silver knife, holding it to a vein in her arm. She pressed in, cutting deep. Blood dripped from the incision, and she held it over the bowl, letting it mix with the ingredients. The greenish broth instantly turned a shocking shade of red as the first drop hit the liquid. Then she withdrew her arm and pressed a cloth over the cut to stop the bleeding. She picked up the baby and plucked something shiny from beside the bowl. A silver pin.

She held out the baby's palm and pricked the centre of it with the pin. The baby squealed and started to cry. My mother rocked her for a moment to soothe her cries. Once the baby quieted, she lifted her hand, holding it over the bowl, and allowed just one drop of blood to fall into the mixture.

The was a flash, like lightning. My mother's voice boomed within the small room. "I bequeath you, Goddess!

Take this blood curse from my child and hide it deep, deep within her so that no one will ever find it. Save her from being hunted like I am hunted. Forever conceal the True Power so that she may live a life of freedom. So that she never knows the suffering of her mother."

She fell silent, and a white light shone from the bowl, so bright that it bleached out the red until it was no longer a thick, viscous liquid, but a clear, see-through fluid.

Tears streamed down my mother's face as she wept. "Oh, thank you, thank you, thank you. Thank you so much." She hugged the baby to her chest, and I felt myself being pulled away.

The scene faded to black, and just as quickly, another began.

A forest in the dark of night. My mother ran through the trees. She was being chased. "I'm going to get you," a disembodied voice echoed in the darkness. "No point running. No point hiding."

A fountain of long dark hair streamed down her back as she ran like her life depended on it. Then a pale, slender hand reached out and grabbed her shoulder, breaking her run. She tumbled backward into someone's arms, and a sense of dread filled me. My mother had been caught, and whoever's hand that was, I sensed they meant her harm.

Something dragged on me, the scene fading away.

Just like that, I was back in Rita's kitchen.

14.

The room shook, and a shelf full of glass jars came loose, smashing to the floor.

Rita rubbed her eyes, and Alvie blinked several times, regaining focus. Wide-eyed, I stared at the two of them, still absorbing the flashbacks of my mother. It took me a second to realise that Rita was staring at me, a mix of fascination and horror on her face.

"You both saw that, right?" I asked, a cold sweat coating my skin.

Rita nodded but didn't speak. I was starting to get really freaked out by her silence.

"That was my mother," I said. "And I'm pretty sure I was the baby. But what was the spell she performed? Do you know what it meant?"

Rita cleared her throat, and she and Alvie shared a concerned look. She swallowed thickly. "Your mother spoke of a blood curse. Something called the True Power. I read about it once in one of my mum's old spell books. As far as I can remember, witches born with True Power blood are extremely rare, mostly because they were hunted almost to extinction. Few people even know about it anymore."

"Do *I* have this blood?"

"If what we saw in the vision is correct, yes. You must've inherited it from your mother. Someone was hunting her in the second vision. I think she created a spell to hide the blood in you, most likely so that you wouldn't be hunted like she was."

My heart clenched. *My mother was hunted?* Dad always said she died from cancer, but now I wondered if that was true. Had the person who chased her in the woods taken her life? I felt a chill just thinking about it.

"But what is True Power blood? What does it do?"

"It comes from the original magical families and is only passed down through the female line." Rita paused as though deciding how to break the news. "Your blood is not only intoxicating to vampires, giving them strength ten times what they already possess, but it's also an incredibly potent magical ingredient, especially in dark magic, which is why your mother wanted to protect you. Witches with your blood are not only hunted by vampires, but also by their own people."

Hearing that, a chill swept over me. I was a witch? This was mind-boggling. "Wait," I said. "Does this mean I'm related to one of the twelve families?"

"You must be. What was your mother's maiden name?"

"Smith," I answered.

"There are no magical families with that name," Alvie said. "It must be an alias."

"If she was in hiding then she'd hardly use her real name," Rita said, her eyebrows drawn in thought. "I could be mistaken, but I'm pretty sure Mum's spell book said that True Power blood can make vampires impervious to sunlight. It's likely the reason their compulsion doesn't work on you. Seems only right that you'd have some form of defence against them."

I swallowed thickly, goosebumps rising as I remembered Ethan's words and his nickname for me. *You smell like sunshine.*

"My God," I whispered. "That's ... insane."

Rita reached out, taking my hand in hers. "Tegan, you're so lucky you came to me with this. Marcel and Gabriel wouldn't have tried to see into the past as I did.

They would've tried to break your mother's spell entirely. You cannot, under any circumstances, allow anyone to break the spell."

"Why not?" I asked, frowning.

"Because it will put a target the size of Everest on your head. The vampires will hunt you to drink from you. The magical families will capture you to use your blood in their spells. And the slayers will kill you so that no vampire can ever get their fangs on the power your blood can provide."

Just like that, the weight of the world settled itself on my shoulders.

"*Fuck.*"

"Yeah," Alvie agreed. "Fuck."

I glanced between the two of them. "You can't tell anyone any about this."

"Of course not," Rita replied fervently. "You have my word."

"And mine," Alvie echoed.

I grew even more tense. "But you both practice magic. Don't you want my blood for your spells?"

"I already told you, we only practice benevolent magic, and the kind of spell that needs your blood is the kind cast to gain power."

"And that's not what we're about," Alvie added. "We're the good guys."

I hoped they were telling the truth. I suddenly felt like fleeing the city and going to live in a cabin in the woods where no one would ever find me. I stared blankly out the window for a moment, information swirling in my brain.

"Your mother must've been a formidable witch," Rita said, distracting me from my panicked thoughts. "As far as I can gather, she created a spell that would hide your blood from predators. I think she used her own blood as the seal, too, so the only way to break the spell may be with her blood."

"But she's dead," I said.

"Yes, and not to sound insensitive, but you're lucky she is. Now the spell can never be broken. Most likely, anyway."

"If my mum had never hidden my blood, would the vampires know what I am simply by smelling me?" I asked.

"I can't say for certain, but they would probably be incredibly drawn to you."

"I think they already are," I said as I rubbed my temples, feeling a headache coming on. "But if my mother managed to hide this thing in me, why couldn't she have hidden it in herself, too?"

"A witch can't cast a spell on herself. She'd need another witch to do that for her. If your mother was in hiding from her family, she likely had no one to help her."

My heart ached as I thought of her all alone with this stupid blood and nobody to help her hide it. Did my dad know about any of this, or had she kept it a secret from him, too?

I looked between Rita and Alvie, feeling desperate. "Nobody can ever find out about this."

"We already promised we won't tell a soul," Alvie reassured. "We're outsiders. We don't align ourselves with any of the divisions in this city, and we certainly wouldn't sell you out."

Rita tilted her head, her expression thoughtful. "Yeah, but how does she know that? Tegan needs something more than a simple promise." There was a pause as she thought some more. "How about a pact spell that seals the information between the three of us, so that we couldn't tell another soul even if we wanted to?"

Alvie nodded, smiling. "I like that idea. What do you think, Tegan?"

"Anything that will put my mind at ease. I suspect it's going to be a while before I can sleep at night."

Rita shot me a sympathetic look as she and Alvie began clearing the table in preparation for the pact spell. Several minutes later, we were sitting in a circle again holding hands. Thankfully, this spell was a lot less complicated than the last.

Rita set a pestle and mortar down in front of her. Into it, she added some cloves of garlic. "To safeguard our secret, I use garlic." The second she crushed the cloves I felt the air thicken around me, the magic coming alive.

"To preserve the strength of our pact, I add frankincense resin," she continued grinding in the next ingredient. "And thirdly, to bring an extra sense of trust and extra strength to our agreement, I add galangal root. This is a secrecy pact. We three vow never to repeat what was revealed in this room tonight to any other person, even on our dying day." She paused, glancing between us. "Repeat after me: We promise to keep this secret forever unspoken until she to whom it pertains wishes this pact to be broken."

We repeated her words and smoke rose from the ingredients, a heady aroma filling the room. I jumped when several sparks went off, like a sparkler at Halloween. Then they vanished, and the smoke disappeared.

"Well, that's that then. Your secret's locked up tight," Rita confirmed.

"Thank you. Both of you," I said. "What you did for me tonight, I'm not sure how to repay you."

"No thanks needed. Magic is my passion. I always welcome the opportunity to practice it," Rita replied as she

141

rose from her seat. "I have something I'd like to give you."

She disappeared upstairs, and I glanced at Alvie. "So, how did you two get into practicing magic in the first place?"

"Rita's mum taught her, then Rita taught me. I'm nowhere near as adept as she is. I can do some basic spells but nothing even remotely like what you saw her do tonight." He paused then, chewing his lip as he glanced at the door and leaned close, lowering his voice. "Don't mention I said this, okay?" I nodded, intrigued. "Rita's always been against the belief that you need to be from a magical family to become a witch. She says she's a prime example of the fact that anyone can practice magic with a little study and determination. But sometimes, well, sometimes I wonder." He rubbed his chin.

"What do you wonder?"

"Well," Alvie went on. "I've been practising for years, but I've never been able to even fractionally reach her level. I think that she might be related to the families but doesn't know it. She's never met her dad—doesn't even know his name. He could be a warlock for all we know."

"It's certainly possible," I replied, thinking of my mother at the same time. Which magical family had she come from?

Before Alvie could continue with his theory, Rita re-entered the room carrying a silver locket on a chain.

"You'll need this," she said, handing it to me.

"What is it?" I rubbed my thumb over the indentations carved on the locket.

"It's been magically infused with saltwater. You'll need to be wearing it whenever you go to work because it'll block Marcel's magic if he tries to unlock your spell. As long as you're wearing it, whatever he tries won't work, which means your secret will be safe."

I smiled at her in thanks. "That's really thoughtful. I seriously owe you one."

She shrugged me off, looking surprisingly abashed. "Like I said, it was no trouble."

At this, my phone buzzed in my pocket. I glanced at the screen, not recognising the number.

"Hello?" I answered curiously.

"Tegan, it's Delilah. I need you to come and meet me at the club."

Delilah was calling me? Weird. Ethan must've given her my number. I glanced at the time. I didn't have long before I had to be at Hagen's for my shift.

"Um, I don't have a lot of time. I have to be at work in two hours."

"I'll make sure you get to work. Please come. It's urgent." The desperation in her voice took me off guard.

"What's wrong? Is Ethan okay?" I asked, worrying Finn Roe might've come after him again.

"Ethan's fine, for now. I'll tell you the rest when you get here. Now hurry."

She hung up, and I found Rita and Alvie staring at me expectantly. "That was a, uh, a friend. I have to go."

Gathering my coat and bag, I said my goodbyes and headed for the bus that would take me to Crimson.

15.

True Power.

The name my mother used kept echoing in my head. I had so many questions, but it wasn't like I could do a Google search for this stuff. I thought of all the dusty old books Gabriel had at Indigo and wondered if I might find some answers in those.

The club wasn't too packed when I got there, probably because it was a weeknight. I sent Delilah a text letting her know I'd arrived, and moments later she appeared, seemingly out of nowhere. I wondered if that was a dhampir talent.

"Come on. We can talk in the staff room," she said, leading me to the back.

We passed by the door to Ethan's office, and I noticed someone was standing outside keeping guard. At first, I thought it was a man, but as I got closer, I saw that it was a woman. She was markedly stunning in an androgynous sort of way, reminding me of a young Leonardo Di Caprio. Her hazel eyes met mine, and I looked away, but not before I caught her smirking.

"Delilah, who's your friend?" she called out as we passed. Her voice was husky and deep.

"She belongs to Ethan, Dru, so you can keep your eyes to yourself," Delilah warned.

Belongs to Ethan? Um, okay. Delilah shot me a look that said I shouldn't argue, so I kept my mouth shut and my head down.

Dru gave a low chuckle. "Fair enough."

"Who was that?" I whispered when we entered the empty staff room.

144

"Dru works for Governor Herrington. She's one of his security guards. Probably the most personable of his bulldogs but also the most lethal. Don't let her charm you."

"Oh. Okay."

"You took your sweet time getting here, by the way," Delilah complained as she pointed to a seat. "Sit down."

I just about managed to keep my snappish reply to myself. *I rode the bus here for you, bitch.*

I sat while Delilah started to pace in agitation, arms folded, face deep in thought. She wore a pair of sky-high red stilettos that almost matched the colour of her hair and a tight black mini dress that seemed painted on. Finally, she stopped pacing and stood facing me. "There's trouble coming, and I need your help."

I tilted my head. "What sort of trouble? And what kind of help?"

Her expression turned grave. "There was an attack on Governor Herrington last night and every high-ranking vampire in the city is under suspicion for it. I need you to give Ethan an alibi."

Say what?! I stared at her, stunned.

"He was with you last night, wasn't he?" she went on.

"Yes," I replied. "But not *all* night. What time was the governor attacked?"

"Just before dawn."

"Ethan left a little before then."

"That doesn't matter. He didn't attack Herrington. That's all you need to know."

"Who did?"

She made an exasperated hand gesture. "Obviously, I don't know that. Herrington is particularly paranoid about other vampires trying to overthrow him. I wouldn't put it past certain individuals to do it, but it wasn't Ethan. I know that for a fact. The only problem is that Ethan was alone in his house after he left you, therefore nobody can vouch for him."

Alone in his house? My imagination ran amuck as I wondered what sort of house Ethan Cristescu lived in. "Can't you or Lucas just lie and say you were with him? I don't get why you need me to do it."

Delilah sighed heavily. "That would work fine if it weren't for the fact that Herrington's people already questioned us before telling us *why*. In ignorance of their true intentions, we told them the truth. So now there's nobody left to say Ethan was with them. Do you understand?"

My gut twisted. I didn't want to get involved in this. I had enough on my plate already after what Rita's spell revealed. Not to mention I was edgy around vampires in general given what I now knew about my blood. I couldn't stand in front of their governor and tell a bare-faced lie.

"Don't you have any human employees who haven't been questioned yet who could give Ethan an alibi?" I asked hopefully.

"You really don't get it," Delilah burst. "We can't just get any old human to vouch for Ethan because Herrington will be able to compel them to tell the truth. But with you, he won't be able to do that. Of course, you'll pretend his compulsion is working on you all the same."

So, I didn't just have to provide an alibi, I had to put on an act as well? My insides turned to ice as I imagined what would happen if Herrington somehow spotted that I was pretending.

"It's too risky."

"Do you want to see Ethan put on trial for a crime he didn't commit?" Delilah asked archly.

"Of course not," I replied, a pain in my stomach at the very thought. There was no denying that, for some inexplicable reason, I cared about him. And I certainly didn't want him put on trial. Vampire court was likely even scarier than the human variety.

"Then please do this. Ethan cares about you, Tegan. I know him better than anyone, and I've never seen him go out of his way to befriend a human. If you care about him, then help him. Winning my brother's trust is a very valuable thing. He goes to great lengths for those he allows into his inner circle."

As I listened to her speak, a trickle of guilt crept in. Would Ethan still trust me if he knew I'd gone to Rita to unravel my spell? I stared at Delilah for a long moment, worrying my lip.

"Okay, I'll do it."

She smiled brightly. "I promise you won't regret this. Now, we just need to get both of your stories straight. I think the easiest route is to tell them that Ethan stayed at your place all night, and also that he remained there today until sunset."

For a moment I was captured by the idea of Ethan spending the entire night at my apartment and what exactly that would entail. I coughed, reminding myself the alibi was fictional. "All right. But where's Ethan now? Isn't he in his office being questioned already?" I figured that was the reason Herrington's guard was standing outside.

"That's the problem. He's been gone all evening, and I can't get hold of him. Herrington and his wife Antonia are in the office waiting with all their bastard bodyguards. Ethan isn't going to have a clue what's going on when he arrives."

Well, that did make things a little more complicated.

Delilah rubbed her temples before grabbing her phone from the counter. "I'm going to try him one more time."

I sat still and waited. It appeared Ethan answered his phone because Delilah began an angry tirade in a language I didn't understand. Romanian, maybe? After a full minute of verbal abuse, she finally calmed down and hung up the phone.

"You got him then," I said.

She gave a curt sniff. "He'll be here in five minutes. Come along, we'll meet him outside."

Delilah didn't seem bothered by the frosty temperatures as we waited for Ethan at the back of the club. I, on the other hand, was absolutely freezing despite wearing my winter coat. I flipped up the collar and pulled it tighter around me. Delilah shot me a look like I was being dramatic.

"You guys must run hot," I said.

"Not really. We just don't feel the effects of temperature change as much as humans."

"Must be nice, living in this city." Tribane rarely experienced nice weather aside from a couple of weeks during summer. A minute later, I spotted Ethan's SUV pull up. He smoothly slid from the car and immediately approached his sister. Again, the two spoke in hushed foreign tones. I was growing a smidge impatient with all the drama and intrigue, especially considering I had a shift at Hagen's to get to.

My annoyance drifted away when Ethan came forward, placing his hand on the small of my back. I remembered how worried I'd been about him when he went after Finn Roe last night, which was ridiculous since he'd survived almost three centuries without me worrying over him so far.

"Are you cold?" he asked, his focus zeroing in on me as his hand came to rest on my shoulder.

"A little."

"Let's get you back inside. I appreciate you doing this," he said, a warmth in his eyes.

"It's no problem."

"All the same, I owe you one."

I glanced at Delilah then back to Ethan. "So, I just need to say that you spent last night and today at my apartment?"

"Yes."

"Seems doable."

Delilah gave a sharp, derisive laugh. "You haven't met the Herringtons yet."

We returned to the club, and Dru was still waiting outside Ethan's office.

"Finally decided to drop by, did we?" she asked, one eyebrow raised.

"I was unaware of the circumstances," Ethan answered her, his voice neutral as we approached.

I glanced at Dru briefly and noticed her nostrils flaring. Oh, great. She was *smelling* me.

"Your human smells … fascinating, Ethan."

"Yes, she does, but I'd appreciate it if you refrained from salivating all over her," he clipped dryly, and Dru scowled. He ushered me into the office, Delilah heavy on our heels. Inside there were two stocky male guards, who I presumed were Herrington's other security personnel. Both wore all black, just like Dru outside. Then I saw Herrington and my eyebrows shot right up. He wasn't at all what I expected. Not a hair over five feet tall, with a round head topped with sparse black hair, he was the spitting image of Danny DeVito.

His wife, Antonia, on the other hand, was tall and slim

149

with pale blonde hair styled into a neat bun at the top of her head. They made the quintessential odd couple. If you didn't look into the cold, cruel jade eyes of Antonia Herrington you'd almost wonder how her husband managed to gain a position of power. I sensed she was the driving force behind the couple.

"Howard, Antonia, so good to see you," Ethan greeted.

Antonia's eyes immediately darted to me. She turned her head to the side, as though sniffing the air. "Why is there a human present?" Her voice was as sharp as a razor blade and I managed not to wince at the sound of it.

"This is Tegan. She's a companion of mine."

"She smells rather—"

"Interesting, yes, I know," Ethan finished for her.

"Where did you find her?" Howard asked, his sharklike eyes taking me in. It was then that I saw past his miniature stature to the wise, possibly scary person who lay beneath.

"We met here at the club," I lied, and Howard shot me a smile that didn't show much kindness.

"Is that so?"

"I understand you've come because of an attack last night?" Ethan interjected.

"Yes," Antonia replied. "We had an intruder enter our home in the early hours of the morning. Somehow this person managed to bypass all our guards, breach our security measures, and enter the governor's study where he was going through some paperwork. If it weren't for the fact that a maid entered and found the masked intruder standing behind Howard with a stake in hand, my dear husband would not be here with us today."

"Was the intruder apprehended?" Ethan questioned, his expression unreadable.

"Sadly not," Howard replied. "He got away before my

guards could catch him, which is why we theorise that he was of our *kind*. Otherwise, he would not have been able to outrun them."

"Ah, so you're here to question if it was I who arranged this … intrusion," Ethan surmised.

"It is necessary," Howard stated blandly. "I mean no offence. My guards have already questioned your staff, most of whom were at home at the time of the attack. Therefore, we now only need to establish your own whereabouts before we can be on our way."

"Very well, I have nothing to hide." Ethan clasped his hands together. "Exactly what time did the attack take place?"

"Between four-thirty and five-o'clock this morning," Howard replied, watching Ethan's reaction very closely.

Ethan glanced at me. "This will all be very easy to clear up then. I was with Tegan all last night. Wasn't I, darling?" At this he tugged me close, wrapping his arm around my waist and allowing me to breathe him in. He smelled like night-blooming jasmine and spice. My heart thudded at his closeness.

"Yes, that's right." I answered, trying my best to keep my voice steady.

Howard studied me a long moment before returning his attention to Ethan. They stared at each other for a long time, as though communicating telepathically.

"May I question her directly?" Howard asked.

"You have my permission," Ethan replied.

Howard turned to me, and I sensed he was about to use his compulsion. I mentally prepared myself to put on an act as though mildly hypnotised. But just as he opened his mouth and focused his eyes on mine, Lucas stormed into the office, pulling a bedraggled, homeless-looking man in by the scruff of the neck.

"What's the meaning of this?" Howard demanded.

"Sorry for the intrusion," Lucas replied, a little out of breath. "I was out front when this guy came running up to the club. I think he's been put under some sort of spell. He accosted me and demanded to speak with you, Governor. He said he's got a message from the sorcerer Theodore."

At this Howard instantly paled. "He's lying. Theodore hasn't been seen in Tribane for decades. He's—he's long dead."

Suddenly the homeless man sputtered and started rambling in a strange, distorted voice that sent shivers down my spine. "Theodore is back. My message is for you, Governor Howard Herrington, Vampire leader of Tribane. The sorcerer Theodore has come to take back the territory that once belonged to him. He has already shown how easy it is for him to gain access to your private home. If you do not surrender your title as governor within the next three days, there will be a mighty war. A war you will lose."

The man fell to the floor and started to convulse in a seizure. A moment later, the convulsions stopped and he jumped to his feet, pulling a stake from his coat pocket. He lunged at Howard, but the two burly guards grabbed him before he could get to the small vampire. They pinned him to the floor.

"Get him out of here!" Howard shouted, glaring at the homeless man with hatred in his eyes. "Drusilla! Get in here now!"

At this, Dru appeared. Howard took her aside to whisper furiously in her ear. She nodded, grabbing the homeless man from the floor and lifting him out of the room. A cold sweat coated my palms as I wondered what would become of the poor sod.

"Did I hear that vermin correctly?" Antonia hissed in a shrill, almost hysterical voice.

"Whoever put the spell on him was probably just trying to spook you by using that name," Delilah said. "Theodore died way back in the sixties, so it couldn't be him who's behind this. Perhaps they imagined the governor would surrender at the mere mention of the name. It's an obvious bluff."

Antonia's jade eyes flicked to Delilah, and I noticed a small measure of disdain. Maybe she didn't like the fact that a dhampir was allowed to live among vampires simply because her father was high status.

"Yes, yes. You are right," Antonia responded. "Our people will discover the true identity of this assassin." She paused, making a sweeping glance over those present, her gaze lingering on Ethan longer than necessary. Clearly, he wasn't out of the woods yet. "And when they are caught, they will wish they had never been born."

Antonia took her husband's hand, who still looked out of sorts after the attempt on his life.

"We will be in touch," Howard said to Ethan as the guards started to escort them from the room. Antonia paused by me, her shrewd eyes taking me in. "She is surprisingly lucid for a blood donor, Ethan. And I see no visible marks on her. I do hope you are not being foolish."

Blood donor? *Wait, what?* Ethan had called me his human companion? Was that the term they used to describe a person they drank blood from?

"Of course not," Ethan replied courteously. "I simply prefer to take my sustenance from a less visible part of the body." He arched a flirtatious eyebrow.

"Hmm," she replied before continuing out the door.

Once they were gone, I exhaled heavily. Something

about that woman seriously terrified me. Delilah sagged down into a chair. Tentatively, I went to sit beside her.

"I'd say thank God they've left, but this last development has me even more worried."

"I thought you said it was only some wannabe impersonating Theodore," Lucas interjected. "If that's the case, then why are you so on edge?"

"I only said that to reassure the governor," Delilah hissed. "Although I don't know why I bothered. Did you see the way that bitch Antonia looked at me? She thinks she's so superior. I heard she has a penchant for young unwilling human males. She uses compulsion to force them to let her feed from them."

"Seriously?" I asked, my stomach turning at the thought.

Delilah nodded. "It's just a rumour, but if it's true then she has no business looking down on me."

"Quiet, everyone," Ethan interrupted. "If Theodore really has returned to the city then it doesn't bode well for us, and it could very possibly be true. It's widely believed that he faked that theatrical death of his."

Okay, now I was way too curious. "Um, who exactly is Theodore anyway?"

"The less you know about him the better," Ethan replied, a little too dismissively for my liking. "Now, come along, I'll take you home."

"I'm not going home. I have to get to work. Also, why did Antonia presume I was a blood donor?"

"It's easier if that's what she believes. Vampires aren't in the habit of spending time with humans for recreational purposes."

I sputtered a laugh. "Recreational purposes?"

"What he means to say is, if we aren't fucking you or

biting you, we aren't interested," Lucas supplied.

"Didn't you go on a date with Amanda?" I countered.

"Yes, and I fucked her good, too."

"Ugh," I grimaced. "Please, spare me."

"I'll drive you to work," Ethan said, casting Lucas a censorious glare as he took my hand and led me from the office.

I was about to protest, but I remembered how tired I was and how much I didn't need vampire drama. We were walking quietly hand in hand down the corridor when Dru appeared, wiping what looked like fresh blood off her knuckles.

"I see you didn't give much heed to the idea of 'don't shoot the messenger' Drusilla," Ethan said, sizing up her dishevelled appearance.

"Just following orders," she shrugged before her gaze settled on me.

"Hey, thought I smelled you there. If you ever get tired of this handsome bastard, come find me."

"Nobody gets tired of me," Ethan shot back. "So, give it up."

"Can't blame me for trying. You got yourself one special girl there, Ethan. You'd better keep an eye on her though." She ran her eyes up and down my body. "Someone just might steal her."

Ethan stared at her with casual disdain, not rising to her taunt. "Go clean yourself up, Dru. Beating up homeless humans isn't a good look." With that, he guided me out the door.

16.

Inside Ethan's car, I was greeted by a welcome rush of warmth, a pleasant contrast to the frosty cold outside. We drove in silence for a few minutes before I noticed he kept stealing glances at me.

"Something's different about you," he stated, his expression thoughtful.

I tensed ever so slightly. Did he know I'd gone to Rita? No, that was impossible. He couldn't read minds. At least, I didn't think he could.

"Different how?" I asked, hoping I came off casual.

"I can't quite place it. You seem—I don't know—enlightened somehow."

Damn. He was more perceptive than I gave him credit for. Then again, I knew next to nothing about his species. His senses could be ten times more heightened than mine, his brain capable of deciphering so much more information. Seeing as vampires lived a thousand years instead of a paltry eighty or ninety, it was only to be expected that they had more senses, too.

"Well, I don't know what you're talking about. I'm extremely tired, but that's nothing new."

"You shouldn't go to work if you're tired. Take the night off. Get some sleep." His voice was gentle, caring, which made me defensive for some reason. Probably because I didn't want to soften towards him even more than I already had. When it came to Ethan, I was having far too many troublesome feelings.

"It's not that easy. I can't just randomly take nights off. I'd get fired."

"I can talk to your boss, convince him you're sick."

I glanced at him. "You mean use your compulsion?"

"Sure."

I had to admit, it was a tempting offer, but I couldn't do it. It didn't feel right. "No, I can't let you do that."

"I'm your friend now, Tegan. You should let me do things for you."

Why did my exhausted brain make that sentence sound dirty?

"I'm still not entirely sure of your intentions."

"You think I'm only sticking around because of the spell?"

"Well, yes, that and how my blood ... *smells* to you. It's kind of obvious."

Ethan went silent, and I cast him a glance. His jaw was tight, his expression tepid. When he spoke, his voice was rough. "Your distrust is highly frustrating to me. What do I need to do to earn it?"

"Stick around? Don't bite me?" I suggested with a hint of humour, hoping to lighten his mood.

His lips slowly transformed into a smirk. "The former I can do. The latter I can make no promises on, but if it does happen, I promise you'll like it."

His flirtatious tone didn't make me feel warm and fuzzy. Instead, I pictured Ethan biting me and all the ramifications that would follow. My blood could make him stronger, more powerful. It could allow him to walk in the sun.

Maybe it was better that vampires could only come out at night. They were so much stronger than humans already. It was only fair that they had some disadvantages. Then I thought of Ethan and the gift I could give him. I could give him something he'd never experienced before. *Daylight.* Something in my heart longed to give it to him, but the logical side of my brain knew it was too risky. I still didn't know enough about what I was.

"Do you ever feel sad that you can't go out during the day?" I asked impulsively.

He glanced at me with raised eyebrows, as though my question surprised him. "Why do you ask that?"

I shrugged. "I was just wondering if vampires ever get seasonal affective disorder."

There was a flicker of emotion in his eyes. It looked a lot like longing. "I'm not sure about seasonal affective disorder, but sometimes I wonder what it would be like to move freely in the world and not have to worry about approaching daylight. And I'd be lying if I said I wasn't curious to see the sun rise. Just once."

"Sunrises can be pretty spectacular."

"Describe them to me," he whispered, and his plea caused emotion to expand in my chest. "Obviously, I've seen pictures," he went on, "but what does it feel like to watch one?"

All of a sudden, the car felt too small, the atmosphere heavy with the longing he seemed to be channelling at me. Sympathy swelled within me. For some reason I felt sad that he'd lived so long but had never enjoyed a sunny day. Never stayed up late or gotten up early to watch the sun rise. "When I was a teenager, my friend, Nicki, and I would climb up onto my dad's roof, smoke cigarettes, and watch the sun come up. It made you feel like new things were possible, like the slate had been wiped clean and the future was bright."

"Wouldn't that be nice," Ethan murmured to himself.

"You want a clean slate?"

His hands flexed on the steering wheel. "I've lived several lifetimes, in human terms at least, and I remember all of them. Memories can be something of a burden. Sometimes I wonder how nice it would be to forget."

"Memories can definitely be a burden," I agreed. The image of finding Matthew still and lifeless in my apartment flashed in my head. "But it's not like the trade-off isn't worth it. I'd give anything to be able to move as fast you can."

"You may have talents you're not aware of. We still don't know what you are."

"I know I'm human," I said, leaving out the part that I was also half-witch. I still wasn't sure whether I wanted Ethan to know that or not yet.

"Human you may be, but that's certainly not all you are," he countered as he pulled to a stop outside Hagen's. Glancing at the dashboard, I groaned when I saw I was ten minutes late. Mr Hagen was inside, glaring daggers at me through the window.

"Crap," I muttered.

"What's wrong?"

"I'm late and my boss looks pissed."

"Let me compel him. It's the least I can do after you were prepared to provide me with an alibi."

I chewed my lip, mulling it over. I really wasn't in the mood to deal with Hagen right now and a night's sleep sounded like heaven. I cast Ethan a glance. "Okay."

He reached out and placed his hand on my knee, giving it a gentle squeeze. The feel of his hand was extremely pleasant. More and more I found myself wanting to be touched by him.

"Don't look so guilty. It's just one night off. You work too hard."

I nodded and watched as Ethan left the car and entered the store. He approached Mr Hagen, and they exchanged a few words. A moment later Ethan returned and started the engine.

"What did you say to him?"

"I told him you were sick and convinced him he'd be more than happy to cover your shift."

That was hilarious and bizarre. Mr Hagen would rather drink his own urine than cover my shift.

"Thanks," I said, closing my eyes for the short journey to my apartment building. I wasn't sure how I managed to let my guard down enough to fall asleep, but the next thing I knew I was lying in bed. Someone had taken off my jeans and shoes. Oh, and there was the unmistakable shape of a body lying next to me.

Ethan Cristescu was in my bed.

Well, sort of. He appeared to be fully clothed and lying on top of the duvet, staring blankly up at the ceiling.

"What are you doing here?" I asked, groggily glancing at the clock. It was the middle of the night.

"I don't trust that slayer not to come back. I thought it would be safer if I stayed until morning. If you're asking why I'm laying beside you in bed, it's because your couch is extremely uncomfortable. I don't know how poor Florence manages to sleep on it."

"The slayer's name is Finn Roe, and I don't think he means me any harm. You, on the other hand—"

"He could try and use you to get to me," Ethan countered. "If he hurt you, I'd have no other choice but to tear him limb from limb, and I'd rather avoid cleaning up the mess."

"So, that's the only reason you're here? You don't want to get blood under your manicured fingernails?"

"That and I find you adorable when you sleep. You drooled on my passenger seat, by the way."

"I did not!"

He chuckled low. "You did. Also, I didn't want to wake you. You were clearly exhausted."

I couldn't believe I'd let my guard down enough to fall asleep in a vampire's car. I'd left myself completely at his mercy. He could've bitten me, but he hadn't. Maybe that was cause to start trusting him a little more.

I swallowed thickly. "In that case, thank you. I don't think anyone's carried me to bed from a car since I was a child."

"You're welcome," Ethan replied before letting silence fall.

Perhaps it was the fact that we were alone in my room and I was in my comfortable little bubble, but on instinct, I reached out and touched my fingers to his. My touch must've taken him off guard because he didn't react right away. Then, after several long moments, his fingers moved, interlinking with mine. His palm was cool but not cold, and I enjoyed the feel of it.

"Ethan?" I whispered, heart beating wildly.

"Yes?"

"Can you hold me for a minute?"

It had been months, almost a year, since I'd last been physically close with anyone, and the need for affection overwhelmed me at that moment. The need to be *held*.

"It would be my pleasure," he whispered before pulling me to him and wrapping his strong, solid arms around me. I sank into the embrace, resting my cheek against his collarbone.

We both emitted a pleasured sigh, and I wondered if he needed to hold someone as much I needed to be held. Did a vampire get lonely after living for almost three hundred years? Did relationships and romantic love still hold meaning? Did his heart yearn to find its match?

"Do vampires fall in love?" I asked quietly as his hand began to rub soothing circles into my lower back.

"Yes, we fall in love," he answered.

"How many times have you been in love?"

"A few."

His answer caused a sharp pang in my chest, and I couldn't resist asking my next question. "Are you in love with anyone ... presently?"

"Not presently, no." There was a small hint of amusement in his response.

"Oh. Have you ever been in love with a human?"

Now he stilled. It took him a moment to reply, and his eyes remained glued to my ceiling. "Once or twice, when I was very young. As vampires grow older and wiser, we tend to avoid falling for humans because it only ever ends tragically. Either we become addicted to their blood, the human becomes addicted to our bite, and inevitably, the human grows ill and dies. Or we manage to avoid the blood addiction and time wreaks his ravages. We're cursed to watch the one we love grow old and eventually pass away while we remain unchanged."

Something about the way he spoke made my chest tighten. "Best not to fall in love with humans then."

"Yes," Ethan agreed, tipping my chin up so that my eyes met his. "Best not."

He held my gaze and I couldn't look away. I was transfixed. Despite all his talk of tragic endings, I wanted him to touch me. He must've sensed my want because his hand reached down, his palm sliding along my outer thigh. I hitched a sharp breath.

"This is a bad idea," I whispered even though my pulse pounded wildly and I definitely didn't want him to stop.

"The worst," Ethan agreed right before he flipped me onto my back. He positioned himself between my legs and began to slowly move down my body. A gasp escaped me when he brushed his nose across the inch of skin between my T-shirt and underwear. Then I felt his lips whisper over my bare stomach, and I hitched another sharp breath.

"You smell incredible," he breathed, his voice a seductive murmur. I exhaled on a shudder, closing my eyes as my head fell back into the pillow. He pressed a hard kiss onto the thin cotton of my boy shorts, causing every tiny hair on my body to stand on end.

"Want me to stop?" he asked from his very intimate position between my legs.

My jaw firmed. "Nope."

He chuckled deeply. "Good."

I gasped and squirmed when he swiftly pulled down my shorts and tossed them aside. A second later I felt the tips of his fangs drag across my hip. A soft sigh escaped me when he pressed his mouth to my stomach, and my insides went haywire. A coil of need formed deep in my belly.

Then he moved up, hovering above me a moment before he gently touched his lips to mine. Unable to resist, I ran my hand down his spine, over his shoulder blades. He reached for the hem of my T-shirt and pushed it up, his knuckles brushing the white lace of my bra and the tops of my breasts. My throat went all strange and ticklish. The ghost of a smile touched his lips when he unclipped my bra, discarding it with my T-shirt in one go. His golden eyes practically glowed as he soaked in the sight of my breasts. He lightly fondled one then the other, toying with the edge of my panties but not lowering them yet.

In the dark of my bedroom, we explored each other with our fingertips. His skin felt as smooth as silk as I ran my hands over his abs. I was kind of fascinated. He seemed so human, yet also not.

"Keep looking at me like that and you'll be in trouble," he whispered in a sultry voice. "Can I keep you?" My heart caught in my throat because there was something so entirely pure about his question.

"Not sure I'm worth keeping," I answered, unable to handle the intimacy in his eyes.

Ethan grinned slowly. "Only a true treasure has no idea of its worth."

He began planting kisses along the curve of my collarbone. Each touch of his lips brought a tiny explosion of pleasure. I hadn't realised just how much I wanted this until now. He moved down my body again, kissing his way up the inside of my leg, and tingles of anticipation filled me. When he reached the apex of my thighs, I let out a quiet moan, and he paused to marvel up at me. "You're nothing like what I expected. I forgot how reactive humans are. And it's confounding, but you smell like ... you smell like every summer day I'll never enjoy."

As soon as the words left his mouth I tensed. All the reasons why I shouldn't be doing this, why I shouldn't be opening up and getting closer to Ethan ran through my mind. A single drop of my blood could give him so much power. Too much, probably. I thought of the night he killed all those slayers in that abandoned industrial estate. How feral and violent he'd been, and I struggled to reconcile that part of him with the protective, kind, flirtatious way he acted around me. He'd done me several favours in the short time I'd known him. Perhaps I could do a favour for him ...

Then the vision of my mother running for her life resurfaced and fear took hold. I couldn't give Ethan the gift of the sun—even if he did deserve it—because my secret might get out and there would be others who'd hunt me like they hunted her.

"Are you okay?" he asked, moving up to brush some messy strands of hair out of my face. His touch was soft, intimate. It made me want to spill my guts to him. Tell him all my secrets and let him decipher the mess.

I stared into his eyes, and a plea stumbled out. "Promise you'll never bite me."

He studied me, his eyebrows drawing together in consternation. "Tegan, you sound frightened. How many times do I have to tell you? I won't hurt you."

"I didn't ask you to promise not to hurt me. I asked you to promise not to bite me."

"My bite isn't something to fear."

"Ethan, please," I begged, my eyes beseeching.

His expression was serious as he tilted his head, a thread of suspicion entering his eyes. "Do you know something I don't?"

I shifted away. "What do you mean?"

"Do you know something about yourself that you aren't telling me?"

Just like that, my blood ran cold. Goosebumps rose on my skin. "No," I replied, scrambling for what to tell him. "It's just that I have a cousin who became a junkie, and I don't ever want to be like that. It's one of my biggest fears." The lie came easily enough, and Ethan seemed to buy it, his gaze turning empathetic.

He swept a hand down my neck, and his touch made me tremble in a good way. "Okay, Tegan, I promise I won't bite you. Not ever. You have my word."

"Thank you," I replied, swallowing tightly. "I appreciate it."

Ethan watched me for several long moments before his

attention went to the window and he swore under his breath. "I have to go. Dawn is approaching."

"Oh," I said, sad that he had to leave. Finding him next to me in my bed was a surprise, but it wasn't an unpleasant one.

He leaned forward, pressing a tender kiss to my lips. "Until next time," he whispered, and then he was gone.

I flopped back onto the bed, my heart pounding. After that little interlude, I suspected I wouldn't be getting more sleep any time soon.

***

The next morning, I couldn't stop thinking about last night with Ethan. His touch. The way he looked at me, taking every inch of me in. I knew I had to be careful. I had to make sure I didn't fall for him because that would be a recipe for disaster.

I was midway through my shift at Indigo and tying little handwritten price tags onto some home-made therapeutic bath soaps. Marcel was out, per usual, while Gabriel manned the cash register. He hadn't said much to me since the meeting at Crimson. Then again, Gabriel wasn't the chatty sort. Remembering all the questions I had about what happened with Governor Herrington, I pulled out my phone and sent Rita a text.

Tegan: Are you free for lunch today? I have some stuff I want to talk to you about.

Her reply came a few minutes later.

Rita: Sure! I know a great place. I'll text you the address.

When I was done with the price tags, I approached Gabriel over by the register.

"Hey."

His eyes flicked up from the book he was reading. "Tegan?"

"Um, I have a request."

"What sort of request?"

"Well, I was wondering if you'd mind me going out back and reading some of your books during my breaks? This magic stuff is all really new to me, and I'm eager to learn everything I can."

His eyes lit up at the mention of his books. "Of course. Knock yourself out. And if you ever have any questions, I'd be happy to answer them for you."

"Thank you. That's so kind."

For a second, I considered asking him about the sorcerer Theodore. I wanted to know who he was and why the vampires seemed so scared of him. But then I'd have to explain the assassination attempt on Governor Herrington, and I wasn't sure if that was something I should reveal since Gabriel was technically not on the vampires' side.

He smiled at me then, and I noticed his eyes linger a moment on my neck and my lips before he shook himself and looked away. "Sorry. I was staring."

I brushed him off. "Don't worry about it."

"It's just that you don't smell at all like other humans. It's a little distracting."

I chuckled, even as I felt a chill at the back of my neck. Gabriel seemed so normal and laidback. It was easy to forget he was a dhampir who drank blood just like vampires did. "Is that a good thing or a bad thing?"

"It's both, really."

"Oh."

"Anyway," he went on awkwardly. "I forgot to mention that Marcel wants to do some spell work at lunch.

Is that okay with you?"

I hesitated. "Actually, I have plans for lunch."

This seemed to surprise him. "You do?"

"Yes, I'm meeting a friend."

"Okay, well, I'll let Marcel know you can't make it." He paused, considering me. "Are you sure you can't put off your plans? Marcel's excited to make a start, and you know how busy he can be. Who knows when he'll next have the free time to do it."

That's what I'm counting on. I shook my head. "Sorry. I'm meeting Rita."

"You're meeting Rita?" Gabriel asked, surprised. "I hadn't realised you two were friends."

I gave a casual shrug. "We got talking when she dropped in the other day and hit it off. She's actually really nice underneath it all."

There was a flicker of suspicion in his gaze, but he didn't say any more and instead returned his attention to the book he was reading.

***

Rita was sitting by the window knocking back a shot of espresso when I arrived at the Mexican restaurant for our lunch date.

"Hey! Tegan!" she called out when she spotted me.

"Hi, thanks for meeting me," I said as I took the seat across from her.

"So," she said, clasping her hands together. "What did you want to talk about?"

I opened my mouth to answer when the waitress appeared to take our orders. I quickly scanned the menu and opted for a quesadilla while Rita ordered fish tacos.

"You were saying," Rita prodded once the waitress left. I took a deep breath and proceeded to give an account of what happened the night before after I'd left her house. I finished with the bit where the deranged homeless guy tried to attack Herrington and spoke of the sorcerer Theodore.

She stared at me, gobsmacked. "Woah. That is ... a lot."

"Definitely a lot," I agreed. "Do you know who this Theodore person is and why the vampires were so freaked by the mention of him?"

Rita's eyes sparkled with knowledge, and I sensed I was in for a good story. "My mum actually told me all about Theodore. She's big into the secret history of this city."

"Tribane has a secret history?"

"Of course! It has a secret population of vampires, dhampirs, witches, and warlocks, so it goes without saying that there's a secret history to go along with them."

"I guess it makes sense when you put it like that," I allowed.

"So," Rita went on. "You know how the city is divided by the Hawthorn river?" I nodded. "Well, it hasn't been like that for very long. Only since, like, the late sixties. Before that, I suppose you could say there was a dictatorship under the rule of the sorcerer Theodore. A sorcerer or sorceress is a very rare kind of warlock or witch. One who has surpassed an extremely high level of magical expertise to the point of becoming immortal through magic and nearly indestructible. I mean, I'm not just talking a thousand years immortal like the vampires, but *immortal* immortal. As in, they *never* die."

My eyes went wide. "Wow."

"Theodore ruled Tribane from the thirties until the

sixties. He had this massive estate on Ridley Island."

"You mean the one just off the coast? The deserted one?" I asked.

"Yes, and you have to wonder why it's been deserted for so long. If you ask me, it's all the bad magical residue left over from when Theodore was there. My mum says you used to be able to see his mansion from the city. Every night it was lit up by all sorts of colourful lights from the carnival rides on the grounds."

"Carnival rides?" I asked, bemused.

"Theodore was crazy for all that fun fair stuff. He collected old rides and antiques, like the big wheel and the chair-o-planes. He had this creepy carnival just inside the gates of his estate, and he used to have his servants turn the rides on every night with music and everything. You know that kind of old piano and accordion fair music?"

Her question sparked a memory, something recent, but I couldn't quite place it, so I brushed it off as random *déjà vu*. "Yes, I know it."

"The rides would come on without anyone ever going on them. Like a ghost carnival."

"That's pretty creepy."

"Very creepy," Rita agreed. "Theodore was a brutal ruler. My mum said he'd kill you for so much as a dirty look. The vampires resented him because he enforced massive taxes on them. He got rich off their hard work. If they refused to pay, he'd make sure their businesses went under with a spell. The magical families resented him, too, but more because he had such powerful magic. They were envious of his power and despised the authority he held over them. The fact that one man could control all of them, as well as the vampires and the dhampirs, really stuck in their craw. And so, all of the resentment led to revolution.

170

People began to get organised. Secret societies formed with the sole purpose of bringing Theodore down."

She paused when the waitress arrived with our food. I took a quick bite out of my quesadilla before nodding for Rita to go on with her story.

"The secret societies banded together to create blocking spells. They started out small, testing them on one street and then another. Before long, all of Tribane was protected by spells that blocked Theodore from using his magic on people. Slowly but surely, Theodore lost his control over the city, and, seemingly defeated, he disappeared off the radar for several months.

"Then came the last day of December when the New Year's festival was in full swing. It used to be a tradition where all supernaturals put their differences aside for one night and welcomed in the New Year together. People were partying the night away and having a good time. But when the fireworks display was about to begin down by the port, Theodore appeared on a giant podium holding a tank of petrol in one arm and a flame-thrower in the other."

A chill crept over me. "What did he do?"

Rita picked up a taco, taking a big bite and swallowing it down. "I can't remember his exact words, but it was something like *You came for a fireworks display, well I'll give you one*, then he poured the petrol all over his clothes before lighting himself on fire and leaping from the podium."

I stared at her, stunned. "Are you serious?"

"It's insane, right? I think the loss of power drove him mad."

"But if he was immortal the fire couldn't have killed him."

"You'd think so, but they found his charred remains

after the fire had been put out, so most people believed he was dead."

"I don't know. If he was a sorcerer, then surely he could've faked all that."

"That's certainly a possibility. He hasn't been seen since. People rarely ever mention him anymore, which is why what happened last night is so strange."

"What happened after he disappeared?" I asked, eager to know more. I couldn't believe there was this whole other history to the city I'd known my entire life.

"Well," Rita said in between bites of taco. "There were a few months of peace before power struggles began to break out between the vampires and the magical families. The dhampirs and slayers weren't involved much because their numbers are so much smaller, but they took the side of the magical families. Eventually, there was a stand-off, and the decision was made to split the city down the middle. The vampires got one half, and everybody else got the other. The rules were drawn up and there's been segregation ever since."

"It just seems so extreme. Surely all supernatural people would want to stick together rather than be pitted against one another all the time."

"You'd think that, but people tend to fixate on small, inconsequential differences and turn them into issues that can't be overcome."

We ate in silence for a few minutes, allowing the bustling lunchtime restaurant noises to drift over us. Finally, I broke the quiet. "What's your opinion on last night? Do you think it really is Theodore come back from the dead?"

Her expression was thoughtful as she took a moment to consider it. "It's possible. But it could just as easily be some fanatic trying to get attention."

For a second, I imagined that it was Theodore. What kind of battle would ensue? The homeless man had said something about a war, and in wars, people always sought power. In that scenario, nothing would be more beneficial than my blood, both for the vampires and for the magical families.

"You seem a little stressed," Rita commented as she dabbed her mouth with a napkin.

I glanced from side to side, making sure no one was listening. "I was just thinking about my blood," I whispered. "If there's a war, people will want it."

"The only people who know about your blood are you, me, and Alvie and we've cast the pact spell, which means the only way anyone will find out is if you tell them, so ..."

"So, I better keep my mouth shut?"

Now she smiled. "Exactly."

17.

Rita walked with me back to Indigo once we'd finished lunch. The place was empty when we stepped inside, but Marcel and Gabriel quicky appeared from the back. Marcel eyed us with no small amount of suspicion, and I started to wonder if I should've kept my budding friendship with Rita a secret.

"Hey, you two. Why the long faces?" Rita asked as they approached us.

Marcel focused his attention on me, not bothering to answer Rita's question. "It's a pity you were busy during lunch today, Tegan. I'll have to try and free up some time tomorrow, or perhaps Friday. We don't want to be falling behind on our little project." There was a subtle edge to his words.

Rita and I shared a glance. I was about to respond when someone else emerged from the back of the store. *Finn Roe.* He sauntered out wearing jeans and a black combat jacket. What on earth was he doing here?

"Nice to see you again, love," he greeted cheerfully.

"Oh, look, it's the Irish Van Helsing," Rita said, rolling her eyes. *Wait, what?*

"How do you all know each other?"

"This city is far smaller than you'd imagine," Finn replied smugly. He clearly enjoyed taking me off guard like this. I looked to Rita, and she shrugged, like Finn's presence was no cause for concern. I, on the other hand, took in the sight of the slayer standing with Marcel by his side and got the distinct feeling *I'd* been the topic of conversation amongst them. And I didn't like that one bit.

"So," Rita went on as she eyed the three. "What is this?

Some sort of boy scout meeting?"

"Finn came to inform Gabriel and me of an important development," Marcel replied. "Although the fact that it's important means it's none of *your* concern."

His dismissive tone irked me, and my gaze narrowed in irritation when I blurted, "Don't talk to her like that." It seemed I forgot for a second that Marcel was my boss. Gabriel's eyebrows rose while Marcel gave a cold laugh, and I saw right past the hippy façade to the cutthroat man who lay beneath.

"What's it to you how I talk to her?" he replied sharply. "You've known her what, a week? You have no clue the kind of woman you're befriending, Tegan."

"Hey! What's that supposed to mean?" Rita interjected.

"It means you're a little girl who goes around masquerading as a witch to dupe silly humans into paying you to cast phoney spells," Marcel shot back.

"Okay, now you're just being rude," Rita replied, but she didn't seem hurt by what he said. Maybe because she already knew this was what he thought of her.

"Have you ever seen her cast a spell?" I challenged.

Marcel glanced at me, looking like my question surprised him. "Well, no, but—"

"Then how do you know she's phony?"

Now his eyes narrowed further in suspicion. "Have *you* seen her cast a spell?"

I folded my arms. "Maybe I have."

Marcel's eyes cut to Rita. "What have you been up to?"

Rita stared him down. "Absolutely nothing. I'm just a silly girl masquerading as a witch after all. Obviously, I'm far too inconsequential for you to worry about."

Marcel's voice turned stony as he took a step closer to Rita, and instinctively, I stood in front of her. "I'll warn you against interfering in my business," he said, eyeing Rita over my shoulder. "You know who I am, and you'd be wise to keep your nose out."

Rita barked a laugh. "I'm not interfering. Tegan and I came in here minding our own business and you three appear like the Spanish Inquisition."

"Listen, just calm down everybody," Gabriel interrupted in a reasonable tone. He pulled Marcel aside and whispered something quickly in his ear. Finn appeared thoroughly amused by all the drama. I sighed as I shook my head at him.

"You're just loving this, aren't you?"

He smiled widely, showing straight white teeth. "Yeah, just a little bit."

"Are you forgetting who saved your life not too long ago?" I shot back.

Finn's smile didn't falter. "Nope. And you'll soon find out that I'm only here to help you."

Rita nudged me, taking my attention away from Finn. "Don't bother fighting with Marcel over me," she whispered. "He's always treated me like crap. I'm used to it. It's water off a duck's back."

Marcel stepped forward, his eyes beseeching. "I apologise, Tegan. I was out of line."

"Um, it's not me you should be apologising to." At this, I linked my arm through Rita's to show exactly whose side I was on. Silence fell as I continued to stare him down. It became clear that Marcel had no intention of telling Rita he was sorry, and something came over me. It suddenly occurred to me that working at Indigo really wasn't worth it. I could get another job somewhere else that didn't involve the pressure and stress of being involved in a supernatural world. A world where a bunch of people were far too eager to discover a secret about me that I had every intention of keeping hidden.

"You know what? I might need the money, but I refuse to work for a bigot. You can stick your job. I'd rather starve than work for a stuck up elitist."

"You can't just quit," Marcel hissed. "We have an arrangement."

"We do? I don't remember signing anything. Come on, Rita, let's go." I turned to leave, and Rita cast me a wide-eyed look as though questioning if I really wanted to walk out of a perfectly good job. And yes, I did. The epiphany came upon me quite suddenly. I couldn't work in a world my mother tried so hard to protect me from. I needed to get out while I still could.

We reached the end of the street before Gabriel came running after us with Finn following behind. There was no sign of Marcel.

"Tegan, wait," Gabriel called. I turned around and noticed he had two books tucked under his arm.

"What do you want?" Rita asked.

Gabriel levelled his attention on me. "I'm not going to try and convince you to come back, because it's clear you've made up your mind, but I just wanted to reassure you that you'll still get paid for the week."

"Thanks, Gabriel, that's very kind of you."

He let out a sigh. "I'll be sorry to see you go. I was getting used to having you around."

"Yeah, well, I was getting used to being around, but I can't work for Marcel. I know he's your friend but I … I don't think he's a good person."

"Maybe you should think about leaving Indigo, too," Rita suggested, eyeing Gabriel. "I know you're not like Marcel."

177

A flicker of frustration entered his eyes. "It's not as easy as that." Now he held out the books. "I thought you might like to take these."

"Oh, right," I said, having forgotten I'd asked if I could check out some of his books. I glanced down, skimming the titles. *A Short History of the Twelve Families* and *The Basics of Magic*. "Thank you."

A moment of quiet ensued as he held my gaze then cleared his throat. "Well, I better be getting back. Don't be a stranger."

I didn't reply because I wasn't sure I could promise that. A part of me was considering leaving Tribane and going somewhere far, far away. Somewhere I'd be safe. Gabriel went, but Finn remained. I shot him an arch look. "What do you want?"

"I know what happened with Herrington at Crimson last night, and I know you were there," he stated, all matter of fact. My heart gave a swift thud.

"How do you know about that?" I asked, stunned.

"I have my informants."

"Okay, well, so what if I was there? What's your point?"

"Two things," Finn said, stepping closer. "One, you still haven't learned your lesson to stay away from the vamps. Bad move. And two, well, there's been a development."

"What kind of development?"

"News has travelled fast that the sorcerer Theodore has returned to Tribane." He paused a moment, eyeing Rita before his attention came back to me. "I assume you've since learned who that is."

"She has," Rita answered for me.

Finn's gaze darkened. "Something else has transpired.

178

Herrington was murdered last night on the grounds of his estate, shortly after he returned home from Crimson. He's survived by his wife, who has taken temporary control of his position as governor."

"Oh, my God!" I exclaimed, gasping. Speechless, I stepped back and sat down on a nearby window ledge.

"You need to be wary of Cristescu. As soon as the sun sets, he'll come looking for you."

"Why?"

"Isn't it obvious? With his governor murdered, he'll be wanting to eradicate all other threats."

"I'm not a threat."

"You're immune to compulsion. Of course you're a threat. The vampires won't want other humans learning how to do what you can."

I glanced at Rita now, fear kicking in. Was it true? Did Ethan consider me a threat? It didn't seem that way last night. He seemed almost in awe of me, and I was certainly in awe of him. But it could be a case of keeping your enemies close …

I noticed Rita kept checking the time on her phone. "Everything okay?" I asked.

Her look was apologetic. "I'm so sorry. It's just that I promised Mum I'd cover one of her appointments today, and if I don't leave now, I'm going to be late."

"Hey, go. I'll call you later," I reassured even though I didn't fancy being left alone with Van Helsing.

"Are you sure?"

"Yes, I'm sure."

Biting her lip worriedly, she nodded and headed off down the street. I turned back to Finn.

"So, you seem to be telling me all this for a reason. What do you propose I do next?" I really hoped he had

179

some good ideas, because I was fresh out of them.

"As far as I can see you have two choices. One is to go home and let Cristescu find you."

"And the other?"

"The other is to come stay with me. My house isn't on vampire territory, so Cristescu won't be able to come for you there, unless he wants to be staked on the spot, that is."

"He's done a decent job of avoiding your stakes so far," I countered.

His eyes flashed in annoyance. "Only because he was on his home turf."

"I think I'll take my chances on my own," I said as I stood from the window ledge and made my way down the street. Finn followed along beside me.

"I'd advise against going home," he warned. "Like I said, that's the first place Cristescu will look as soon as the sun goes down. You'll have to think of somewhere better than that."

"I'm not going home. I have a friend I can stay with."

"And that's the second place he'll look. Come on Tegan, you're smarter than that," Finn chided.

I stopped walking swiftly and stood in front of him, our faces mere inches apart. For a second, I was thrown by how handsome he was up close. "I don't trust you," I stated simply.

"Well, that hurts my feelings. Why not?"

"Because you're a zealot," I answered honestly. "And you look at me like I'm something you can use to your advantage, not as a person."

"That's bullshit. I want to help you. If you look past all the vampire slaughtering, I'm actually a nice bloke."

"I haven't seen you slaughter any vampires yet," I taunted.

180

Now he grinned. "Is that a challenge?"

"No. Now will you please quit following me? It's starting to get creepy."

He threw his hands up. "Fine. It's your funeral. But if you come to your senses you have my number. Don't hesitate to use it."

I didn't respond as I continued down the street, my mind racing as my anxiety increased. Everything was becoming a little too dangerous, and I was beginning to wonder if I should get out of the city for a while. I could go stay with my dad. He didn't live too far from Tribane, but at least it would put some distance between me and all the people who had an unhealthy interest in what I was. And maybe I could quiz him about my mother and whether or not he knew she was a witch.

I pulled out my phone and sent a quick text.

Tegan: Hey Dad! Any chance I could come stay with you for a while? Need a little break from the city.

His response popped up a minute later.

Dad: Of course, honey. You know you're always welcome here. x

All that was left was to talk to Mr Hagen about taking a few weeks off, which I wasn't looking forward to. He'd likely fire me, but I'd already walked out of one job today so what was another? I could stay with Dad for as long as it took to find somewhere else to work that wasn't a soul-killing night shift.

Deciding to bite the bullet, I pulled up Hagen's number and hit call. As expected, as soon as I mentioned taking a few weeks off I heard the dreaded words, "That's it. You're sacked." Where was Ethan's compulsion when you needed it? With a lump in my throat, I hung up the phone and headed to my apartment to pack a bag.

In my heart of hearts, I didn't want to leave, because I had all these new and confusing feelings for Ethan that I longed to explore. But logically, I knew it was the right choice. The vampire governor had just been murdered in his own home. Things were about to get even more dangerous in this city. I could feel it in my bones.

When I reached my building, I felt a funny sensation in the pit of my stomach urging me not to go in. I shrugged it off, putting it down to the spicy lunch, and headed inside. Just before I reached my apartment, I bumped into Florence. She looked well, much better than usual. Her hair and clothes were clean, and she seemed less burdened somehow.

"Tegan, there are some scary looking men hanging around outside your apartment," she warned, and I froze. It was still light out, so it couldn't be vampires. I peeked my head around the corner and spotted two tall guys dressed in black. They were the same ones who'd been with Herrington last night. His bodyguards. But what on earth were they doing here? I'd thought they were vampires, but they must've been human. There was no other way they could be here right now.

"Is your dad home?" I asked, turning back to Florence. She shook her head. "Good. Can I hide in your apartment for a minute?"

"Sure, come in."

I stepped inside, and the place reeked of old cigarette smoke. All the furniture was battered and worn, but other than that it was clean. I suspected that was Florence's doing. My mind went back to Herrington's guards and panic seized me. Did they think I had something to do with his murder?

"There's something strange about them," Florence

commented, breaking me from my thoughts.

"Strange about who?"

"The men outside your place. They don't seem normal."

What she said caught my interest. It reminded me of how she'd reacted when she met Ethan. "Do they seem not normal in the same way my friend Ethan seemed not normal?"

"No. They're a different kind of, um, not n-n-normal."

Oh. Well, that was interesting. If they weren't human and they weren't vampires, then what exactly were they? Werewolves? Demons? Ghouls? The possibilities were endless. And also terrifying.

I was about to question her further when the door opened, and Terry walked in. I fully expected him to yell at me and demand to know what I was doing in his home. Instead, he carried a bag full of groceries into the kitchen and began unloading them onto the counter.

"Have you told Tegan the good news, Flo?" he asked casually. He sounded oddly friendly and at ease. Had someone given Terry Vaine a lobotomy? Because this was bizarre behaviour from him. He didn't even seem drunk.

Florence looked back to me, a smile brightening her face. "Right, I forgot. Dad's s-sending me to live with my grandmother in Chesterport."

My eyebrows shot up. "Really?"

"This city's no place for a teenager. My mother will take good care of her," Terry said.

"Gran's the best. I haven't seen in her in forever though," Florence added.

"Well, that's actually great news, and weirdly coincidental. My dad lives in Chesterport and I'm going to visit him for a few weeks."

183

Her eyes lit up at this, and Terry didn't seem at all phased. What happened to the man who threatened me to stay away from his daughter? "That's amazing. We'll be able to hang out."

"Yes, we will." I glanced over my shoulder, still worried about the men waiting out there for me. I needed to avoid them. Then I noticed Florence's balcony outside. I could climb down the fire escape to the street. So much for packing a bag.

I stepped closer to her, speaking low so that Terry couldn't hear. He seemed oblivious as he put his groceries away. "Do you mind if I sneak out down your fire escape? I don't want to bump into those men."

Florence's eyes, wise beyond her years, took me in before she nodded. "Yes, go ahead. I'll call you when I get to Gran's house."

"Great. See you soon. And take care of yourself," I said, giving her a quick hug before I approached the balcony door and slipped out. The apartment was several stories up, and my stomach quivered a little at the height. I closed my eyes, swallowing tightly before I began the climb down. I blew out a relieved breath when I reached the street, walking swiftly from the building just in case anyone else was hanging about.

Hairs on the back of my neck stood on end and I got the distinct feeling I was being followed. Acting on instinct, I rifled through my bag looking for Finn Roe's number. If the vampires thought I had something to do with the murder of their governor, then accepting the protection of a slayer made sense, right? Either way, I was eager to get off the south side.

"Hello?" he answered. "Who's this?"

"Hi, Finn," I replied, clearing my throat. "It's Tegan,

184

um, I've reconsidered your offer."

"Oh, yeah?" I could hear the smug smile in his voice.

"Yes. Some of Herrington's guards were outside my apartment just now—"

"What did I tell you about going home?"

"I just went back to grab some things before I went to stay with my dad, but now I'm wondering if that's wise. I don't want to bring any trouble to his door if the vampires are after me for their governor's murder. I also suspect that the men outside my place weren't human, which just makes things all the more worrying."

"They're probably shapeshifters," Finn said. "There's only a tiny population of them in the city, and they often work for the vamps or the magical families as security because of their strength."

"Shapeshifters?" I said, stunned.

Finn ignored my question, his voice serious. "Look, you need to get off vampire territory fast. Meet me at Macken's Bridge in ten minutes."

He hung up, and I quickened my pace. By the time I reached the bridge, Finn was already there. I spotted him leaning against the ledge.

"Come on," he said when he saw me. "I'm parked this way." I followed him to a side street, where a nondescript black van was parked. It bore a similar licence plate to the green van from before, the letters DOH clearly visible. I felt strangely traitorous climbing into it, but needs must. Surely Ethan would understand ...

Finn drove in silence towards a residential area on the north side of the Hawthorn river. The row of houses was similar to where Rita lived, though the neighbourhood was a little nicer.

"Here we are," he announced as he pulled up outside a

185

red brick house with a brightly painted blue door.

"You own this place?" I asked curiously.

"Nah, it belongs to my friend, Noel. He lets me rent a room. He's higher up in the organisation than I am."

"Oh." I replied, monosyllabic. I felt a little out of my depth. Finn turned his key in the lock, pushed the door open, and an unusually large German Shepherd came running at us, barking and huffing happily when he spotted Finn. I went still because big dogs made me nervous.

"Hey, Wolf," Finn greeted, petting the dog's head before he noticed my anxiety. "Don't tell me the girl who hangs out with vampires is afraid of a pup like Wolf here," he said mockingly.

"He's almost the same height as me," I shot back.

Finn chuckled. "Ah, don't worry about that. Wolf's a big softie."

"He doesn't look like a softie. He looks like he takes after his namesake."

Finn gave another chuckle as he stepped inside the house, Wolf hot on his heels. "You hungry?" he asked the dog, heading into the kitchen and opening the fridge to retrieve an airtight container full of red meat.

"You don't feed him biscuits?" I asked, watching as he spooned the meat into a large silver bowl.

"No way. That stuff is crap. Wolf needs his protein."

Once he was finished feeding the dog, Finn offered me a cup of tea, and I nodded, still wary of Wolf. He just didn't seem like a normal dog. There was too much wisdom in his eyes. Though maybe I was just on edge because of the day I was having. A lot had happened in the last twenty-four hours, and now here I was taking refuge in the home of a vampire slayer.

When he was finished making the tea, Finn carried two

cups alongside a plate of biscuits into the living room. He was strangely hospitable given his occupation. The furnishings were old but homely, and I took a seat on the couch.

Finn offered me a cup, and I took a sip, my thoughts still jumbled.

"You made the right choice coming to me. I know you don't trust me fully yet, but you will."

"I didn't come here because I'm afraid of Ethan, you know. He's not a bad person."

Finn glowered. "He's not a person at all."

"You're wrong. He has good in him." Finn didn't look convinced. "Anyway," I went on. "I came because of Herrington's goons lurking outside my apartment. Do you think they were there just to question me, or was it something more sinister?"

His expression turned thoughtful. "Hard to tell. But you had the right idea getting out of there, just in case."

Wolf plodded into the room and curled up on a rug in front of the fireplace. The house really was quite cosy. My thoughts went to my own little apartment and what would become of it. I had enough to cover rent for the next month or two, but after that I was screwed. Walking out on two jobs in one day really wasn't the smartest idea I'd ever had. What had come over me? I felt like discovering all this new information about my mother and my blood had me acting in a bizarrely self-sabotaging manner.

I glanced at Finn and found him studying me. His eyes traced my mouth, the line of my jaw, making me self-conscious. "So," I said, clearing my throat. "How did you get into the slaying business?" I picked up a biscuit and dipped it in my tea before taking a bite.

"Why do you want to know?"

"You want me to trust you, right? In order to do that I have to get to know you better. Besides, we might as well talk. What else are we going to do to pass the time?"

Suddenly, his eyes took on a sultry gleam. "Come upstairs with me. I know a couple of fun things we could do."

I tilted my head, arching a cynical eyebrow. "No, thank you."

He winked. "It was worth a try."

My stomach fluttered at his wink. Wait a second, did he fancy me? Was that why he was helping me? I really didn't have time for that right now. I was trying to decide what to do to stay alive. Romance, or well, sex, seemed superfluous.

Finn eyed me. "What's that look for?"

"It's nothing."

"No, go on. Tell me."

"I just have this suspicion you might have a little bit of a crush on me, so I'll tell you upfront I'm not interested."

Now he barked a laugh. "Modest, aren't we?"

"I don't see the point in beating around the bush." I folded my arms.

"Well, you can relax. You're not bad looking, but I don't have any designs on you. I'm helping you purely out of the goodness of my heart."

"Right," I scoffed cynically and took another sip of tea.

"You've an attitude. Bit of a thick shell, too. Why's that?"

"The why is none of your business," I shot back and motioned to some framed pictures on the mantelpiece. One looked like a class photo, except all the men and women wore strange black uniforms. Slayer uniforms, I realised belatedly. "Do slayers have graduation ceremonies or something?"

Finn's eyes flicked to the picture. "Or something."

There was another photo of Finn grinning into the camera with an older man beside him. "Is that Noel?"

"Yeah. He's my superior in the DOH. He's also one of my closest friends, in a fatherly kind of way."

In the picture, Noel wore his uniform, several medals pinned to his breast. "What's with all the medals? Please don't tell me they award them to you for killing vampires." I bristled at the thought.

Finn set his mug down and eyed me a moment. "Don't waste your sympathy on them. Vampires have killed far more humans than humans have killed vampires."

"Oh? Can you point me to some material on that statistic?"

"Don't be smart. My job is to protect humans. You should be on my side."

"I'm not on anybody's side but my own. Think of me as a slightly grumpy version of Switzerland."

"Sometimes it's impossible stay neutral, Tegan," he replied, staring me down. A long moment of silence fell between us before he blew out a sigh. "I came here about three years ago. Tribane has one of the largest centres for vampire slayers in the world."

"You moved here to join the DOH? That's a fairly drastic life decision."

"Yeah, well, I had my reasons," Finn went on.

"And those were?"

His expression darkened. I didn't think he was going to respond, but then he spoke, his voice subdued. "A vampire back home killed my mother and my sister, the only family I had. He'd developed some kind of sick obsession with the two of them and messed with their heads for a while before

189

he finished them off. Exactly what Cristescu will do to you in the end. He might toy with you for a little longer than usual since you're an anomaly and he can't use his compulsion on you, but believe me, once he gets bored, and they always do, he'll drain you until you're nothing but a shrivelled old corpse."

"Lovely," I replied, my blood running cold at the imagery. A knot of dread began to form in the pit of my stomach as I wondered if he was right. Ethan claimed vampires didn't kill, but that could very well be a massive lie. I looked back to Finn. "So, you think I should stay away from Ethan altogether?"

"If you want to live long enough to see your next birthday, yes, that's what I'd recommend."

An icy tendril wrapped itself around my chest at his warning just as my phone vibrated in my pocket. I pulled it out and saw Rita's name on the screen.

"Hi, Rita," I answered.

"Tegan!" she replied, breathless. "You need to get down to the port right now."

"Why? What's going on?"

"The whole city's running wild on a rumour that Theodore is going to show himself there after sundown, which is approximately twenty-five minutes from now."

I looked at Finn, and his eyebrows shot up. The volume on my phone was loud enough for him to hear what Rita said. In fact, he was already standing and grabbing his jacket.

"Okay, I'll see you there."

"See you soon," Rita replied before quickly hanging up.

"Come on," Finn said. "We need to get a move on. We don't have much time."

18.

Before we even got close to the port, we were slowed down by crowds of people all going in the same direction as us. Rumours travelled fast in this city, it seemed. There were so many people that Finn eventually had to park the van so we could get out and walk the rest of the way.

"Stay close," he urged as we joined the crowd. I nodded, but only because the people I was surrounded by struck me as not quite … normal. These weren't humans. At least, most of them weren't. These were witches, warlocks, and dhampirs. The average person might not recognise the difference, but I was starting to sense "otherness" in people the more entrenched I became in this world.

When we reached the port, I spotted a crowd of vampires gathered on the other side. I worried about what would happen if the two sides mixed. Would there be a fight? A riot? Was Ethan among them?

My heart rate picked up just thinking about him. Would he be angry if he saw me with Finn? Did I care?

If the squeeze in my chest was anything to go by, then yes, I did care.

"This isn't good," Finn muttered to himself, and I agreed with him. Everyone was on a knife's edge waiting to see if Theodore would show his face, the air markedly tense. And a tense atmosphere amongst sworn enemies was not a good combination.

As I took in the very evident divide between the two sides, I remembered how I was supposed to present myself in front of the two governors and declare my position as neutral. I had a funny feeling that wouldn't be happening now, especially since Herrington had been murdered.

Something buzzed around my head. I swiped at it, thinking it was a fly, before noticing a tiny gold speck of light, like the tip of a very small torch.

"Do you see that?" I asked Finn.

He glanced at me, perplexed. "See what?"

Before I could reply, Rita and Alvie appeared. Rita caught the speck of light between her thumb and forefinger and it blinked out of existence.

"Hey," she said with grin. "Cool trick, huh? We couldn't find you in the crowd, so I used a little locating spell."

"Very cool," I agreed. "How come Finn couldn't see it?"

Now she winked. "I cast it so only you could see. Can you imagine what would happen if every misfit here saw the light? They'd think it was Theodore and chaos would break out." Her gaze travelled to Finn. "What are you doing with him anyway?"

I bit my lip. "Herrington's guards were waiting outside my apartment when I got home this afternoon. Finn's been helping me stay safe."

Her eyes narrowed in suspicion. "Has he now?"

"Oh, don't look at me like that. I can be trusted," Finn said in protest.

"Anyway," I went on, changing the subject. "Do you think it really is Theodore behind all this tonight?"

Her expression sobered. "I don't know. Only time will tell. Come on, let's try to find a spot with a better view."

We managed to squeeze our way to the front of the pier, and I spotted Marcel and Gabriel nearby. Marcel nodded to Finn, but didn't bother to acknowledge my presence. Guess he was still pissed at me for quitting.

"I'll be back in a minute," Finn said, lightly touching my elbow before he went to join the two men. The three of them huddled together to talk, but I couldn't hear what was said. Rita and Alvie stared out at the water, anticipation in their eyes. I stepped close to Rita and linked my arm through hers. She accepted it wordlessly and continued staring.

"What are you two looking at?"

"The Island," Alvie answered, nodding to Ridley Island, which lay in direct view of the port. It was probably less than a mile out, and it seemed so empty in the dark.

"Why?"

"It's too obvious," Rita said. "We were all instructed to come to the area of the port with the best view of Ridley. Something's going to happen over there. I can feel it."

I gazed out again, noticing that other people's attentions were drawn to the island, too. Suddenly, I understood what Rita meant about being able to feel it. There was a buzz of electricity coming from the direction of Ridley, even though the entire place was cloaked in darkness.

A cold shiver tiptoed down my spine.

I sensed someone's attention and glanced over to where the vampires had gathered. There stood Ethan, his eyes boring into mine. His expression was stony, his entire demeanour tense.

Why the hell are you standing over there with my enemies? His face seemed to ask.

I frowned, my stomach twisting, because I felt like I was betraying him despite having made no pledges of allegiance. He never dropped my gaze, and my attention wandered to those he was with. Beside him stood Delilah and Lucas. My chest constricted when I spotted the recently

194

bereaved Antonia Herrington standing to Ethan's left, alongside Dru and the guards who'd come to my apartment.

Well, shit.

I slid my arm from Rita's and positioned myself behind her and Alvie, hoping Antonia didn't spot me. She had an air of sorrow and fury about her tonight, making a potent mix. Even from a distance, she looked severe with her white hair pulled back into a bun. She wore a black pantsuit with pearls around her neck, along with a small mourning hat and veil shielding her face. Dru stood close beside her, scanning the area for threats. I tried to make myself as small as possible in the hope that she wouldn't notice me either.

Finally dragging my eyes away from the group of vampires, I brought my attention back to the island. It was completely barren, just a bare expanse of land. Rita had mentioned that there was once a mansion there surrounded by carnival rides, but that had been decades ago. Now it was flat, lifeless, and dead.

Anticipation filled me, along with a certain degree of dread. I wondered what Nicki was up to right now. Life would be so much simpler if I were with her, drinking a bottle of wine and talking about mundane, average things, instead of standing here waiting for a fearsome sorcerer to appear.

In an instant, everything and everyone grew silent. Rita gripped my hand in hers. As our palms met, music started to play. Where was it coming from? Something about it tickled at my memory, and then it occurred to me. This was the same music I'd heard walking home from Crimson that night when the street had suddenly emptied, leaving me completely alone with the sense that someone, or *something,* was watching me.

Had it been Theodore? And if it was him, why was he interested in me?

The thought that he somehow knew about my blood gave me chills. But no, that was impossible, wasn't it?

I glanced at Rita as the music grew louder, the circular tune reminding me of a merry-go-round. Rita closed her eyes as though trying to sense where the music was coming from. When she opened them, they were round with shock.

"It's him," she breathed. "It really is him."

"Where is he, Rita?" Alvie asked urgently.

Before she had the chance to answer, the ground began to shake. I looked around, my gaze drawn out to the water. It was rippling violently, and I gasped when I saw the island. Objects rose miraculously from the ground. Gravel and mud and rocks shot up into the air as something pushed its way to the surface. The music grew louder, so loud it hurt my ears. I closed my hands over them to block out some of the noise.

"It's his house," Rita said as we watched the building rise from the ground like an enormous zombie rising from a grave. Goosebumps pinched at my skin. I'd never seen anything like it.

Tangled vines and mud coated its exterior. It was huge, taking up a large part of the island. "That's Theodore's old mansion, the one that disappeared after he died. I'm certain of it," someone commented close by.

I turned to look over at Marcel, Gabriel, and Finn. The three of them stood frozen in shock. How much magic would it take to pull off a stunt like this? Perhaps more than all the witches and warlocks present held combined.

I jumped when my pocket began to vibrate. It was just my phone though. The mundane sound snapped me out of my fear, and I laughed involuntarily. I lifted my phone to my ear, chest thrumming when I spotted Ethan's name on the screen.

"Hello?" I answered, glancing over to where he stood. He was staring directly at me, his expression sharp, and chills once more skittered down my spine.

"What on earth are you doing over there?" he growled. I didn't like his accusatory tone.

"I'm here with my friends," I answered, gesturing to Rita and Alvie.

"I can see the slayer with Gabriel and Marcel. Have you been in league with him all this time?"

"What? No, of course not. He's been helping me."

"Helping you how?"

"Well, I heard about what happened to Herrington. Then I arrived home to find his guards lurking around outside my apartment. It was daylight, so I had no other choice but to ask Finn for help."

"*Finn,*" he seethed. "You're on first name terms with him?"

"Does Antonia think I had something to do with her husband's death?" I shot back, not bothering to answer his question.

Ethan went silent then, but I noticed his attention go to Antonia for a moment.

"They probably just wanted to question everyone Herrington was in contact with last night," Ethan explained, but there was no mistaking the worry in his voice. Crap, if Ethan Cristescu was worried, then I should definitely be worried.

"Anyway, is this really the time to be calling me? I think there are more pertinent issues at hand," I said, gesturing to the mansion that had miraculously risen from the ground.

"That's why you need to come to me now. I can't protect you if you're over there."

I scoffed loudly. "I'm not going anywhere near Antonia Herrington."

"Antonia is not going to—"

My focus was pulled from Ethan when all around me people began making noises of shock and astonishment. Even a little bit of awe. I looked back to the island and saw that more objects had now risen to the surface. Carnival rides. Dirt spilled off them as they spun around, lit up with colourful lights. There was the chair-o-planes, a large merry-go-round with horses, and a giant big wheel.

"Tegan, come to me now," Ethan ordered.

I was about to respond when the music suddenly stopped, and everybody fell silent. The only sound was the click and whirr of the motors working the fair rides across the water. The cold strengthened, and I pulled my coat tighter around me. The distinct tap of footsteps echoed as someone walked down the empty aisle dividing the vampires from the witches, warlocks, and dhampirs. All heads turned in the direction of the lone individual. It was a man with chalky white skin and jet-black hair that was slicked back to highlight a severe widow's peak. He was dressed all in black, his patent leather shoes shining under the light of the moon. He reminded me of Mr Mistoffelees from *Cats*, which somehow rendered him even more terrifying.

"Is that Theodore?" I whispered to Rita.

"I've never seen him in the flesh before, but from my mother's description, I'd say that's him. He has a bit of a unique appearance."

"You can say that again."

Theodore turned to face his audience, and he seemed to

relish the attention, not to mention the shock and fear on the faces of those gathered.

"Vampires, dhampirs, warlocks, and witches of Tribane," he announced in an eery voice. "I thank you for your attendance at my homecoming this night. I see some new faces and some old ones, and some very, very interesting ones." I could swear his dark eyes fell on me for the briefest second and my skin crawled.

"I have been gone for quite some time, yet it feels as though I have never left. I'm very pleased to be home, and I'm ready to take back the territory I left behind." He eyed Antonia now, and she looked like she was seconds away from violently attacking him.

"What makes you think you can do anything of the sort?" she hissed.

"Would you like a demonstration?" Theodore responded blandly, the threat clear in his eyes. "Although I do believe you've already witnessed exactly what I'm capable of. My condolences on the loss of your husband."

"It was you!" Antonia roared. "You murdered him! We vampires will not submit to you, Theodore. There will be war before you ever control us again."

"Let there be war then, and once you have perished, I will take my territory. I've already made a deal with Siegfried Pamphrock. I will stay away from North Tribane, but the south, well, I believe there is a vacancy there for the position of governor, is there not?"

"Over my dead body," Antonia seethed.

"That might very well be the case," Theodore replied. I didn't fail to notice the flicker of fear in Antonia's eyes, but it was gone in an instant. "Although I do hope we can come to a more amicable arrangement. I don't want to turn my happy homecoming into a blood bath. Now, be a good little vampire and submit. No number of guards can protect you if I decide to take your life."

Ethan surprised me when he spoke up on Antonia's behalf. "Are you so confident, Sorcerer, that you believe you can take on the entire vampire population of this city?"

Theodore chuckled. "I'm sure my warlock friends will be more than happy to assist me if push comes to shove."

"Is that true?" Ethan shouted. "Will you let this tyrant speak for you all? Declare war against your enemies on your behalf?"

"We will follow the orders of our governor. If he has made a deal with Theodore, then we accept that decision," a warlock with long grey hair responded.

"Spineless bastards," Rita muttered under her breath.

"Blind obedience as usual," Ethan said dismissively, shaking his head.

"I thought everyone hated Theodore. Why would Pamphrock make a deal with him?" I whispered to Rita.

"Pamphrock would do anything to get one over on the vampires, even if it meant allying himself with an old adversary."

That didn't sound good. Not good at all. I was starting to regret not taking the opportunity to flee to my dad's house when I had the chance. But no, I couldn't bring danger to his door. Not before I figured out exactly what was going to happen now that Theodore was in the mix.

The tension heightened, and I didn't want to be stuck in the middle of things if a fight broke out. We needed to get out of there soon.

"Let's make some tracks," Alvie suggested quietly, echoing my own thoughts. Rita nodded in agreement, and the three of us huddled together, slowly making our way through the crowd.

"Do you actually think we'd ever join forces with you parasites?" One warlock shouted. "We'd rather have Theodore on our side than fight alongside vermin."

At this, Rita, Alvie, and I quickened our pace, though it didn't do much good. We hardly made it a few feet through the crowd before someone among the vampires launched a flaming petrol bomb in our direction. There were several screams when it landed, and all hell broke loose. People began to scatter in every direction, and moments later it was full-on mayhem. I'd been holding onto Rita's hand, but we got separated in the chaos.

"Rita! Alvie!" I called before I was shoved to the ground. I landed on my side and pain shot up my hip. I quickly ran my hands down my body to make sure I wasn't bleeding. Losing blood during a melee like this would be unfortunate.

Next to me, a dhampir and a vampire fell to the ground in a struggle. I was getting good at differentiating one from the other. The dhampirs were less statuesque and had more of a human aspect to them. Most of the vampires looked like they were built from solid marble, and they seemed almost too beautiful to be real.

The dhampir had his hands around the vampire's throat, but the vampire was able to rip out of his hold and scamper away. I'd thought a vampire would be stronger than a dhampir, and yet this one fled for his life? Perhaps it was all down to age, with the oldest being the strongest. The dhampir rose to his feet and chased after his opponent, disappearing out of sight.

I struggled to stand and tried to get as far away as I could from the fighting. Rita and Alvie appeared to be long gone. Something danced in my vision, twisting and twirling in a swirl of black and purple. The next thing I knew,

201

Theodore was there, his face directly in front of mine. I almost fainted from the shock of it. In front of the crowd earlier, he'd just about passed for human, but up this close, he seemed absolutely alien. His face was bizarre, like it'd been painted with white clown make-up.

He tilted his head as he studied me, his lips curving in a chilling grin. Something about it reminded me of the child-catcher from *Chitty Chitty Bang Bang*, a character who'd terrified me as a kid. I was just as frightened now.

"I haven't found one of your kind in a very long time. Lucky, lucky me."

"My k-kind?" I asked, pulse racing.

"You have True Power blood, my child. Quite the find, I must say." He gave a cruel laugh.

"How do you know that?"

"I always know," he replied, reaching out to take my hand. His skin was cold as ice. "You're coming with me."

I tried to jerk away, but his eyes found mine. I saw madness in their deep brown depths and inwardly shivered.

"Let go of me!" I protested, yanking my arm, but his grip was like steel. Theodore raised his other hand and made a small pushing motion. Suddenly, it felt like somebody had stuffed a sock in my mouth. I heaved and choked on it, unable to make a sound.

My eyes bugged as I saw a metal chain sail through the air towards Theodore, the kind used to dock ships. The chain wrapped around Theodore's neck, and his grip fell away. I stumbled backwards, spotting Ethan pulling the chain tighter around him.

"Run now!" he roared.

Theodore grabbed hold of the chain. His lips moved as he muttered a spell, and the metal melted to liquid. Ethan swore, his hand burning as he let go of the melting chain. I

202

didn't stick around to see what happened next. I ran like the wind, my stomach a storm of anxiety. I'd thought Theodore had the upper hand, but then I heard him wail in agony. I turned to look back and saw Ethan had somehow managed to break the sorcerer's hand. The same hand he used to cast spells. That would keep him out of action long enough for us to get away at least.

Ethan's eyes met mine, and I gestured wildly. "Leave him. Let's go!"

He seemed to come to his senses because he dropped a weakened Theodore to the ground and ran towards me. Without a word, he picked me up, threw me over his shoulder, and the world became a blur.

19.

I was dizzy when Ethan finally lowered me to the ground. He used his vampire speed to get us away from the fighting, and we stopped just down the street from Crimson. As soon as my feet hit the pavement, I winced in pain. It must've been the adrenaline, but I didn't feel how badly I had injured my hip until now. I gritted my teeth as I tried to walk, but my limp was evident.

"Are you hurt?" Ethan asked, eyeing me in concern.

"I fell when the fighting broke out. I'm a little sore, but I'll survive," I lied.

He moved fast, appearing in front of me as his eyes surveyed my body. "You're in pain," he stated plainly.

I waved him away. "I'll be fine."

"I can give you some blood to heal it."

I blinked at him, stunned by the suggestion. "Your blood heals?"

Ethan nodded. "It's really quite useful."

I hesitated. There had to be a catch. "I remember you saying it was addictive."

"Not if it's only once."

"Oh," I breathed. "Well, um, thanks, but no. It's not that bad." I tried to take a step away, but pain shot through me.

"Let me see," Ethan said, his voice gentle as he placed his palm on the small of my back and guided me down a deserted side alley. His hand slid along my hip, and I hissed in pain. His brow furrowed. "I think you might've fractured a bone. You really should take some of my blood, Tegan. Don't suffer unnecessarily."

I glanced up at him, falling into his golden eyes. Under

204

normal circumstances, I'd never even consider taking him up on his offer, but what if he was right about my bone being fractured? I could hardly afford a hospital bill now that I was unemployed.

I glanced at him, worrying my lip. "How much would I need to take?"

"Not a lot." There was a flash of heat in his eyes like he was excited by the prospect of me drinking from him.

My stomach heaved in protest. I remembered having nosebleeds as a kid, and the taste of blood in my mouth wasn't pleasant. "Does your blood taste the same as human blood?"

"Don't worry about the taste. I assure you, you'll like it."

I stared at his neck for a second, swallowing nervously. "Would I have to … bite you?"

He chuckled low and deep, the sound vibrating through me. "Would you like to bite me?"

"What? No, of course not. I was just—"

He reached out, his hand clasping my shoulder. "Relax, Tegan. I'll do the biting. You just need to drink."

There was something in his eyes that seemed a little calculating, but maybe the pain was messing with my perception. In the distance, I could still hear the fighting. I hoped Rita and Alvie got away safely. And okay, I also hoped Finn, Gabriel, and Marcel were safe, too. I might not have been Marcel's biggest fan, but that didn't mean I wanted him hurt.

I brought my attention back to Ethan. "Right, let's get this over with."

He raised an eyebrow in amusement. "I'll try not to be offended."

"You know what I mean. We don't have much time," I

said, worried the fighting would spread this direction.

Holding my gaze, Ethan revealed his fangs, and my stomach somersaulted. They looked sharp and were so white that they practically glistened in the dark. He lifted his wrist to his mouth, and without preamble, he sank his fangs in. I gasped. His eyes flashed darkly. I spotted a trickle of blood and became mesmerised. There was a draw to it, a strange allure. I found myself moving unconsciously closer to him, and I suddenly felt ravenous.

Ethan held out his wrist, his words a seductive murmur, "Drink."

Eagerly, I leaned in and pressed my mouth to his wrist. His skin was like silk against my lips, and when the tang of his blood hit my tongue something came over me. I let out a pleasured moan as I drank it deep. The liquid slid down my throat, tasting like nothing on this earth. It was heaven, the ambrosia of the Gods, and as I drank, I could feel my injury knitting itself back together. My body was healing within seconds, all because of his blood.

Wow.

I felt him pet my hair, his voice a raspy caress. "That's enough now, Sunshine."

I didn't want to stop. I gripped his wrist tight and refused to let go. Ethan emitted a low, guttural sound of pleasure, like he didn't want me to stop either. Before I could react, he backed me up against the wall, his hard, unyielding body pressed into mine as I continued to drink from him. I welcomed the connection, wanted it with every fibre of my being. Every cell in my body came alive, exhilaration coursing through my veins. I felt like I could conquer the world.

"Easy, easy," Ethan murmured as his other hand came up to cup my jaw. Very gently, he extricated my mouth from his wrist, and I whimpered unhappily. His lips curved in a smile. "You liked that more than I thought you would." A pause as his smile turned contemplative, then he spoke in a whisper, almost to himself. "I liked it more than I thought I would."

"I feel ... I feel incredible," I breathed. If I looked in a mirror, I was certain my pupils would be dilated. I'd experimented with a few recreational drugs in my time, but they had nothing on this.

"It will fade," Ethan assured me, using his thumb to wipe my lower lip. I stared at the drop that came away with his thumb and without thinking captured his thumb in my mouth. What he said about it not being addictive was obviously horseshit because I was already fiending for more. This wasn't good. Not good at all.

His eyes glittered in what looked like arousal, and my cheeks flamed bright red as I drew away from him, realising what I'd done. "Sorry. I don't know what came over me."

"Don't worry about it. Do you feel healed?"

"I feel like I'm made of titanium," I answered honestly, and he chuckled.

"I should've given you a little more warning. The first taste of vampire blood can be quite ..." He paused as his eyes held mine, a sensual promise in their golden depths, "... intense."

Feeling overwhelmed by the effect he had on me, I stepped away, turning around and taking a moment to gather myself. I was embarrassed by my behaviour. His blood had momentarily turned me into some sort of crazed addict. I ran my hand over my hip and there was no pain at all. I felt brand new, energised, and alive.

Turning back to Ethan, I sent him a sincere look.

"Thank you."

He smiled dashingly. "Don't thank me. The pleasure was all mine."

Seriously? I'd practically molested him right out in the open. Then again, he had seemed to enjoy himself. I cleared my throat. "Right, well, I'd better get going."

I made a move to leave, but Ethan blocked my way. "You're not going anywhere. I still want to know what you were doing with that slayer."

"I already told you. He was protecting me. He doesn't mean *me* any harm."

"You don't need him to protect you. You have me."

"Not during daylight hours," I countered, and his expression grew perturbed.

"Antonia's guards won't bother you again. I'll see to that. Besides, it's clear now that Theodore was the one who killed the governor."

I felt cold, thinking of the way Theodore had looked at me, how he knew what I was. I couldn't tell Ethan, because he still didn't know the truth about me, and I wasn't sure yet if it was safe to tell him.

Ethan held his hand out. "Come. We'll be safe back at the club."

In the distance, I heard a loud pop and a bang. Things were still crazy and sticking with Ethan seemed like the smartest option. For now, at least. I took his hand, and he led me out of the alley.

20.

When we stepped inside Crimson, the place looked like the casualty section of a war zone. Antonia was laid out on one of the tables, her trouser leg ripped off, revealing a gaping wound that one of her guards was working to clean up. It appeared to be slowly healing before my eyes. One of the club's bouncers was attending to Delilah and Lucas, both of whom sported various scrapes and wounds, which were also healing miraculously fast.

My eyes widened when I spotted Finn and Gabriel. *What on earth were they doing here?* They didn't appear to be held hostage, which was even odder. I met Finn's gaze for a moment, a question in my eyes. I was about to walk over and ask why he was here when Ethan led me away, striding across the room to check on his sister.

"Are you all right?" he asked with worry.

"I'm okay," Delilah replied. "You should see the other girl."

"And I'm just peachy, thanks for asking," Lucas put in wryly.

Ethan's lips curved in a smirk as he glanced at his friend. "Glad to hear it."

"You seem different," Delilah remarked as she eyed me. I stiffened self-consciously.

"Tegan was badly injured," Ethan interjected. "I had to give her some of my blood."

Delilah's eyes grew round. "Oh."

I tensed. "What's that look for? What am I missing?"

Ethan reached out, pushing my hair over my shoulder. "You're not missing anything."

"Yes, she is," Delilah muttered under her breath.

209

I stepped away from Ethan, worried now as I eyed him suspiciously. "Out with it. What is she talking about?"

He blew out a breath, casting his sister a beleaguered look. "There may have been one or two things I didn't tell you."

I arched an eyebrow and folded my arms. "Such as?"

"Such as the fact that since you drank my blood, we will now be connected for a time."

"Connected how?"

"I'll be able to sense you. I'll know if you're in danger. I'll also be able to locate you, wherever you are."

I gaped at him. "What?"

"It won't last forever, just for a few months."

"A few months!"

Ethan stepped close, clasping my shoulders in his hands. "Don't make a scene. Is it such a bad thing? If you find yourself in trouble, I'll know and will be able to come to your rescue."

"I don't need rescuing," I argued, unsure how exactly I felt about this. Right now, I felt pretty damn mad.

"Did I not rescue you from Theodore tonight? And I do recall assisting you on one or two previous occasions."

"It doesn't matter. I don't want you always knowing where I am. It's an invasion of privacy."

His expression darkened. "Why? Do you have something to hide?"

Only the fact that my blood could turn you and every vampire here into super vampires.

I stared at him, not replying. He held my gaze, not backing down. Finally, I released a sigh. "Look, I'm going to find out what Gabriel and Finn are doing here."

Suddenly, Ethan became aware that a slayer was in his night club. "Who the hell let *him* in?" he demanded loudly.

"The slayer and the dhampir have temporarily come to our side," Antonia informed him from where she lay waiting for her leg to heal. "You will not harm either of them, Ethan Cristescu. That's an order."

Ethan's jaw hardened. He looked furious, but he obviously couldn't object to Antonia's command. "I'll go talk to them," I said quietly, then turned and went over to where Finn and Gabriel, both looking uncomfortable and out of place, sat in one of the sumptuously appointed club booths.

"Well, this is unexpected," I whispered as I slid in next to Gabriel.

"Neither of us agrees with Pamphrock's decision to side with Theodore," Finn explained reluctantly. "We made the difficult choice to team up with the vamps for the time being. Everyone in North Tribane agrees with Pamphrock's decision to allow the sorcerer to take over the south. They think he'll stop once he has the vamps under his rule, but as soon as that happens, he'll be setting his sights on our territory. Pamphrock is a fool to not see that."

"So, siding with the vampires is the lesser of two evils?" I surmised.

"Pretty much," Gabriel said, his expression tense. He didn't like being here, that was for sure.

"And Antonia has agreed to let you fight for her? That's surprising."

"We're not fighting for her," Finn cut in. It was clearly killing him to be anywhere near his sworn enemies. "We're fighting *against* Theodore. There's a difference."

I almost smiled. "Is there now?"

"Oh, you can wipe that smile off your face, Missy."

"I just find it interesting how the vampires are no longer the evilest beings in the world. Maybe now you'll reconsider your obsession with wiping them out."

"I'm taking a brief hiatus, that's all," he stated irritably.

I glanced between the two of them, noting the absence of a certain warlock. "What about Marcel? Is he happy to side with Theodore?"

"Marcel is old school," Gabriel replied. "No matter how bad things get with the sorcerer, he'll always prefer his own kind over the vampires. That's just his way."

I felt bad for Gabriel. He looked so disappointed in his friend. "Well, I think it's very big of you to put your differences aside to fight for the greater good. I know it must be difficult. You don't like Ethan much do you?"

"No, I do not."

"Hey," Finn whispered. "This isn't easy for me either. I do kill these people for a living." He peered over his shoulder, glancing uneasily at the assembled vampires.

"They do sort of look like they want to jump you," I agreed, spotting a male vampire who was glaring in Finn's direction.

Finn picked up the glass of whiskey he'd been nursing and downed the last of it. "Had a bit of a scrape with that one a while back. If we manage to get rid of Theodore, he'll be the first one to rip my throat out. We called a truce before you got here and agreed to put our differences aside, but I have a feeling the truce will end the second Theodore is defeated."

"*If* he's defeated," Gabriel added just as my phone vibrated with a text.

Rita: Are you okay? Alvie and I couldn't find you anywhere after we got separated. We managed to make it to my house unscathed.

Tegan: I'm okay. Ethan helped me get away. Glad you both got out of there safely!

212

When I finished sending the text I glanced up and found Delilah standing in front of the booth, one hand on her hip while the other twirled a red curl around her finger.

"Mind if I join you, Tegan?" she asked, her bright green eyes levelled on Finn with a hungry intensity. He swallowed visibly.

"Sure," I said, wondering what she could want. She sat next to Finn and directly opposite me. Finn looked tense as she scooted close, clearly trying to rile him.

"I'm sorry Ethan didn't warn you of the full repercussions of drinking his blood," she said to me, her look apologetic.

"You drank his blood?" Gabriel questioned, his brows furrowing.

"Hey! I didn't have a choice," I defended. "I took a bad fall when the fighting broke out and injured my hip. Then Theodore was all up in my face trying to take me away with him. To be honest, I'm grateful Ethan was there to save me. I'm not sure what I would've done if he hadn't shown up." I paused, glancing at Delilah. "Yes, it was sly of him not to tell me what it truly meant to drink his blood, but I was in agony and he took the pain away. Though I'm pissed at him for withholding all the facts, I'm grateful for his help."

"Wait a second, what do you mean Theodore was going to take you away with him?" Delilah asked, and I realised belatedly that I probably shouldn't have mentioned that part.

I shrugged and tried to play it down. "I don't know. I fell and the next thing I knew Theodore was crouched before me, saying he was bringing me with him. Maybe he needed a hostage."

Gabriel and Finn regarded me with interest now, too.

"Why would he take a human hostage? Nobody would care what happens to a human," Delilah said thoughtfully.

"Jeez, thanks."

"I bet Theodore knows what's different about you. That's why he wanted to take you," Delilah went on, her voice quiet, face tense. She slid out of the booth and went directly to Ethan, where she was no doubt relaying the details of what I just told her.

"Shit," I whispered, my stomach in knots.

"Tegan, what is it?" Gabriel asked, his voice low and concerned.

I didn't answer because Ethan had turned to look at me from across the club, his expression unreadable. My skin tightened and my stomach was in knots as my fear of him discovering the truth built.

"I wouldn't fancy being you right now," Finn said. "Cristescu looks mad."

"Shut up, or I'll tell Delilah you want to volunteer some blood for her next meal."

"Don't you dare," Finn threatened. "It's hard enough being around all these vamps. I don't want any of them thinking I'm a fan."

"Delilah isn't a vampire. She's a dhampir. She lives with the vampires because her father was apparently a big deal," I told him.

"Really?" Finn asked, suddenly looking at Delilah in a whole new light.

"Yes, really," I answered, noticing Gabriel had suddenly grown very still. "Are you okay?" I asked him.

"Yes, I just need to use the bathroom," he said as he left me alone with Finn, who was now staring over at Delilah.

"Not a vampire, you say," he murmured quietly to

himself.

"Right everyone," Ethan announced, going to stand in the centre of the club. "Gather round. Some plans need to be made if we're going to successfully take on Theodore." His eyes rested on me for a moment, and I desperately wished to know what he was thinking. What did he make of the fact that Theodore wanted to take me with him?

All of the vampires went to gather around him, while Antonia climbed off the table she'd been lying on and went to stand next to him. Finn and I remained seated at the booth. There had to be at least fifty vampires present and neither of us fancied getting too close to them. Gabriel returned from the bathroom and silently retook his seat.

A woman with short brown hair raised her hand to speak. Antonia inclined her head to grant permission. "I have at least forty of our people working in my warehouse," the woman said. "All of them will be willing to fight if it comes to that."

"Thank you, Olivia," Antonia replied. "That is a very generous offer, and I'll keep it in mind should it be needed." Olivia smiled and bowed her head.

"That's all very well and good," Ethan interjected. "But unfortunately, as vampires, we are at a distinct disadvantage when it comes to taking on Theodore since we have no magic to contend with his vast supply."

"Yes, but we have numbers," Lucas added. "And although he may have hundreds of warlocks and slayers willing to help him win the south, we are physically stronger than each of them as individuals."

I heard Finn make a derisive grumble. Luckily, none of the vampires heard. It clearly irked him to listen to Lucas talk about how much stronger vampires were. I brought my attention back to Ethan and found him staring at Gabriel in a strange way. He looked like he was concocting some sort of plan.

"I'd almost forgotten," Ethan said, still eyeing Gabriel. "We do have at least one trick up our sleeve when it comes to fighting magic with magic."

"Oh?" Antonia questioned.

"Our new ally, Gabriel Forbes, is quite a talented warlock."

All the vampires turned to look our way. Antonia's eyes were curious as she took Gabriel in. "Of the Forbes magical family?"

Gabriel stiffened. "Yes, but I'm merely one warlock. I wouldn't stand a chance against Theodore."

"True," Ethan agreed. "But you are extremely well-read. I'm sure you could consult your books. If you still collect the way you used to you must have a better collection than all the magical families combined by now. Perhaps you can discover a way to get rid of Theodore with a spell or a ritual from one of your tomes. If you're successful, you'll be richly rewarded for your effort."

"I can second that," Antonia put in, still eyeing Gabriel with interest.

"There's no way to defeat a sorcerer unless you become a sorcerer yourself," Gabriel argued. "And that would take a lot more time than we've got. Decades, in fact."

Ethan stared at him even more intensely than before. "There are always loopholes. After all, the supernaturals of Tribane managed to banish Theodore in the sixties. Why not again?"

"You overestimate my abilities," Gabriel replied.

A challenge flashed in Ethan's gaze. "Find a solution and I'll give you your rightful share of what was left in our

216

father's will."

Just like that, the room was thrown into silence. Did I hear him correctly?

"You two are brothers?" I asked Gabriel in a stunned whisper.

"Half-brothers," Gabriel corrected, but it seemed that this wasn't quite the shock to everyone else as it was to me and Finn. It seemed we were the only two who didn't know that Gabriel and Ethan were related. That meant Delilah was his half-sister, too. Finn and I shared a look of disbelief. I finally understood what Ethan and Gabriel's history was, why they were always so tense around one another. They shared a father, but while Ethan and Delilah had been raised by him, Gabriel had been cast out. I wondered just how much their father left them when he died. How much he didn't leave to Gabriel because he was a dhampir.

Antonia made a noise of impatience. "Are we here to discuss the fact that Alin Cristescu enjoyed the company of human females, or are we here to plan a war?"

"I apologise," Ethan said with a deferential lowering of his head.

Antonia turned to address Gabriel. "Am I to believe that you have the knowledge to devise a spell that will defeat Theodore?"

Gabriel seemed frustrated now. Reluctantly, he replied, "I can make no promises, but I'll try my best."

Antonia peered at him through a narrowed gaze. "Very well then. We will see what the bastard, half-breed son of Alin Cristescu can do. In the meantime, I'll prepare our people for a battle. I'll return here tomorrow just after sundown to see what you have come up with."

Gabriel looked like he wanted to tear his hair out. I was

sure when he woke up this morning, he never imagined he'd end up working for Antonia Herrington come nightfall. Antonia rose from her seat, and with her guards, including Dru, she exited the club with a graceful flourish.

After that, the rest of the vampires started to leave. Some went to Ethan and spoke with him in earnest, hushed tones before heading out, probably wanting to be reassured of Gabriel's merits and trustworthiness. As I watched them, an idea sprang to mind. I glanced from Finn to Gabriel.

"I think there's someone who can help you figure out how to fight against Theodore."

"Oh yeah, and who's that?" Finn questioned.

"Rita," I answered simply.

Gabriel shook his head. "Look, Tegan, I know you two have become friends, but I don't think Rita can help. Fighting Theodore is a big task, and she isn't even a member of one of the magical families."

His immediate dismissal bothered me. "Can you just put your stupid prejudices aside for a minute? You haven't even seen what she can do yet. I have, and no offense, but in comparison to what I've witnessed you and Marcel do, Rita far surpasses that. You're all so blind that you can't see a powerful witch when she's standing right in front of you. If you could look past your preconceived notions, I think that you and Rita might make a formidable team. Your book smarts combined with her raw talent could be unbelievable."

Gabriel eyed me for a long moment. He still didn't look convinced. Crossing his arms, he seemed a little defensive, and I understood. If his father was a vampire and his mother a human, then that meant his mother came from a magical family. He'd grown up being told he was special, and it was obviously a blow to hear that someone like Rita might actually be more talented than him.

"You know, Gabe," Finn said, breaking the silence. "I think Tegan might be right. When we arrived at the port, Rita cast a spell to locate Tegan out of the crowd."

Gabriel considered him. "She did?"

Finn nodded. I rolled my eyes. "Why are you so against believing in her? She knows how to do all kinds of cool stuff. Finn has no reason to lie to you, and she even helped me …" I went silent, realising I'd been about to blurt that Rita helped me discover what was different about me.

"She helped you what?" Gabriel questioned.

"Nothing. Never mind. My point is, you can ask Rita for help, or you can spend the next twenty-four hours searching for a solution in your books that you might never find."

A long stretch of quiet elapsed before Gabriel finally relented. "Fine. Call Rita and fill her in on the situation. Tell her to come to my apartment in the morning. She knows where it is. I'll try to work with her, but I can't make any guarantees on results."

I smiled wide. "I knew you'd see sense." With that, I stood to go use the bathroom and call Rita. It only took me a few minutes to fill her in on everything, and she enthusiastically agreed to help us. I was beginning to realise that underneath her Goth style and slightly bitchy facade, Rita was a positive, sunshiny person.

Finn and Gabriel were gone by the time I left the bathroom, and I guessed they wanted to spend as little time in Ethan's club as possible. The place was empty, only Ethan and Lucas left sitting by the bar.

"Not opening up for business tonight?" I asked as I took the stool next to Ethan. I was still supremely annoyed at him for not disclosing how drinking his blood would form a connection between us, but I was too tired to fight with him about it right then.

"Not tonight," he replied.

"Do you mind if I pour myself a drink?" I asked, and he nodded for me to go ahead.

I reached for the nearest vodka bottle and poured some into a shot glass. Ethan and Lucas both watched as I knocked it back and poured another. I didn't think I'd ever stop finding it weird that all they consumed was blood.

"Have you seen Amanda again?" I asked, focusing my attention on Lucas because Ethan was channelling some serious brooding vibes my way. I could tell he wanted to talk about the whole "connection" thing, but it would have to wait for another time. I was *so* done with this day. Now that Antonia was no longer after me for her husband's murder, I could go home and sleep in my own bed, then think about my next steps in the morning.

Lucas's smile showed the barest tip of a fang. "Yes. I've grown particularly fond of her."

I poured another shot. "Well, be warned, I'll hunt you down and torture you if anything even remotely bad happens to her when she's with you. Got it?"

Lucas rose from his stool, looking mildly amused. "Got it."

He and Ethan shared a glance before he turned and left. As soon as Ethan and I were alone the tension thickened. I was hyperaware of him, and the image of me taking his finger into my mouth and sucking the drop of blood away was etched in my mind. I was so embarrassed over how crazy I'd gone.

"You know," he said, breaking the quiet. "I've had nothing but trouble since you walked into my life."

"If I remember correctly, it was you who walked into

mine. And besides, I'd walk away from all this right now if you'd only let me." I shot back defensively.

His gaze heated. "I'm afraid I can't allow that."

I lifted an eyebrow in challenge. "You think I need permission?"

He reached out, gently caressing my jaw. "I would hope you'd choose to stay of your own accord."

My heart skipped a beat. If things were different, I might choose to stay here with Ethan forever. He captured a part of me I didn't know existed, made me feel alive in a way I hadn't before. Sadly, though, things weren't different, and all the time I spent with him put me at risk. I was walking a tight rope, and one single misstep could lead to the truth being discovered. If that happened, I'd have to run just like my mother did.

"Delilah spoke of the sorcerer wanting to take you hostage from the port," Ethan said then, drawing me from my thoughts.

"I'm not sure why," I lied. "Maybe he figured out my connection to you and thought I'd be good leverage to get the vampires to stand down."

Ethan studied me, several thoughts flashing behind his eyes. "Maybe," he finally said. "Come. I'll drive you home."

"I can walk."

"There could still be fighting going on. I'm not letting you walk," he insisted.

Exhausted, I followed him out to his car. Silence fell as we made the journey to my apartment, and I didn't protest when he followed me into my building. When we reached the door to my place I stopped and turned back to face him. "Thank you for bringing me home."

Ethan looked somewhat forlorn. "You're not going to

invite me in, are you?"

I shook my head. He let out a sigh. "If I'd told you about the connection, you wouldn't have drunk my blood, and if you hadn't, you'd still be in agony right now."

"I know that, and I understand why you did it, but I'm not ready to forgive you yet."

Ethan reached out and tucked some hair behind my ear. "I hope you can forgive me one day. Sleep well, Sunshine." The second the tenderly spoken words left his mouth, he was gone. I stared down the empty corridor, noting his absence, and suddenly feeling far too alone. A part of me wished he insisted on staying.

Then, as I entered my apartment and climbed into bed, I noticed a strange, new feeling in my chest. It wasn't unpleasant, but it was certainly odd. There was a tightness, a kind of a pull, and I realised that this was the connection Ethan spoke of.

I fell asleep with a vague thought of how odd it was that the connection seemed to be wrapped around my heart.

**

I slept late the next morning. Drawing the curtains, I found the city looked perfectly normal. You'd never have guessed a tyrannical sorcerer was trying to take over. I checked my phone and found a new message.

Dad: Are you still coming to visit?

I quickly typed a reply.

Tegan: I have a few things to take care of here first. I'll let you know in the next few days when I'll be arriving.

I still planned on seeing my dad. I could kill two birds with one stone because I wanted to check on Florence when I got there and make sure everything was okay at her grandma's house. The woman was Terry's mother after all and that meant she could be just as much of a sociopath as he was.

Besides, it was probably wise to get away for a while. I wasn't a murder suspect anymore, but whenever I thought of how Theodore had looked at me, how he knew exactly what I was, anxiety took over. Rita said witches and warlocks used my blood for dark magic, and I shuddered to think what Theodore could do if he managed to capture me.

I completed a few chores around my apartment before packing a bag in preparation for my visit to Dad's. As I was going through my wardrobe, my attention lingered on the shoebox where I kept Matthew's songbook. Some instinct had me pulling the box out and flicking through the notebook again. Maybe I enjoyed torturing myself. Heaven knew reading his lyrics wasn't going to bring him back.

I flicked to the page where I left off last. The next song was called "The White Queen", and something about the title gave me a tiny chill at the back of my neck.

The white queen comes
And finds me sometimes
She takes away a piece of me
Bit by bit
Drop by drop

I stopped reading and frowned. Who was the white queen? Was she some kind of metaphor for drugs? I moved on to the second verse:

The white queen comes
And makes me forget sometimes
That she had ever come at all
A black cloud fogs my mind
But pictures I recall
Of bleeding and of biting

I hope for her
Never to return

Now I swallowed in alarm, because it almost sounded like he was talking about a vampire. Two lines, in particular, stood out, *makes me forget sometimes* and *of bleeding and of biting*. These were things that vampires did to humans. They bit them and made them bleed, then they used their compulsion to make them forget. Suddenly feeling sick, I pushed the notebook away. The thought was almost too awful to consider, but had a vampire been preying on Matthew? Had she visited him again and again, drinking from him and turning him into an addict the way Ethan had described could happen? Had he turned to illegal drugs to dull the pain of being preyed upon?

I started to flick through the rest of the notebook, searching for more clues, when a loose page fell free. It looked like a piece of sketching paper. The side facing up was blank, but I could see the outline of a face drawn in pencil on the other side. My hands shook as I picked it up and turned it over. Matthew had drawn a close up of a woman's face. Music had always been his passion, but he'd been a good artist, too. The drawing was so detailed, but the feature that most caught my attention was the fangs peeking out of the woman's mouth. Then, as I took in the entirety of her face, I startled, because I recognised the vampire in the drawing.

It was Antonia.

My pulse pounded as I remembered something Delilah said the night I first encountered Antonia and Howard at Crimson. She said there was a rumour that Antonia liked to take her blood from young, unwilling human males. The realisation that Matthew had been one of her victims made everything inside of me go cold.

I'd been so busy working every hour I could that I hadn't realised my boyfriend was being used as a blood bank by one of the most powerful vampires in Tribane.

Rage filled me. If Antonia hadn't preyed on Matthew, then he might not have taken his life. Did he see it as the only route of escape? The thought was heart-breaking, causing a tear to trickle down my cheek. I wished to turn back time, so I could go back and help him, stop Antonia from preying on him somehow.

I hated her.

Hated her with everything I had inside me. A dark resolution began to form. Antonia would pay for what she did.

I'd bide my time, but the first chance I got I was going to kill the steely-eyed, pale haired vampire who'd driven Matthew to suicide.

My phone vibrated loudly, snapping me from my murderous, vengeful thoughts.

"Hello, Rita," I answered, unable to help how angry I sounded.

"Someone got out of bed on the wrong side this morning," she commented. "Everything okay?"

"Actually, I got out of bed on the right side. It's what followed that pissed me off."

"Sounds bad. You want to talk about it?"

"No. It's probably better if I don't. What were you calling me for?"

"Well," she began, her voice hushed. "I've been at Gabriel's all morning."

"And?" I prompted, wondering why she was beating around the bush.

"Sorry," she went on, whispering now. It sounded like she closed a door behind her. "Marcel just showed up so

I'm hiding in the bathroom. He's already suspicious of Gabriel's allegiances, so we can't afford him finding out what we're up to. Anyway, I'm calling you because I think I know a spell that will get rid of Theodore. It won't exactly kill him, but it will banish him into a hell dimension for a couple of decades. It's just, I haven't told Gabriel about it yet."

"Why not?" I asked curiously.

"Because one of the ingredients for the spell is sort of impossible to get. Well, not *impossible*. I could get it, but then Gabriel will want to know how I got it and that's something I can't tell him."

"Well, spit it out. What is it?"

A long stretch of silence dragged on before she answered, "I need a vial of your blood, Tegan."

Time stilled and my insides were thrown into a tailspin. "Right," I breathed, heart racing. This was too risky. I couldn't give her my blood … could I?

"I'm sorry. I should never have asked. We'll just have to find another way."

"No, don't do that. Just give me a couple of hours to think about this."

"Okay. We'll talk later," she whispered before quickly hanging up the phone. I said a prayer that Marcel didn't find her hiding in Gabriel's bathroom. Going to sit down on my sofa, I dropped my head into my hands. Just when I thought things couldn't get any more stressful Rita threw a spanner in the works and made things even worse, though I knew she was just trying to find a solution to our sorcerer problem.

If I gave her my blood, then Gabriel would want to know how she found such a rare ingredient. And if he discovered that I was the source of said ingredient, my secret could get out and every vampire, witch, warlock, and slayer in the city would want to capture me. But perhaps … perhaps Gabriel would agree to keep my secret, too. Maybe I could trust him with it the same way I trusted Rita and Alvie.

He was just so difficult to read. I knew he sided with the vampires against Theodore, but would the lure of my blood override his loyalty to the cause? He was, after all, a member of the magical families.

I wasn't sure how long I sat stressing and mulling things over when the solution suddenly occurred to me. In order to restore peace to the city and get rid of Theodore, I needed to give Rita the blood she needed, then disappear somewhere nobody would find me. My time in Tribane was running out anyway, and I'd already been planning to get away. I could simply make it a more permanent departure. Besides, with Theodore knowing what I was, it was only a matter of time before others discovered the truth, too.

Yes, it'd be hard to leave my friends behind, Ethan especially, but sometimes sacrifices had to be made. Determination sat like steel in my gut. I finally had a plan, and once it was completed, I was going to leave this city forever.

21.

After I was fully packed, I headed out to meet Rita before she and Gabriel were due at Crimson. It was icy cold out, so I wrapped up tight in my winter coat and scarf.

I was almost at the club when an eery sensation crawled across the back of my neck. My ears pricked when I heard the tinkling of piano music and noticed the street was suddenly empty of people. A wave of *déjà vu* hit me as I looked around, on edge. Even cars were missing from the road.

Suspicion and fear took over as I glanced behind me and quickened my pace. The sound of my footsteps echoed as the music grew louder. I knew it was him. Theodore had come for me.

I broke into a futile run and ran straight into someone's chest. I looked up and was greeted by Theodore's soulless eyes. Turning, I ran in the opposite direction. Again, I was stopped in my tracks when he magically appeared in front of me.

"What do you want?!" I demanded, fear and adrenaline coagulating in my gut, my breaths coming hard and fast. His slim, pale hand reached out to caress my cheek, and I recoiled. "Get away from me!"

He laughed darkly at my poor attempt to escape, and a shadow rose behind him. Out of it, a form took shape, becoming a massive, black, human-sized crow. I trembled when its wings spread wide and Theodore pulled me to him. The giant crow's wings wrapped around us both, and I felt it take flight before everything went black.

I woke up to the sound of glasses clinking and liquid being poured. A piano played a light and cheerful tune nearby. The next thing I noticed was that I was lying on a fancy velvet couch, no longer wearing my own clothes. I peered down at myself, scanning the red evening gown, black silk gloves, and diamond bracelets. I reached up and felt a similar diamond necklace resting against my throat.

A large, ornate mirror hung above an open fireplace. I stared at my reflection, barely recognising myself. My hair had been styled into set waves, like that of a silent movie era actress. My make-up was perfect, my eyes heavily shadowed, and my lips matte red.

Sitting up, I looked around and took the place in. I was in the middle of a party. Everyone was dressed in stylish evening wear, laughing and joking as they sipped their drinks, not even noticing the random woman who'd just woken up on one of their couches.

Something seemed … off.

The people were strange. For a start, their clothing wasn't modern; it was straight out of the 1930s, and secondly, though they smiled and appeared to be having a good time, there was something dead in their eyes, something tortured behind their smiles. Their happiness seemed forced. Plus, they weren't speaking English. They spoke in German.

Where the hell was I?

"Would you care for a drink?" a waiter asked, brandishing a tray of glasses filled with champagne. I looked at him, wide-eyed, and shook my head. Standing, I walked by the waiter to a nearby window to peer outside. Carnival rides stared back at me, and at that moment, I knew exactly where I was. I was in Theodore's mansion on Ridley Island. But why was his house filled with German people dressed for a dinner party with a 1930's fancy dress theme? And who the hell undressed me, did my hair, and

229

put me in an elegant evening gown?

A shiver crept over me at the thought that it was Theodore.

"Are you enjoying yourself?" a familiar voice asked.

Speak of the devil. Theodore's cold breath washed over my bare shoulder, making my skin crawl.

"Not particularly." I turned my head to meet his gaze and my stomach twisted when I found him smiling down at me.

"I hope you don't mind, but I took the liberty of having you dressed for the occasion. Do you like my party room? I've had it for more than eighty years now."

"What do you mean?" I questioned, still taking in my surroundings in confusion. I glanced back at Theodore, and for a second, he seemed familiar. His eyes reminded me of someone, but I couldn't tell who. It niggled at me, the information just out of reach.

"I held a party in this very room in Berlin in 1938, just before the war broke out," Theodore explained. "I decided that I enjoyed it so much I would keep it frozen in time for so long as it entertained me."

How could this same room have been in Berlin in 1938? I wondered in confusion. Then the image of the house rising from the earth flashed in my mind, and I realised just how powerful Theodore was. This was his home, and he could seemingly magic it anywhere in the world.

"So, you're telling me that these people have been trapped in this room since the thirties, living out an endless party?"

"Exactly."

I looked around, both in awe and in horror. "How have you frozen them?"

"I'm a sorcerer, Treasure. Freezing people in time is just one of my many talents."

A chill skittered down my spine at the way he called me Treasure. I took a small step back because he was clearly a psychopath. How could he justify this? How could he live with himself knowing that he was keeping these poor people trapped for his amusement? They should all have grown old and grey and most likely passed away by now. Instead, they were held prisoner inside of their youthful bodies. Forced to endure the same party over and over.

Theodore went and sat down on the velvet sofa I'd woken up on. He patted the space next to him, but I remained standing. He frowned and made a motion with his hand, and my body was propelled forward, forcing me to sit next to him against my will. He magicked a glass of red wine, seemingly out of thin air. He swirled it around, inhaled the aroma, and took a sip.

"You know," he said, his tone nostalgic. "I have lived for a very long time, but this," he gestured around the room, "has always remained my favourite era. Such extravagance at war with poverty. The world is a cutthroat place, is it not?"

"I suppose it is," I replied, my pulse pounding as I tried to think of how I could escape.

He turned to study me. I felt his eerie gaze traverse my profile and cold trickled into my bones. "Do tell me, Treasure, what is your name?"

I considered lying, but then again, what was the point? Theodore sensed the power in my blood just from looking at me. Withholding my name wasn't going to do me much good. I forced myself to meet his gaze. "My name is Tegan Stolle."

"Tegan Stolle," he repeated, a flicker of a frown crossing his features. Perhaps he'd been hoping I'd have one of the magical family surnames, which would make my origins much easier to determine. "Do you know it's been over twenty years since I last came across a female of the True Power bloodline? What a surprise to find you in this city that I used to call home."

I swallowed down what felt like a hard lump of rock in my throat because it was around twenty years ago that my mother died. A memory of the vision from Rita's spell surfaced, of the pale, long-fingered hand reaching out to grab her as she ran through the woods. "And what did you do to the last woman when you found her?" I asked though I could hardly bear to hear the answer.

Theodore studied me for a long moment, then said, "I hunted her down. She had been evading me for quite some time. I finally tracked her to some woods in a back-water town, a town not too far from here, in fact. She gave a good chase." He paused, a reminiscent smile on his lips. "But I caught up to her in the end. I kept her for a while, and then, well, quite inevitably she died."

My chest constricted. His story was hauntingly similar to the vision, and I knew without a shadow of a doubt that Theodore had been the one my mother ran from. He'd captured her and killed her, and now he was going to do the exact same thing to me.

"How did she die?" I whispered.

Theodore stared at the red wine in his glass before taking another sip. "The liquid that runs in your veins is a highly powerful magical substance, and when used in a spell it can achieve almost anything the caster wishes."

I already knew this, but I didn't interrupt, instead allowing him to talk. The longer he talked, the longer I had to figure out an escape.

"I hadn't planned on killing her. In truth, she was far more valuable to me alive than dead. But I eventually drained her of too much blood and she expired. Quite tragic, really. We could've achieved so many more wonderful things together. But that doesn't matter. Now that I have you, I will be far more careful."

"What was her name?" I croaked. I needed to hear it. I needed to know for definite.

"Who's name?"

"The woman you captured."

"Oh." He furrowed his brow as though trying to recall it. "Well, now, let me see. I think it was Doreen? Dorian? I'm sorry, I don't quite remember." Fury burned inside of me. He'd killed her and couldn't even be bothered to remember her name.

Tears filled my eyes and my hands began to shake as I stared at him. "Dora," I whispered angrily.

Theodore slapped his hand down on his thigh. "Why yes, I do believe that was her name." He stopped and a sickening satisfaction filled his eyes. "She wasn't any relation of yours, was she?" His nostrils flared like he was savouring my heartache.

I jumped up from my seat, grabbed a tray of drinks out of the waiter's hands, and threw them directly at Theodore. "She was my fucking mother, you evil monster!" I screamed. My voice seemed to echo through the room. The spilled wine and smashed glass magically fell away from Theodore, not leaving a single stain or scratch. I let out an almighty wail, but none of the party-goers seemed to hear me. They continued to chat and enjoy themselves; the pianist over in the corner continued to play. Theodore stared me down, his expression empty.

Finally, he blinked and a faint smile returned to his lips. "You should think about where you direct your anger, my dear. The next time, I will not be inclined to overlook such behaviour."

Then he called on the waiter to clean up the mess I'd made. No more than a minute later, Theodore tilted his head to the side, his ear sticking out as though listening for something far away. He rose and went to peer out the window. A quiet expletive escaped his lips before he turned back around.

"I'm afraid we must cut our enjoyment short tonight," he said, addressing me pointedly. "We have some unwanted guests on the premises." His eyes turned purple for a moment as he lifted his right hand, making some bizarre gestures. I immediately found myself outside in the freezing cold, sitting on a seat on the big ferris wheel as it made its rotation around and around. I looked down in time to see a group of people crowd around the front door of the mansion. One person used a gun to shoot open the lock before they disappeared inside.

I managed to spot Ethan and Gabriel, but I seriously hoped Rita was among them. She was the only one with a chance of outwitting Theodore. A yacht floated on the shore just off the island. I wondered who it belonged to, although the style had Antonia Herrington written all over it.

Nothing happened for several minutes. The icy cold cut through me, the fabric of the evening gown I wore far too thin. I needed to get off this ride and find Rita because I knew she still needed my blood for her spell. I pulled my legs up through the bars and kneeled in a crouch as I neared the platform. Then, when I was closest to the ground, I jumped. It wasn't a graceful jump, given my outfit, and it hurt when I hit the platform, but at least I was off the dizzying ride.

A second later, every window in the mansion shattered outward, glass shards flying everywhere. A blinding, multi-coloured light poured out of them like a dazzling rainbow. Then a stream of people came running out. The rainbow vanished and was replaced with a horde of flying, rabid crows that cawed and snapped at those they were chasing. Was the crow Theodore's totem animal? These small ones were even more frightening than the giant one. They seem crazed and ravenous.

I spotted Ethan, Lucas, and Delilah first, then Rita, Gabriel, and Finn. Antonia and her guards, along with some of the other nameless vampires who had been present in the club last night, followed.

"Rita!" I shouted as she ran toward the big wheel. She looked over at me, clearly relieved. It was the relief of a person who feared you were dead. She carried a heavy-looking bag over her shoulder as she ran to me while the others used whatever weapons they had to fight off the crows.

Finn was crouched over by the chair-o-planes, a bow and arrow stretched out in front of him as he shot at the small flying monsters. I watched as one of his projectiles darted straight into the centre of a crow's chest, his aim perfect. Dru and Antonia's other guards shot at the birds with their guns as they maintained a protective circle around the evil bitch they were paid to keep alive.

I wouldn't forget what she'd done to Matthew, but now wasn't the time for my revenge.

Ethan and Lucas swung swords at the crows, their vampire speed allowing them to slice the birds with startling efficiency. Delilah's method of defending herself was perhaps the most ingenious and strange. She sat on a horse on the merry go round, her swift arms swinging out and grabbing the birds as they flew by, and quite plainly snapping their necks. I shuddered at the violence of it.

"What on earth are you wearing?" Rita asked breathlessly when she reached me.

"Never mind that. Do you have what you need for your spell?" I asked.

"Yes," she answered, still trying to catch her breath. "Everything except for your blood."

"Okay. Good. Let's get down underneath the platform and make a start."

I hadn't noticed until that moment, but Gabriel, with a look of confusion, stood right behind Rita. I knew exactly what he was wondering. Why did Rita need my blood to perform her spell? He didn't voice the question though, instead dutifully following Rita as she crawled into the shallow space beneath the big wheel.

When I joined them, Rita withdrew a wooden board from her bag, on which she placed a variety of intricate looking spell ingredients, and not just the herbal kind I'd seen her use before. Gabriel clicked on a torch to illuminate the space, and my gaze scanned the items laid out before me. There was a small container of what appeared to be dead spiders and another containing slimy earthworms. They wriggled in the bowl, still alive. Another container held a mixture of maggots and dead cockroaches. There was also a dead rat and a sharp blade made of silver.

"Don't be alarmed," Rita said, gauging my reaction. "I know this looks a little sinister, but opening up a portal into a hell dimension requires slightly darker magic than what I'm used to."

"I thought you didn't practice dark magic?" I said in

236

concern.

"I don't, but dire circumstances call for dire actions. I can make an allowance just this once."

"Thank you," I said, truly grateful. She was making a sacrifice by being here, and she had no clue how much I needed Theodore gone. I could run to the other side of the planet, but he was so powerful he was sure to find me no matter where I hid.

Rita handed me the blade. It looked almost exactly like the one my mother had used to cut herself when she cast the spell to protect me. "Is this silver?" I asked, my eyes tracing the carvings on the handle.

"Yes," Rita nodded. "It needs to be silver for the spell to work."

I turned it over in my hand, the light of Gabriel's torch glinting off it and transfixing me.

"Are you okay, Tegan?" Gabriel asked gently, speaking for the first time.

"Yes, I'm just a little out of sorts," I answered nervously. "It's only to be expected."

"Yes, it is," Rita agreed as she handed me a small glass vial. "Here," she said. "I need you to fill this with your blood. Cutting down the centre of your palm will probably be easiest." I nodded and braced myself for pain.

Gabriel coughed to clear his throat. "Um, why do we need Tegan's blood?" he asked, looking slightly worried. Rita and I shared a glance.

"You might as well tell him," she said. "We might not survive the night anyway. If we do, well, we'll figure something out when the time comes."

I glanced at Gabriel, but no words formed. I was terrified of telling him, of having anyone else know the truth about me. "I have True Power blood," I finally managed to whisper. "That's why Rita needs it for the spell. It's what you and Marcel and all the rest of them have been so eager to find out about me. You were right. It was my mother who cast the spell when I was a baby. She made it so that my blood would be hidden from everyone."

I expected Gabriel to exclaim his shock, or be angry at me for going behind everyone's back to find out what I was on my own. But he didn't. Instead, he looked ashamed. "I'm sorry I allowed Marcel to convince me to help him unravel the spell. Your bloodline, well, it's not something people should know about you. For your safety."

I swallowed down a thick ball of emotion at Gabriel's sincerity. Rita had been right about him. He could be trusted more than Marcel. I brought my attention back to the blade in my hand. We were running out of time, and I needed to do this before Theodore had a chance to send more crazed crows our way. Without further ado, I sliced down the centre of my palm like Rita instructed, sucking in a sharp breath at the pain. Then I squeezed my hand tight and allowed several drops of blood to drip into the glass vial before handing it over to Rita.

She took it from me, and I tore a strip of fabric off the end of my gown and wrapped it around my hand to stem the bleeding. Glancing up, I found Gabriel staring at me with marked hunger in his eyes. A chill crept over me. Then he blinked, looking embarrassed.

"Sorry, it's just … your blood smells …"

"Delicious, yes, she knows," Rita finished for him just as a violent scream cut through the air.

"I'll go check what's happening. You two start the spell," I said, needing the excuse to get away. Gabriel was the least aggressive of the blood drinkers I was acquainted with, and if my blood could make him look so ravenous, I shuddered to think about how a full-blooded vampire would react.

I crawled out from under the platform, making sure to stay hidden. Theodore stood atop the steps leading up to his mansion. He had Delilah's red hair twisted around his fisted hand, and I knew instantly she was the one who'd screamed. He violently pulled her down each time she struggled to get away from him.

I watched as Ethan stepped forward, addressing Theodore. "Let her go and we will leave. It's clear we are no match for you."

"I'll let her go as soon as you return my human to me," Theodore replied, his eyes going to the vacant seat on the big wheel. "I can see she has been taken."

"What human?" Ethan asked. "We didn't find any human."

"You know exactly who I am talking about," Theodore went on. "Tegan is her name, and she is of great value to me. I had transported her to a safe place, and now she is gone. Return her and I will return this one," he finished, pulling down hard on Delilah's hair. She let out another scream.

A look of grim anger and determination crossed Ethan's features. "Tegan does not belong to you, and if you have harmed her, I will make sure you suffer." His bravery on my behalf was touching. My heart gave a swift, emotional thud.

"Ah, so you're aware of her value," Theodore said. "I have always found that True Power blood tended to evade those of the vampire species. It's ironic, really, since it is vampires who have the most to gain from finding it."

"That's what she is?" Ethan whispered in awe, a stunned look in his eyes as the puzzle pieces finally fit together.

"Excuse me," Antonia interjected. "Did I just hear you correctly? Am I to believe that this girl is one of the power-blooded females?"

"True indeed," Theodore answered with false sincerity and an even falser smile. "But you can wipe that hungry expression off your greedy face. I discovered her first, therefore she belongs to me."

"She belongs to nobody but herself," Ethan countered grimly and again my heart pounded. He was defending me and my personal sovereignty. He didn't claim I was his, didn't talk like I was a piece of property to be owned. Whatever fondness I already had for him grew in intensity, and it pained me because, if by some miracle we managed to defeat Theodore tonight, I would most certainly have to run away. The sorcerer just announced what I was to a group of vampires, and the news would spread fast. I could practically see their eyes glowing with want.

"What is this now?" Theodore asked in wry amusement. "A parasite defending a human? I thought they were all just blood banks to you."

I didn't have time to hear Ethan's response because Rita was whispering my name. "Tegan, come quick," she urged. "We need you to complete the circle."

I crawled back under and sat down in between Rita and Gabriel before taking a deep breath. I looked between the two of them. "Okay, let's do this."

Rita nodded, an air of calm confidence about her as she instructed Gabriel to pour the vial of my blood into the spell bowl only when she told him to. He agreed, and we joined hands, forming a circle.

Rita began the spell speaking in what sounded like Latin. I remembered Marcel speaking a similar language when I'd watched him do magic. I had no idea what she was saying, but I did make out Theodore's name here and there. The spell was nothing like the one she'd cast before. Instead of swirling, the concoction in the bowl began to pop and crackle.

Rita raised her head, looking first at Gabriel, then at me. There was a fire in her eyes, and at that moment, I saw just how powerful a witch she would one day become. "*Aperiesque ostium inferni dimensionem.* And you shall open the door to the dimension of hell."

Then she gave the signal for Gabriel to pour my blood into the bowl. He lifted up the vial and tipped it in. Nothing happened. The three of us sat and stared at each other for several moments. No change in the air. It certainly didn't feel like the door to a hell dimension had been opened. The three of us crawled out from under the big wheel.

Theodore still had Delilah in his grip. He spoke with Antonia now, who had taken several steps closer, standing only a few yards away from him. The gravel crunched under my feet and Theodore's eyes flashed to me. A slow, satisfied smile spread across his lips when he saw me. Rita looked up into the sky, probably wondering where her hell door had gotten to. My chest deflated. For whatever reason, the spell hadn't worked. Theodore was very much present and accounted for.

"Ah, my human was not taken after all," Theodore declared. "Come here, Tegan, so that I may return this wench to her rightful owners." Everybody's attention came to me. I didn't fail to notice the eager gleam in the vampires' eyes. Well, all except for Ethan. He simply looked relieved to see me alive and well, and my heart didn't know what to do with that information.

"Don't go near him," Ethan warned, holding my gaze. I

thought of how he'd defended me, and my chest warmed. A moment passed between us, some kind of silent communication.

Let me protect you, his eyes said.

He didn't need to ask twice. I had absolutely no intention of going anywhere near Theodore. I stepped back to stand behind Gabriel. Theodore's eyes flashed purple and I braced myself, anticipating being transported to some other place again like the last time they turned that unnatural colour. It was only when I saw everyone's eyes go wide in shock as they stared behind me that I realised someone, or *something*, was there.

I tensed, really, *really* not wanting to turn around.

Some sixth sense told me Theodore had summoned that monstrous crow again. It was waiting to lift me up and fly away with me clutched in its enormous talons. I felt its wings wrap around me, readying for flight, when Ethan suddenly appeared. With lightning speed, he raised his sword and chopped the crow's head clean off. Blood spattered everywhere. I stared in horror as its giant head rolled on the ground, my mouth agape.

"Are you hurt?" Ethan asked, pulling me to him and enveloping me in his strong arms. I sank into the embrace, absorbing his strength. I was about to answer him when I spotted something big and gaping form several feet above Theodore's head. At first I thought, *Oh please no, not another of his monsters.* But then I realised that Theodore had no clue there was a giant hole hovering above him.

Rita's doorway finally came through.

22.

Rita stared up, seemingly stunned that her spell worked. Disbelief coloured her expression as she slowly walked toward the hole in the sky that she created. Finally, Theodore turned around to see what everybody was gawking at.

He put his hand out. It was curled into a fist except for the baby finger. He pointed it at the hole and gave a calm order, "Close."

The hole didn't close. He whipped back around to glare at us. Rita stood directly in front of him, and Theodore appeared to realise that she was the one responsible for the dimensional door. His cold eyes cut into her.

I watched the two of them in a standoff when it suddenly occurred to me—when I'd thought Theodore reminded me of someone, I couldn't put my finger on who it was. Now I realised it was Rita. They had the same eyes, but while Rita's held kindness and humanity, Theodore's contained nothing but malevolence and concentrated dark magic.

Another memory sprang forth, of the time I'd been in Rita's house and Alvie had confided in me, theorising that Rita was so good at magic because her unknown father might be a warlock. Or perhaps even a sorcerer? I shook my head at myself, shaking off the idea. It couldn't be …

Theodore's smile lacked warmth as he took Rita in. "I didn't realise there was a budding young witch present." There was tightness in his voice that told me he was quietly enraged. How dare a novice cast such a powerful spell against him? "Tell me, child, to which family do you belong?"

Rita folded her arms and gave a laugh. It sounded confident, but I was certain she was quaking in her boots deep down. She put up a good front. "I don't belong to any of them, thank you very much. You snobs aren't the only ones who can do magic, you know."

Theodore was silent. He studied her for a prolonged moment.

"Well, isn't that interesting," he mused. He was about to say more when tendrils of dark mist began to lick out of the dimensional door, swirling around him like a shadow. The tendrils slithered about Theodore and his eyes went wide. He struggled against them, zapping one with a bolt of purple magic that shot directly from his hand. In his struggle, he released Delilah, and she ran over to the safety of the vampires. A rush of fear flooded me at the thought that he might actually be able to fight Rita's spell. He threw all of his magic at the dark mist as it continued to pull him into the hole in the sky, impervious to his power.

Theodore refused to give up, struggling against the pull. Rita rushed forward and shocked everyone when she pushed Theodore into the hole. He fell but grabbed hold of her wrist just in time. Their eyes locked, and some kind of communication took place. I started forward, my instinct to save Rita in case Theodore pulled her into the hole with him. But somebody else got there just before me. Gabriel.

He looked powerful as his hands moved about him, casting a spell of his own. Suddenly the shadowy tendrils multiplied, ripping Theodore's grip from Rita. Then the hole consumed him, and a moment later it disappeared completely. Theodore was gone. I emitted a breath of sheer relief. I wondered where exactly he'd end up. Was it literal hell? With fire and brimstone and eternal suffering?

Rita fell back into Gabriel's arms, her breath coming

out in rapid bursts. I thought she might be in shock. She'd almost fallen into the hole with Theodore. Then I thought of the split second when they'd stared into each other's eyes. Had he said something to her? And if so, what? My theory about him being her father seemed farfetched, but then, didn't it make sense that the only person who could defeat Theodore was his own daughter?

I brushed the thought aside. I had no proof, only a hunch.

A warm hand touched my shoulder, and I turned to find Ethan's concerned face peering down at me. I was about to pull him into a hug when the stark realisation hit that he knew what I was now. I jerked away nervously. *All* of the vampires knew what I was.

"Don't be frightened," he pleaded.

I licked my suddenly dry lips. "Can you blame me?" Antonia, in particular, looked like she wanted to sink her fangs into me as soon as possible.

Ethan ran a hand through his hair, a look of consternation on his face as he shot Antonia a warning glare. His expression said, *touch her and die.* At least he seemed willing to fight to protect me. Judging by how the vampires were still eyeing me with marked interest, I needed all the protection I could get.

I needed to get off this island, though, and fast.

Ethan slid his arm around me, pulling me tight to his body, his mouth hovering by my ear as he whispered, "I won't allow anyone to touch you. You have my word."

Strangely enough, I believed him. The trouble was, he was one vampire, and they were many.

I met his gaze, searching. "Don't you want what they want?"

His eyes flickered back and forth between mine. "I

want you safe. That's all I want."

So, he didn't want my blood? That was ... surprising. Then again, Ethan had always insisted he wanted to be my friend, an ally. Maybe he'd actually been telling the truth.

Ethan's hand slid down to my hip, his fingers making contact with my bare skin where the dress was torn. "That's really all you want?" I asked, a hitch in my voice. His touch was very distracting.

His mouth moved close to my ear again. "Not all. I'm also extremely interested in getting you out of this dress." He gently squeezed my hip and my eyes widened, cheeks heating.

My throat went dry. "That sounds like an interesting proposition."

He laughed throatily, and I clenched my thighs at the sound. What was I doing standing here letting him flirt with me? By all rights, I should be diving into the ice-cold water and swimming to shore before Antonia could sink her fangs into me just like she'd done to poor Matthew.

Ethan pulled me closer so that half of my body was flush against his. I looked deep into his eyes, feeling a pull to lean in and let him kiss me. Something in my gut told me he wanted to.

"Have I ever told that your eyes are quite marvellous?" he asked. "They're as blue as the Mediterranean."

"Oh." I flushed. "Uh, thanks."

He gave another laugh and pressed a kiss to the top of my head. "Compliments, Tegan. You need to learn how to take them."

I was about to reply when one of the chairs from the big wheel came crashing down, landing just a few feet in front of us. Yikes! To my left, the merry-go-round disintegrated before our eyes until it was nothing but a pile of dust.

"This place is falling apart now that Theodore's magic is no longer powering it," said Gabriel. "We need to get out of here." Ethan nodded, and without missing a beat, he scooped me up into his arms. Gabriel helped Rita to her feet as Ethan carried me to the boat, just barely dodging another falling chair.

I looked back over his shoulder just in time to see the mansion begin to crumble, the bricks disintegrating into nothing. Quickly, we all boarded the yacht. The engine started, and we sailed away from Ridley Island. I couldn't say I was going to miss the place.

Ethan sat down on a bench, still holding me tight. It was cold, so I didn't mind the possessive gesture. I sat on his lap, and he wrapped his arms around me, both of us looking at the island as it grew smaller and smaller in the distance. At that moment, I remembered Theodore's party room with all of those people trapped inside. I startled and tried to stand, but Ethan pulled me back to him.

"What is it, Tegan?" he asked in concern.

I didn't answer as I stared at the pile of dust that was once Theodore's mansion. The people he'd trapped were gone, too, disintegrated to dust just like everything else that had been there. A sense of sadness filled me up as I mourned for the lives the sorcerer stole.

"Nothing," I answered finally, falling tiredly back into his arms as a single tear fell down my cheek.

Ethan watched its descent, reaching out to wipe it away. "You're sad?"

"Yes, but not because of you."

He tilted his head, his eyes roaming my face, focusing on my mouth. "I like having you close to me." His hand moved to my outer thigh, causing tingles to spread through me. I looked away shyly and met Rita's gaze. She'd clearly been watching us, and she looked concerned. I understood why. What she saw was a woman with True Power blood getting far too close to a vampire. A recipe for disaster if ever there was one.

Antonia, who was sitting on the other side of the yacht, eyed me closely, and I grew unnerved.

"You will bring her to my house once we get to shore," Antonia said to Ethan. It sounded like an order. His hold on me tightened.

"I think Tegan would prefer to go to her own home and rest," he replied, his voice resolute.

Antonia didn't waver and fear coiled in my stomach. "You will bring her to my house, Ethan Cristescu," she stated, her words broaching no argument. I anxiously scrambled to figure out a way to evade Antonia long enough to get out of Tribane and away from her.

I could see that Ethan was about to argue when I placed my hand on his arm. "It's okay. I'll go with her." His face was a picture of confusion as I turned back to Antonia and bowed my head slightly. I moved out of Ethan's hold and went to her, kneeling before her in supplication. I gazed at her, my eyes beseeching, and hoped my timid act worked. "Antonia, would you mind if I made a brief trip to my apartment before I go with you. There are some things I would like to get, and I'd like the chance to wash off all of this dirt." Something like a smirk graced her lips. She clearly thought I was a fool to go with her so easily, but that was fine. I needed her to underestimate me. While she was busy being smug, I plucked a stray white hair that had fallen onto her black coat, closing my fist over it tight.

"Very well," she answered after thinking it over. "But Drusilla will go with you, and when you are done, she will escort you back to me."

"Thank you," I replied graciously, before getting up and going back over to sit with Ethan.

When we arrived at the shore, Ethan and Dru escorted me to my apartment in Ethan's SUV. Ethan instructed Dru to wait in the car, but she insisted on coming up with us and keeping guard outside my door to make sure we didn't try anything. Ethan agreed, but it was clear he was pissed when he reached my apartment and slammed my door in Dru's face, making sure she didn't follow us inside.

"You don't need to be so rude to her," I told him. "She's only doing her job."

Ethan stood in my tiny kitchen, hands fisted in agitation, his forehead furrowed. "Why are you doing this? Going with Antonia is a death sentence, and you know it."

I came to stand in front of him, taking his hand into mine. "I'm not going with Antonia. I'm leaving Tribane. I just needed time to get my things. I'm still trying to figure out a way to get rid of Dru though."

Ethan's agitation immediately disappeared, and a smile shaped his handsome mouth. "Why didn't you say so?" he beamed, lifting my hand to his mouth and pressing a kiss to my knuckles as his eyes met mine. "Where are we going?"

"We?" I asked in surprise. "You want to come with me?"

"Why not? Delilah can take care of the club while I'm away."

Butterflies filled me at the thought, but at the same time my heart clenched in sadness. I pulled my hand from Ethan's hold. "I don't think you get it. I'm leaving Tribane for good. Not just for a holiday. I won't be coming back. Ever."

Ethan shook his head. "Antonia will not be in charge

249

for much longer, Tegan. Soon she'll be overthrown and it will be safe for you to return."

"It's not just about Antonia. There are a whole bunch of vampires who know what I am now, and that information is only going to spread. I don't think you get the enormity of my situation. I'm going to have to hide for the rest of my life." Saying it out loud made the reality of what I faced come crashing down on me. "You might not be interested in me for what my blood can give you, but I can guarantee you that's not the case for the rest of the vampires who were there tonight. They'll all want a piece of me, and they won't stop taking and taking until I'm dead."

The same as what Theodore did to my mother.

Ethan pulled me into his arms. They were so warm and strong and protective. I wished I could stay in his embrace forever, but I couldn't. I moved away and met his gaze. "I'm sorry, Ethan, but you can't come with me. This is something I need to do alone. I need to get away from this world, a world to which you belong. If you come with me, then I'll never escape it."

He stared at me, a multitude of pain in his eyes because he knew what I said was the truth.

"I'm going to take a quick shower," I said because I couldn't stand there and look at him any longer. If I did, I'd only embarrass myself by crying or getting overly emotional. I hadn't known him long, but our chance meeting at Hagen's had upturned my entire life. Maybe we were always supposed to meet. Maybe it was destiny. But it was a short-lived destiny, and now I had to go.

I showered quickly, discarding the gown but keeping the diamond jewellery. If I was going on the run, then I'd need every bit of cash I could get, and hocking the bracelets and necklace would provide me with a tidy sum.

Thanks Theodore! I hope those hell flames aren't singeing your backside, you evil prick.

Holding onto humour right now was the only thing that would keep me together. I dressed in jeans and a T-shirt before carefully folding Antonia's strand of hair in a piece of tissue paper and placing it carefully in the side compartment of my bag. I'd need it later.

With everything sorted, I sat on my bed and considered my next move. I stared at the four walls that surrounded me. Perhaps it was for the best that I got away from this place. Far too many painful memorics permeated in the air since I lost Matthew. He took his life in this apartment to escape Antonia's predation. The stain of his death would always linger.

With a sigh of resignation, I placed my key on the bedside table, hitched my bag up onto my shoulder, and went out to face Ethan.

He watched me enter the room without expression, but I sensed his conflict. He didn't want to let me go. The feeling was mutual because I was going to need nerves of steel to walk away from him, from the possibility of *us*.

I held his gaze and exhaled nervously. "Is there any way that you could, I don't know, knock Dru out or something? It's the only way I can think of getting out of here without her following us."

Ethan nodded. "Leave it to me." With that, he rose and went to the door. I heard him make small talk with Dru before everything went silent. Then he was dragging her unconscious body back inside my apartment.

"She'll be out of action for a couple of hours," Ethan said, leaving her lying on the sofa. "Come along, you need all the head start you can get."

I wasn't going to argue with that. We hurried down to his car. Ethan started the engine before looking to me for instruction. "Where do you want me to take you?"

"To the bus station," I answered soberly.

Ethan eyed me now, a soft look in his eyes. "Do you need money?"

I shook my head, thinking of the diamonds tucked away in my bag. "No, I should be okay for a while." A pause as I considered him. "How much longer will the blood connection between us last?"

"A month or two, but don't worry. Wherever you end up, I won't tell anyone where you are. You have my word."

"Thank you. I've come to learn that your word can be trusted."

Something about what I said caused a flicker of emotion to enter Ethan's eyes. It meant something that I finally trusted him. A moment of quiet ensued before I spoke again, "Actually, I know this is a lot to ask, but could you bring me to Rita's house first? There's one last thing I need to ask her to do."

"Does she live on the other side of the river?" Ethan asked, his brow furrowed.

"Yes, but I need to see her. Please, I'll be eternally grateful."

Ethan was silent a long moment before he finally put the car in gear and moved off. "What's her address?" he asked reluctantly. I reached out and hugged his neck. "Thank you," I whispered, and some of his stiffness subsided. I knew he was taking a big chance driving me across the Hawthorn. I rattled out her address, and Ethan drove pensively. He seemed on high alert as he entered enemy territory on my behalf.

He remained in the car when we reached Rita's house,

scanning the street as I went and knocked on her door, praying she was home. Noreen answered and brought me into the living room where Rita was sprawled out on the couch. She wore a pair of pink wool pyjamas and matching fluffy slippers. I stifled a grin at how different she looked not wearing her usual gothic ensemble.

"What? I've had a long day," she griped. "These are my comfiest PJs."

"They do look terribly comfortable," I said, my grin breaking through.

"I'll leave you two to talk," Noreen said, closing the door behind her.

I went to sit on the arm of the couch, my expression sobering. "Listen, I need you to do something for me."

Rita raised an eyebrow as she sat up. "Have I not done enough for you yet? Because I think banishing a sorcerer to a hell dimension is quite a lot for a day's work."

I placed my hand on hers, my voice sincere. "You have done so much for me, Rita. You're an incredible witch, but I do need one more favour."

She sighed even as a smile tugged at her lips when I called her an incredible witch. "I guess one more can't hurt. So, what do you want me to do this time?"

I pulled my bag up onto my lap and retrieved the piece of folded up tissue containing Antonia's hair. "I need to know if there's anything you can do with this." I held it out to her.

"What is it?" she asked, opening the tissue to reveal the single strand of white hair.

"It's hair," I answered. "Antonia Herrington's to be exact."

She arched an eyebrow. "And what, pray tell, do you want me to do with it?"

I inhaled deeply, preparing my explanation.

"You don't know this about me, but earlier this year, my boyfriend Matthew committed suicide. I thought it was depression, but the other night while I was going through his things, I discovered the real reason he'd killed himself. Antonia had been feeding from him against his will. She'd messed with his head so much that he'd decided he'd rather die than continue to be her victim."

Rita's mouth fell open as she reached out to place her hand on mine. I continued speaking. "I can't allow her to get away with what she did to him. I saw this hair on her coat tonight and took it because I wanted to have something of hers so that maybe you could put a hex on her."

Rita stared at me, her eyebrows crawling all the way up her forehead now. "Hexes are serious business, and they're derived from dark magic. I'm not sure I want to dip my toe into those waters again so soon."

I frowned, guilt twisting inside me. "No, you're right. I shouldn't have asked."

I reached out to take the hair back, but Rita stayed me with a hand. "Wait. You're sure this is what you want?"

"Positive," I replied.

She worried her lip. "Okay, then. I'll create a hex. To be honest, I'm quite impressed you thought to take one of her hairs. I keep forgetting you're half magical since your mother was a witch. The inclination toward spells comes somewhat more naturally to members of the magical families."

I didn't know what to say to that. I'd never felt particularly magical, though I did sometimes have a sixth sense when it came to danger, a nagging voice in my brain that warned me it was close. Other than that, I'd never done anything even remotely close to the magic Rita, Gabriel, and Theodore possessed.

"Any idea on what sort of hex you want?" Rita asked.

Steel formed in my gut. "I don't care what it is. I just want her to suffer."

Her expression turned thoughtful. "Well, I do know a certain spell. Actually, it's more of a curse. It's supposed to make bad people suffer for their sins. Like a guilt curse. The person you put it on feels the guilt of every single crime they've committed for the rest of their lives. If I curse Antonia, then she'll suffer for every life she's ever destroyed. Including your boyfriend's."

That sounded … perfect, really. I felt vindicated to know that Antonia would feel guilt. There was a fury in me, one that made me want to take her down. She'd ruined Matthew and clearly planned to drain me of my blood for the power it could give her. As far as I was concerned, Antonia deserved everything that was coming to her.

Rita must've seen the resolution in my eyes because she quietly rose from the couch and left the room. When she returned, she proceeded to set up her spell ingredients for the curse. When it was done, the air around me felt different, like something I needed to release had finally been set free. I hugged Rita tight, thanking her for the spell. When she pulled away, she looked suspicious.

"Why exactly were you in such a hurry to get this done?"

I frowned, not seeing the point in beating around the bush. "I'm leaving, Rita. I can't stay here now that there are vampires who know what I am. Not to mention Finn. He'll be reporting back to his slayer buddies any minute now and they'll be coming for me, too."

She looked sad, and if I wasn't mistaken, her eyes seemed a little glassy. We hadn't known each other long, but we'd bonded fast. "Do you think you'll ever come back?"

"To be honest, I don't know. Probably not."

She nodded and this time she was the one to hug me. "Good luck, Tegan. I'll cast a spell tomorrow that will help you to stay hidden, if you'd like? It might not throw them off the scent forever, but it'll cause some confusion long enough for you to find somewhere safe to stay."

Do. Not. Cry. What had I done to deserve her? "That would be great," I managed, my voice cracking slightly. I was going to miss her so, so much.

"Tell Alvie I said goodbye."

"I will."

***

The walk from Rita's front door to Ethan's car seemed like the longest I'd ever taken. Saying goodbye to him was going to be rough, but it had to be done. No matter which way you spun it, I couldn't stay in Tribane. The reality of my situation made me want to go out and buy an army bunker, an arsenal of weapons, and a lifetime supply of non-perishable food so I could hide away forever.

I opened the door and slid into the passenger seat beside him. We sat in silence for several seconds before I spoke, "You won't have to worry about Antonia punishing you for helping me escape," I said.

"Oh?"

"I had Rita cast a spell," I replied, and he nodded, a distant look in his eyes. I felt like he was already withdrawing from me and it broke my heart.

"I'll take you to the bus station now," he said, starting the engine.

"Right, thanks," I whispered.

The sudden tension stifled me, and the drive to the bus station was one of the tensest I'd ever endured. When we arrived, Ethan parked in a spot close to the entrance, and I checked the time on the dashboard. It was very late. I hoped there were still buses leaving. I didn't care where I went. I just needed to get out of this city.

Ethan's hands fell from the steering wheel and came to rest on his lap. He clenched one fist, not looking at me when he said, "You could always stay. We could fight."

"I can't." I reached out, pressing a hand to his cheek and forcing him to meet my gaze.

"I don't want you to go." There was a potent sadness in his otherworldly eyes.

"If you were in my shoes, what would you do?" I asked softly.

He didn't answer, instead bringing his face closer to mine, so close his mouth was only a whisper away. His intoxicating scent surrounded me as I focused on his lips and told him, "I wish I was brave enough to stay."

He gripped me softly by the wrist. "You are. You just don't know it yet."

I shook my head, still unable to look away from his mouth. "I wish I could believe that."

Ethan exhaled a heavy, frustrated breath. "Do you know that I've never felt for any human the way I feel for you? It will kill me to let you go, but I won't force you to stay."

At this, I lost any semblance of self-control. I closed the small distance between us and gently pressed my lips to his. A rumble emanated from him as he gripped my face and deepened the kiss. His tongue danced with mine and tingles encapsulated my entire body. His fingertips grazed

257

the skin beneath my T-shirt and a burst of desire shattered through me. I let out a quiet moan as he whispered in my ear, "You're beautiful."

I wanted to melt.

"So are you," I said, breaking the kiss and pulling back to take him in. I would never forget him. He was the most stunning man I'd ever laid eyes on. Something in him called to me from the very first moment we met. I reached out and brushed a strand of his messy blond hair away from his face, the gesture sad but affectionate. This goodbye was agonising, but I couldn't help prolonging it because as soon as it was over I'd have to go and face the fact that I was never going to see him again.

He brought his mouth to mine once more and slipped his hand farther under my top, running his fingers over the lace lining of my bra. My breathing quickened, my thighs clenching at his touch.

"Let's go to my place," he rasped, and just like that, reality came crashing back down. I was being cruel by kissing him. All it did was give him hope. I should've gone already, should've said my goodbyes and left. Yet here I was, shoving my tongue down Ethan's throat. This was wrong, all wrong. I needed to find the strength to walk away.

This was one of the most difficult things I'd ever done. My heart was screaming at me, urging me to go home with Ethan and face whatever consequences came in the morning. But my heart was fickle and didn't think long-term. My brain was logical. It told me the correct course of action.

"I have to go now," I said, drawing away from Ethan.

Several emotions flitted across his face. Then finally, stoic resignation.

A lump of grief formed in my throat. "Tell Delilah I said goodbye and tell Lucas to be kind to Amanda."

He nodded, looking away, his jaw working. I fixed my T-shirt and buttoned up my coat before opening the car door and stepping out. I was just about to leave when I turned back.

"Just go," he said, voice rough. Tears filled my eyes as I hitched my bag over my shoulder and started walking toward the station. I tried to snap out of it, but it was no use. I pulled a crumpled tissue from my bag and wiped at my tears. When I turned to look back once more, Ethan's car was gone.

Grief clutched at my heart.

Inside I found the nearest ATM and withdrew some money. Catching sight of myself in the window, I hurried to the bathroom to clean myself up. I looked a mess, my eyes red from crying.

I gazed at my reflection and hardly recognised the woman who stared back at me. She looked sad but also resilient. I'd been through so much in the last year and it had toughened me, made me stronger. I could survive this, deep in my heart I knew I could. And one day I'd find a way to thrive.

I left the bathroom and walked to the middle of the station, staring up at the destinations all lit up on the screen. Around me, people hurried this way and that, all with places to be.

I clutched my bag tightly as I scanned the list, picking a place at random, somewhere far, far away from Tribane. A voice whispered in my ear, chilling me to my core. It sounded a lot like Theodore, but that was crazy because he was gone.

You can run as far as you want, but this isn't the last

you've seen of this city, Treasure.

I shook off the chill, telling myself it was merely my imagination, as I stepped up to the counter and bought a ticket.

Thank you for reading *Nightfall*. The story continues in *Moonglow*, book #2 in the Blood Magic Series.

Meet the Author

Greetings! 'Tis a pleasure to make your acquaintance. My name is L.H. Cosway and I wrote the book you just read. I hail from Dublin, Ireland, where I live with my husband and two tiny dictators of the canine variety. My favourite things in life include daydreaming about fictional characters, eating in fancy restaurants, looking at dresses online that I'll never buy, having entire conversations with my dogs, listening to podcasts and of course, reading books. I happen to believe that imperfect people are the most interesting kind. They tell the best stories.

Here is my website where you can find various and sundry information about me and my books: **www.lhcoswayauthor.com**

Want to chat about my stories with like-minded readers or pick my brain? You can join my reader group by searching for the Blue Queens

You can also keep up with all my latest book news and goings on by subscribing to my newsletter: **www.lhcoswayauthor.com/newsletter/**

Books by L.H. Cosway

Contemporary Romance
Painted Faces
Killer Queen
The Nature of Cruelty
Still Life with Strings
Showmance
Fauxmance
Happy-Go-Lucky
Beyond the Sea

The Cracks Duet
A Crack in Everything (#1)
How the Light Gets In (#2)

The Hearts Series
Six of Hearts (#1)
Hearts of Fire (#2)
King of Hearts (#3)
Hearts of Blue (#4)
Thief of Hearts (#5)
Cross My Heart (5.75)
Hearts on Air (#6)

The Running on Air Series
Air Kiss (#0.5)
Off the Air (#1)
Something in the Air (#2)

The Rugby Series with Penny Reid
The Hooker & the Hermit (#1)
The Player & the Pixie (#2)

Manufactured by Amazon.ca
Bolton, ON